Wakefield Press

TAKING DOWN EVELYN TAIT

Poppy Nwosu is an Australian YA author. Her debut novel, *Making Friends with Alice Dyson*, was shortlisted for the 2018 Adelaide Festival Unpublished Manuscript Award, and for the Readings Young Adult Book Prize 2019. Growing up in central North Queensland, Poppy enjoyed a thoroughly wild childhood surrounded by rainforest and cane fields. After studying music at university, she moved overseas to Ireland, where she spent two years exploring Europe. These days Poppy and her husband still love to travel, but they also like to come home again to their house in Adelaide near the sea.

Visit Poppy at www.talltaleswithpoppynwosu.com.

TAKING DOWN EVELYN TAIT

Poppy
Nwosu

**Wakefield
Press**

Wakefield Press
16 Rose Street
Mile End
South Australia 5031
www.wakefieldpress.com.au

First published 2020

Cover designed by Liz Nicholson, Wakefield Press
Edited by Margot Lloyd, Wakefield Press
Typeset by Michael Deves, Wakefield Press
Cover illustration by Rory Brockman-Tanham
Text illustrations by Gus Nwosu

ISBN 978 1 74305 697 4

NATIONAL
LIBRARY
OF AUSTRALIA

A catalogue record for this
book is available from the
National Library of Australia

Government
of South Australia

Department of the
Premier and Cabinet

CORIOLE
McLAREN VALE

Wakefield Press thanks
Coriole Vineyards for
continued support

It's for you, Guscake

1

HOW TO LOSE YOUR BEST FRIEND AND YOUR BREAKFAST. EXCELLENT!

To be honest, it wasn't excellent. I just said it so this would seem like an upbeat story. But surprise! It isn't.

Also, I had vegemite toast and banana for breakfast. Obviously the banana wasn't actually on top of the vegemite toast. They were separate. Only complete deviants eat those things together. Like my stepmum. She's disgusting. In the end, though, everything gets mixed together in your belly. There's nothing you can do about it. So it isn't my fault.

Not really.

It's Grace's fault.

She tells me this thing on the train that really winds me up, and then I just can't get it out of my head no matter how hard I try. I'm sitting there and the carriage is jerking and wiggling beneath me, and Grace is sitting across from me all innocent like. As if she hasn't just told me she's in love with my literal mortal enemy, Miss Perfect herself, Evelyn Tait.

The tracks are uneven and the seat is swaying and I'm starting to get real sick. Like, feel it rising inside my throat kind of sick. But Grace keeps prattling on and on about Evelyn, like everything is wonderful. Except it isn't.

I shake the stunned expression off my face. 'But you know how I feel about Evelyn!' I hiss this real soft and quiet, because the train is filled with other students all going where we're going, and I have no interest in being today's biggest topic of gossip at school. Not that anyone is listening. The girls in the next booth are going on and on about some mad party one of them went to on the weekend. I try to block them out.

A flicker passes across Grace's face. 'Is this because she's a girl?'

'No,' I splutter, 'it's because it's *Evelyn Tait*.'

Grace *knows* how I feel about Miss Perfect. She knows. And besides, Grace has been obvious about liking girls since we first met. The fact that this is her first time *dating* a girl makes no difference. She's hooked up before. She knows it's not a big deal. I shake my head. 'I just … seriously?'

My best friend bites her lip. 'I know. I know it's awkward, Lottie. I really do. And I'm sorry. I get why you're upset.' She hesitates and then the rest of it leaves her in a rush, 'But I can't help who I like. I can't. I tried, I did try. Because of you. But I like her.' She draws in a deep breath and then drops her next bombshell. 'And she likes me back.'

'No, she doesn't,' I say automatically. 'She's using you.'

Grace laughs, but there's a sharper edge to it now. 'Using me for what, exactly? My super rich family?'

Well, no.

'My in-depth academic knowledge? To help with her grades?'

Mmmh. No. Evelyn doesn't need anyone to help with her grades.

'So what then?' Grace lifts her chin just as the girls in the other booth burst into squeals of laughter. One of them is talking about the neighbours calling the cops on the party for being too wild. I raise my eyebrows at Grace, because it's funny. The girls look about twelve.

She's having none of it. 'Lottie, I'm trying to talk to you about something important.'

I sigh. 'I know, I know. But I just don't like her.'

It's not the truth. Or at least, not the whole truth. But Grace gets it. She knows, and she doesn't care. Her face twists and she peers out the window at the wide slow river flashing by, reflecting orange morning light like fire. The girls behind us laugh again, giggling as the speaker finishes her tale by saying, 'Then I woke up.'

I roll my eyes so hard I give myself a headache. It matches my nausea perfectly. And the more I think about it, the more irritated I feel. Not because of the misleading-party-dream idiots, but because of Grace. Because she knows me. Or at least she should. Her being with Evelyn isn't some small deal. It's an infringement. And she should have tried harder to avoid it.

The train rattles onwards through the suburbs, past old crumbling houses with big overgrown lawns and wild myrtle wattle peeking through the fences, straining to get out. I press against the glass, thinking of that scent, wattle and salt from the ocean, anything to keep my mind off Miss Perfect. The houses whizz by and we come to a patch of big freshly painted McMansions, line upon line of them, all the same.

My mum must be living happily in one of those in Sydney by now. Shiny mansions are her thing. Not that she's invited me to visit her. I turn away, feeling sicker.

By the time we reach the station I'm really wired. I'm buzzing, nauseous, and I'm pissed. We stash our bags in our lockers and

I'm considering swinging by old Jerry's office just for a quiet sit on his threadbare couch, because that always calms me down. Except Grace nudges me and I glance up to catch Sebastian's eye as he walks by. He smiles and I'm pretty sure I don't smile back. I guess I must be staring, because Grace nudges me again, harder this time, her elbow in my rib cage.

'Ow,' I mutter, rubbing my side as Sebastian and his cloud of friends float away down the hall. I lean back against the metal lockers and feel even sicker. How can one boy be so pretty? I sigh and Grace gives me a very pointed look.

'It's not even remotely the same,' I mutter.

She raises her eyebrow and says nothing, but I read the message loud and clear.

Grace has never liked Sebastian, not since we first started high school and he laughed when Jamie Gorecki made fun of her bright pink hair on the oval. I remember that day a whole lot more fondly than Grace, because it was the day she and I first met. We've been best friends ever since, so I guess I should thank Jamie Gorecki. Besides, Grace's hair has only gotten brighter and pinker, and Jamie Gorecki learned the hard way not to mess with Grace Singh.

But still, my best friend never forgave Sebastian. Or me it seems, for liking him.

'That was ages ago,' I mutter. 'And a lot's happened since then. He's different now.'

Grace grins sweetly. 'Yeah, he got prettier.'

'He was always pretty,' I argue.

'He's gross.' She shrugs, then this dreamy expression crawls over her face. 'Unlike Evelyn.'

That hits me right in the stomach. I huff and puff and slam

my locker shut. Whatever. Me and Sebastian are never going to happen, but this thing with Evelyn? My blood boils. The girl's a witch. I'm sure she's seducing my best friend just to get back at me for last time. She's evil and she's going to break Grace's heart.

And the worst thing?

Everyone thinks she's perfect. *Everyone*. They think she's kind and smart and sweet. I'm the only one who knows the truth.

And there she is. I grimace, showing teeth.

Evelyn Tait.

With her thick luscious hair and her pretty pointed face.

School hasn't started yet but she's already in the lab, working away with her oversize safety glasses and stupid science tubes or whatever. I press my face against the big glass window separating the labs from the public access area. It's getting busier in the corridor, students swelling through the halls on their way to class, jostling me and Grace. Not that my best friend notices. She's watching Evelyn with a big goofy grin plastered on her face. I'm going to puke.

Instead I scowl at Evelyn through the glass, but she doesn't even notice. She's smiling back at Grace and waving shyly, smoothing her hair. Disgusting.

She's not chaperoned. Only Evelyn would be allowed to do lab work unattended before school. Such a suck-up.

I don't try to stop myself. And one good thing about me is that usually I do. Try, I mean. I always *try* to stop myself.

It rarely works, but whatever.

I push open the lab door, even though Grace is grasping my shoulder saying, 'Lottie, we've got class. Come back!'

I shake her off. Inside the lab I stand frozen beside the door, no idea what I'm going to do, but feeling pretty vicious, like I'm definitely about to do *something.*

'Hi Evelyn.' I sound nasty.

My mortal enemy smiles shyly, like she doesn't hear my tone. 'Hey Grace.'

I huff again. She totally ignored me.

Grace squeezes into the lab behind me, giving a dumb little half wave.

I'm going to puke.

I turn away and startle, because someone else is in here, sprawled over a desk, tongue sticking out of his mouth as he does ... some lab thing, I don't know. Writing calculations in a crazy scrawl across a lab book. He pokes his freckled explosion of a face up and blinks at me. 'Lottie, you can't be in here.'

I roll my eyes. 'I already *am* in here, Jude.' He is such an idiot sometimes. 'I'm just saying hi to Evelyn. You know Evelyn, of course. She's a friend stealer and suck-up.' I glare at her for effect.

'Lottie!' Grace isn't happy.

I don't care.

'I do know Evelyn, yes,' says Jude very seriously. 'She's my lab partner.'

I blink at him.

I'm pretty sure he's joking.

I glare at him too, for good measure, but he just smiles.

'Lottie.' Grace has my arm again. 'Let's go to class, okay?' Except then she's distracted because Evelyn is smiling at her again, sweet as pie.

'Do you think you could help me reach that beaker, Grace?' Evelyn points high to a set of shelves fixed to the wall beside the whiteboard. 'I'm not tall enough.'

Oh kill me now. She's playing the damsel in distress. Disgusting.

I share a look with Jude but he just shrugs. He's plenty tall and Evelyn is *his* lab partner, as he so nicely pointed out, and yet he stays where he is, bending to continue his work.

Grace skips across the room before I can stop her, reaching for the beaker. I bark out a laugh because she can't reach it either. In fact, she's even shorter than Evelyn.

Something nasty is rolling in my belly as I stalk across the room. 'Poor tiny Evelyn. Here, let me help you.' I start dragging one of the desks over, the lab equipment shaking and rattling, the glass violently clinking.

Jude is paying proper attention now, unfolding himself from the desk and scuffing his sneakers across the laminate floor as he takes faltering steps towards us. 'Uh, Lottie, maybe you shouldn't ...'

I throw him a silencing glare. He's dusted in so many freckles his face is an entirely different colour from the rest of his skin, all of it crowded together like a bomb went off.

I'm taller than both Grace and stupid Evelyn, but there's no way even I could reach the dumb beaker. Still, I'm determined to help. The desk I'm dragging slams against the shelves and all the little bottles and tubes rattle and shake, glass on glass.

'Lottie,' Grace is focused on me now. 'Seriously, what the hell are you doing? Get down.'

Sneakers on the desk, I'm towering over them all, Jude frozen just behind Evelyn who gapes at me. The desk shakes beneath my feet. It's not entirely stable.

But I can't help myself.

'Get down, you'll break it!' Evelyn's cries just urge me onwards.

'Lottie, stop it!' Grace steps away. 'Please!'

I lift the beaker from the shelf. Hold it above Evelyn's head, grinning wildly. I'm rather enjoying myself. I raise my eyebrows and she realises what I'm about to do.

I drop the beaker and she slams to her knees, grasping it just before it smashes against the floor.

I laugh and Grace squeals, down beside Evelyn now.

And that would have been it, I swear. I might have a problem with knowing where the line is, but seriously, I know when to stop.

Mostly.

Suddenly I realise the hallway is crowded with students, faces and noses pressed against the lab glass, all of them gawping. Boys push each other to get a better view, school bags and shoulders slamming against the glass.

All at once I feel very exposed, like maybe this wasn't such an excellent idea after all. Like maybe I do have a problem with my behaviour like my dad says I do.

The thought of my dad makes my stomach turn.

I'm already on my millionth warning.

'Get down,' Grace hisses. She's holding the desk steady, or at least trying to. 'I don't want to get in trouble right now, I told you, my ...'

Hoots and cat calls sound through the door.

But that's okay, I'm about to hop onto the floor anyway, one foot already lifted. I'm done. I'm less pissed off now, just sick. It's erupting in waves in my belly, rising into my throat. Probably because I've just realised Sebastian is standing out there in the crowd, beautiful green gaze locked onto me. Of all the days for him to notice I exist.

The door swings open and Ms Peters walks in, red in the face, sweaty and harassed by the crowded students outside. She's shouting at them as she enters, round glasses flashing and hair a mad tangle of red.

She stops. Gazes from me, frozen in the air, to Grace clutching the desk steady beneath my feet and then to Evelyn huddled on the floor. Jude raises his hands like he's being arrested.

I roll my eyes at him. 'Oh come *on*—'

The desk slides sideways, jerked from beneath my feet, abrupt and violent. I slam my hand on the shelf for balance, and the plastic gives way, down, down, the shelf slides from its slots. I grab wildly for another, a shower of beakers and bottles glittering in the air, a cacophony of screams and excitement from beyond the labs. I scream too. And then I hit the floor hard, my knee smacking the desk leg, which has flipped over, and I'm lying breathless in a pile of Evelyn and crushed beakers and broken glass.

Tangled and gasping.

And then silence.

'Don't move,' screams Ms Peters. Her sensible heels crunch over the floor, but she's not reaching for me, it's Evelyn she extricates from our puddle of science mayhem, Evelyn who has a bright red stripe across her palm. Blood.

'You're injured.' Ms Peters's face is as red as her hair. 'Oh my god, Evelyn.'

'A teeny tiny cut,' I mutter, dragging myself to my feet. Glass tinkles onto the linoleum floor. A shower of sparkles and glow. Grace has backed away to stand next to Jude now.

'You ... you ...' Ms Peters is sure looking at me now, tangled hair slicked unusually flat against her brow. She turns around wildly, hand still gripping Evelyn's wrist and displaying the miniature, minuscule, barely there scrape on Miss Perfect's palm. 'All of you! To the principal's office. Now!'

Grace shoots daggers at me. More like machine gun bullets. So does Evelyn, except hers are little atomic bombs. She's almost as red as the teacher.

I gulp.

Jude just stands there. 'But I didn't *do* anything.'

'*All* of you,' screams Ms Peters. She reaches for my elbow, dragging me in a much rougher way than she's dragging Evelyn. And that's when I see it, right there on Miss Perfect's pretty face. A curling of her lips, a twitch of her mouth, half-hidden by her wave of long sweeping hair.

Evelyn is smirking at me.

And I think about the desk, the way it jerked so suddenly to the side.

My stomach swells and rises.

I chuck up. Banana and vegemite mixing with the pretty flowers printed across Ms Peters's blouse.

2

AN APPLE A DAY KEEPS THE ...

I flop onto the threadbare couch, bag to the floor in a heavy thump.

Jerry looks up from his computer, glancing at me over the top of his glasses. He frowns. Excessively, if you ask me. Considering it was only a teeny tiny cut.

'Back again, are we, Charlotte?'

The man is bald on top and it's very distracting. So shiny. So round. Reminds me of one of those gobstopper lollies. The ones that never budge, never change, no matter how hard you try to wear them down. Like my stepmum, now that I think about it. I wrinkle my nose.

On the upside, Jerry definitely is a good listener. I'll give him that.

'You know you can call me Lottie,' I tell him generously. 'Don't be shy, Jerry.' I slouch further on the couch into a classic patient pose, head on the arm rest, feet hanging over the far side, ratty sneakers bobbing in midair. It's a little small if I'm honest but still quite comfortable.

Jerry grimaces. 'Charlotte, please sit straight. And it's Mr Virk to you. Is that clear?'

I nod absently. 'Sure. No worries.' I don't move.

He's clicking away on his mouse with at least three green apples spread across his desk, which is pretty strange. I wonder if I should have brought him an apple. Would it cool his anger? Is that what the other students are doing these days?

I watch from the corner of my eye as he sighs loudly and does ... whatever it is that principals do on their computers. Peek at student files? Browse the internet? View the school's CCTV? Does our school *have* CCTV? Interesting. I'm about to ask about it when Jerry rubs a hand across his face and says, 'So, you entered the labs without a teacher—'

'No,' I protest. 'Evelyn was there.'

'Evelyn Tait isn't a teacher, Charlotte.'

'Yeah, but she will be one day. I mean, look at her. She's made for it. Ordering everyone around all day, all bossy and filled with knowledge. Gross.'

He blinks. 'You know that *I'm* a teacher, don't you, Charlotte?'

I'm shocked, swinging my legs off the couch to sit straight. 'You're a *principal*, Jerry. It's completely different. A king among teachers.' I pause, thinking. 'Or at least like a prime minister. I guess the *actual* prime minister would be the king in this scenario—'

'Charlotte. *Charlotte*. Can we focus, please?' He sighs and his bald shiny head catches the light. 'I need you to take this seriously.'

'Sure, Jerry. Anything for you.'

He puffs his cheeks out as he rests his chin on his hands, peering at me over his shimmering glasses. The morning light drenches his desk in gold. We stay like that for a few moments, and he moves one of his green apples across his desk and then immediately moves it back again. He sighs. 'It's not even nine am yet.'

He didn't used to sigh this much. He used to yell at me a lot instead. Until I single-handedly wore down the material of his couch into a perfect Lottie-sized shape. Wore him down, too, I suppose. These days we don't bother with the theatrics, we just enjoy some nice conversations together. Sometimes he even lets me sit here quietly while he clicks away on his computer watching the school's CCTV. Or whatever it is he does. Probably footage of the teacher's lounge. Those teachers are out of control.

'Why are you smirking, Charlotte? Do you really have no understanding of how serious this situation is? A student was *injured*.'

I slouch a bit more. 'It was a teeny tiny cut. It was nothing.'

'You can't cut people, Charlotte.'

'I didn't!' I protest. 'Evelyn was just in the way of an accident. A total accident.'

'It was an accident that you climbed on a desk and pushed over the lab shelf?'

'Yeah.' Now he gets it. 'A total accident. I don't know what Ms Peters told you, but it wasn't my fault.'

Jerry rests back in his chair, hands behind his head, assessing me. He's quiet for a long time. Which feels like a bad thing. I realise I'm holding my breath.

Finally, I can't stand it any longer. 'What are you thinking about?'

'Suspension. Five days.'

'No!'

'Yes. And I'm calling your dad.'

'No!' Disaster. My dad will kill me. Or he'll kill me with kindness, even worse. 'Please, Jerry, I'll be good. I swear. Don't call my dad! Don't suspend me.'

He does the huffing, puffing, sighing thing again. 'Why don't I believe you? Why? I give you a warning, you're back on my couch. I give you extra homework, you're back on my couch. I give you detention, where are you?'

It takes me a beat to realise he's waiting. 'Oh! Well, I guess I'm back on your couch.'

'That's right, Charlotte. You're back on my couch. No matter what I say or do, you always end up back here and the cycle begins again.' He's getting worked up now, the skin on his head growing shinier by the moment. Blood flow rising, I guess.

'So this time it's suspension.' He holds up a hand to stop my protests. 'No. No! And next time it'll be expulsion. Do you understand me?'

I hesitate. 'Yes, Jerry.'

'Good. You've got two years left in this school. Make them worth something. You detest Evelyn Tait so much but maybe you should try *emulating* her instead. The world outside these gates isn't kind and people like Evelyn do well and people like you ... well, sometimes they just get chewed up and spat out. Unless you make a change, I truly think you'll regret it.'

I gape at him. Chew me up? Spit me out?

'You have to take responsibility for your actions, Charlotte. You're not a child.'

'I'm sixteen,' I point out, trying my luck. 'That's kind of like being a child.'

He waves his hands around, like he's shooing invisible bugs. 'No, that's kind of like being an *adult*.'

It's my turn to sigh now. 'I do try, Jerry. It's just that I find it difficult sometimes to know where the line is, you know? Like I just can't help myself. I have to go where the situation leads me. It's not my fault.'

He does a double take. 'Yes. It is.' He frowns. 'That's absolutely your fault. If you do the thing, then it's your fault that you did it. That's how this works.'

'Oh.'

I swear he rolls his eyes. 'Suspension. Five days.'

'One day.'

'Four days.'

'One day.'

He sighs. 'Three days. That's it. It's done.'

I beam. 'Okay, Jerry. Deal.'

'It's not a deal, Charlotte! This isn't a negotiation ... Oh, never mind. Sit there and be quiet while you wait for your dad. Not a sound out of you.'

And there it is. The point he gives up.

I sink back on the couch. Three days off school. Not so bad, I suppose. The lecture from my dad will be less nice, but I suppose I should take old Jerry's advice and be responsible for my own actions. So I'll listen to my dad and be good or whatever, and in three days I'll be back at school and stuff will go back to how it's always been.

Excellent.

Sort of.

I think back to the vomit smeared across Ms Peters's blouse, to Evelyn's smirk and Grace's sword eyes.

Not excellent exactly. But fixable, I reckon.

Hopefully.

Jerry gets off the phone to his secretary, asking her to call my dad probably. I wasn't listening. Then he reaches for his mouse and there's this fantastic moment when he grabs a shiny green apple instead, trying to click it with no effect. A hilariously shocked expression blooms on his face and then he scowls at the apple in his hand before glaring at me like this is also somehow my fault.

I don't say anything, just smirk quietly to myself, which of course makes him sigh. Again. I lean back and get comfortable while we wait for my dad, legs folded beneath me and stupid school uniform unbuttoned to reveal my much more comfortable t-shirt beneath.

'Feet off the couch, Charlotte.'

I comply, but only because he gave me three days instead of five. But then my t-shirt catches his attention.

'What's that?'

I glance down. 'It's a t-shirt, Jerry.'

'But what is it?'

'A face. Obviously.'

'A face? It looks like a murder victim.' He doesn't sound pleased.

'Well, that's true. It's a band shirt, see, and they have this song about—'

'You can't wear that to school, Charlotte. How many times do I have to tell you? Take it off.'

My eyes bulge. 'Here?'

'No, of course not here.' He puffs out his cheeks again. 'Just wear your school uniform properly, please. Do the buttons back up, will you.'

'Yes, Jerry.'

'You can't wear those band shirts. It's against school rules.'

That irritates me. 'I'm expressing myself.'

'Maybe so, but that shirt is offensive. It's too negative.'

'It's not negative.' I frown. 'It's a band I love. It's really positive. You let Evelyn wear that orchestra t-shirt last year.'

'That's because she competed in the youth orchestra, Charlotte. And it didn't have a corpse on it.'

'That's discrimination. It's favouritism, Jerry. I'm disappointed in you. I didn't think you operated like that.'

The door creaks open and Jerry's secretary pops her head in, interrupting us. 'Charlotte's dad is here, Mr Virk. Is Charlotte ready?'

Jerry waves his hand desperately. 'Yes, thank you, Geraldine. Please. Take her away. Hurry.'

Frowning I stand and heave my bag onto my shoulders. 'Think about it,' I tell him. 'Imagine if I told you that something you loved was too negative. Maybe I should send you some music, you might find you enjoy it. Would you like that?'

'No, thank you, Charlotte. I'm quite all right as I am.'

I shrug. 'If you're sure.' I hesitate, swaying on my feet. 'Well, I'll see you in three days I guess, Jerry.'

'Sure. Three days, Charlotte. Great. Wonderful.'

I don't think he means it.

3

SIX TIPS ON COUNSELLING (FROM A COUNSELLOR)

It's hot. Like, skin stuck to the car seat kind of hot.

That scenario is my dad's fault, of course. He insists on driving around in this shiny old 1960s model, painted powder blue with wings like fins at the back of the car. We cruise home from school and I basically have my entire head stuck out the window because the stupid car was made pre air-conditioning and I'm slowly dying. My hair slicks to my forehead, sweat trickling down my back until my t-shirt is sticking to my skin. I've already ditched my school uniform blouse. Kicked my sneakers off too and put my feet on the dash.

Dad is having none of it. He had to cancel appointments because of me, a fact that he's quick to let me know. Over and over as we drive home. I don't listen too closely, just sit with my hair streaming in the wind, watching the world go by.

My school isn't far from home, so it only takes about ten minutes for us to wing through the suburbs, cruising along the seafront, heat and salt heavy in the air and the ocean glimmering deep aqua blue on the horizon. Beautiful. I wiggle my toes on the dash and block my dad's voice out.

A summer afternoon free of classes?

Not so bad.

The car slides onto a wide bridge, long and smooth, stretching over the sparkling river, a factory settled like a nightmare at the water's edge. I stick my fingers out the window into the sun, hand moving like a sail through the rushing wind as the factory passes by, all red bricks and open gaping windows, glass shattered like wolves' teeth in deep dark mouths.

Dad's still talking at me but I steadfastly ignore him as he turns the car into the back streets towards home. The lanes here change to old chipped cobblestone, lined with the jagged stone walls of old warehouses. The buildings are huge and European and peeling paint.

Dad loves that stuff. Cars with no air-conditioners. Buildings with big useless spaces. Anything old and idiotic. It's his thing.

And I guess our neighbourhood is his thing too, the Port, a little suburb built forever ago, curled around the river. He loves it even though the streets are sometimes spray-painted with swastikas, and the shadowy pubs are filled with old blokes, fleshy cracks visible over their bar stools.

Still, it's the kind of place that creeps beneath your skin.

We turn the corner near our street, full of empty dilapidated warehouses next to newly built flash apartments, and curl along the cobblestones towards home.

I glance across at Dad. He's still talking, hammering on and on about me and my future and my stupid choices, and all the appointments he's missing. I breathe deep, salt and heat. I'd never admit it to him, but maybe I love this place as much as he does, because if you live here long enough you become part of the fabric of it. The big barred basements and old decaying sailing ships. The seagulls wheeling over the river and sunsets that soak the whole world in orange. You can feel the stories crackling beneath the pavement, beneath your feet as you walk over the cobblestones.

This place has history.

It's perfect.

Or at least it was until my stepmum moved in with us.

And there she is, stomping from the stairwell of our flat in all her glory, hair frizzing and chest heaving. My smelly barely born brother is nestled tight against her chest and I'm pretty sure her blouse has more sick on it than Ms Peters's.

Dad slides from the sticky car and smiles at them through the beating sun. 'How's Leo?' He's left the car parked on the sidewalk, which means he's planning on heading back to work.

My stepmum squints in the bright light of the great outdoors, moving from the dark stairwell through the overgrown communal backyard, a Hills hoist creaking in the hot wind. Since Leo came she's been stuck inside with him twenty-four seven. It almost makes me feel sorry for her.

Almost.

'Leo's fine,' she answers with a tight smile, gaze flicking across to me. 'But, Donal, what happened?'

Dad doesn't get the chance to tell her what happened, because the shared garage door rolls up as a car drives round the corner, halting beside us. The man in the front winds his window down, scowling at me and then stiffly greeting Dad, totally ignoring my stepmum. 'How's it going, Donal?'

Dad smiles. 'Good, good. You, Ed?'

Eddie Carillo glares at me again and I wither away on the sidewalk. Even more so when I peer through the glass into the backseat and notice Jude perched inside the air-conditioned car, freckly frown very pointedly not facing me.

Eddie clears his throat loudly. 'My son got sent home from school because of your daughter.' He says this in an extremely provoking way. 'You need to keep that girl away from him.'

'Now, now,' Dad holds his hands out like he's trying to calm a bear. All fluttery and useless. 'I'm sure Lottie didn't—'

'I don't care how often he makes moon eyes at her through the window, you hear me? You keep her away from him.'

I blink. Peering through the glass I wrinkle my nose at Jude, who is desperately poking at the back of his dad's car seat. 'Daaaaaad,' he whines.

Moon eyes?

Dad's still trying to calm the situation, saying stuff like, 'Can't we talk about this like adults, Ed?' in his best counsellor voice, but Ed's already rolled his window back up and his car is creeping onwards into the dark gaping garage. Soon the roller door has come down again, leaving us outside in the baking heat, the heavy sun on my black t-shirt about to give me a stroke.

Dad glares at me. My stepmum glares at me. Even little smelly Leo sort of glares at me. Dad ushers Celeste into the stairwell we share with the new flash apartment complex next door and fills her in on my glorious morning in the school lab. I wince as the truth is lost in translation. The teeny tiny cut on Evelyn's hand morphs into something huge and gaping.

'That's not exactly how it happened,' I mutter, but they're both lost in their own world. I trail behind them into the flat. We've lived here forever, one of those warehouses that's all open spaces and no privacy, a complex built above an Afghan restaurant that always smells of spice and tabouleh. When my parents bought it way back when, no one wanted to live in the Port at all, so it was a cheap crumbling hovel until Dad fixed it up. It's only recently people act like my family's rich when I tell them where we live. Like everything else in the Port, it's complicated. Like two sides of a coin.

Kicking off my thongs at the door I follow the family into our kitchen, glaring at my dad. He's not telling the story right. And of course my stepmum is gasping, clutching little stinky Leo closer as if I might try to gouge his hand with lab equipment too. I roll my eyes.

'What about Evelyn?' The stepmum's voice is dripping sugary concern. 'Where is she?'

'Still at school. They patched her up, Celeste. She's fine.' Dad leans over and kisses her cheek.

Puke.

He whispers something against her skin, all sweet and soft, like I'm not here, except then he turns to me, frowning. 'And you, kiddo, you're with me. In the study, now.'

I nod miserably, dragging my feet to the 'study', which is actually just a corner of our flat near the glass doors to the balcony, which has no privacy whatsoever. Stupid open plan living. Dad leans his bum on his huge dark wood desk and motions for me to sit in the stupid velvet armchair opposite. Celeste is close by, clinking away in the background doing whatever it is she does here all day. I clasp my hands in my lap and sit primly, waiting.

'I'm going to give you some wisdom, kiddo, and you can listen or you can ignore me. It's up to you.' He smiles his counsellor smile, the one he uses on the teens who come through his office.

Our cat winds her way around my ankles. Black soft fur and sharp claws. Very sharp.

'Ow!'

'Come on, Lottie, just try and pay attention for once.'

I'm wounded in more ways than one, and I glare at D'Angelo as she saunters off and then glare at Dad as he smooths his expression back into his calm counsellor face. He shifts his bum on the desk, ruffling a bunch of papers and edging a crusty old coffee cup even closer to the corner of the desk.

'Lottie, what happened today, it's got to stop.'

Counselling 101: State the bloody obvious. See how they react.

I sigh, feeling defensive. I don't like when he tries to use his counselling powers on me. 'I know that, Dad.'

He raises his eyebrows. 'Do you?'

'Yes.'

'So, let's go over this again. Was your experience today good or bad?'

'Bad,' I mutter.

'Okay. Why was it bad?'

Counselling 101: Ask the bloody obvious.

I roll my eyes. 'Obviously because I got suspended. Because I'm sitting here talking to you, which is just ... awful. And because ...'

I hesitate.

He leans closer. 'Because ...?'

Counselling 101: Cut to the very heart of the problem.

My voice is barely a whisper. 'Maybe Grace isn't talking to me anymore.' The look she gave me at school before I left was pure poison, and she hasn't answered any of my messages since.

My dad scrunches his face, sour as a lemon. 'Well, I admit I was hoping you'd say it was because Evelyn actually got hurt this time, Lottie, but okay, let's go with this instead. Why do you think Grace might not want to talk to you anymore? And how does that make you feel?'

Ugh.

'It doesn't make me feel anything. Can we just drop it?'

'No, we can't just drop it. Tell me how you *feel*.'

'Like shit, Dad.'

'Don't swear.'

'You *asked* me.'

'Why do you always have to make things so difficult?'

Counselling 101: Drop the counselling approach and just become a regular angry dad again.

I don't say anything, just clamp my mouth shut as he leans close and lowers his voice. 'Look, there's a line, Lottie, and you are the only person I know who consistently crosses it. Maybe you secretly enjoy being in trouble, I don't know. Maybe it's a cry for attention.' He glances across our open living area towards the stepmum, who's rolling around with Leo on a mat with a bunch of lego. He's way too young for lego. I could've told her that. Babies love to swallow weird stuff. It's their favourite thing.

Dad clears his throat and my attention flicks back to his face. 'I know things haven't been easy for you, Lottie. There's been some big changes around here over the last year, I get that, but you've got to at least try. If you can't stop yourself from crossing the line, at least try to be a bit more careful about it, okay?'

I blink at him. 'Are you saying not to get caught, Dad?'

He blusters. 'No. No, of course not.'

'Celeste! Celeste,' I yell over my shoulder. Both my stepmum and Leo stop rolling around, heads perked up. 'Celeste! Dad says if I want to break the rules I shouldn't let myself get caught. Then it's okay. Do you agree with that philosophy?'

I turn back to Dad, who is attempting to shush me. 'I don't think she agrees with your view on things, Dad. Maybe you should've discussed your values and fundamental differences before you married her. I mean, you guys are virtually strangers.'

Dad is pissed now. I'm good at that. It's a skill I have.

'This isn't about Celeste. This conversation is between you and me. *I'm* your father.'

'Right. And she's *not* my mum.' I cross my arms over my chest, not making eye contact. 'And she never will be.' D'Angelo is sniffing at the closed fridge in the kitchen now, looking suspicious.

'No one's asking her to be,' Dad hisses, leaning forward so Celeste can't hear. I bet he's wishing his study had a door right about now. 'Just be civil, Lottie. That's all I'm asking.'

'Civil?' I huff. 'Like how you gave me two minutes notice that an entirely new family was moving into *our* house? Was that civil?'

Dad takes deep breaths, and suddenly his counselling expression, kind and understanding with a hint of fun, is plastered sickeningly across his face. 'That's not what we're talking about right now, Lottie. This conversation is about you and what you did at school today. Okay?'

'Yeah. Sure. Whatever.'

'Did you wear that t-shirt to school?'

I glance at my band shirt. The bloody face stares right back at me. I blink. 'Yeah. So?'

His eyes flutter closed. 'But under your uniform, right? Where no one can see it. We've talked about this.'

I nod enthusiastically. 'Yeah, of course. Under my uniform. No one saw it.'

'Good.'

'Except old Jerry, of course.'

'Old ... who? The principal? Mr Virk? Lottie!'

I shrug. 'It's not a big deal. It's just a t-shirt. Besides, you're the one who said I should find something I'm passionate about and pursue it. So I did.'

'I didn't mean this.'

I frown. He hates my music, and last week I overheard him assuring the stepmum that it's just a phase, something I'll grow out of. Except I don't want to grow out of the things I like. Or the way I am.

It seems unfair that everyone expects me to.

'What about Leo?' Dad continues. 'He's growing up in this house too. There's too much death and noise.'

I flinch, wounded. 'Noise?'

I hate when people say that. Dad's never said it before. He must have heard it from Celeste. 'I suppose Evelyn would never listen to noise,' I mutter.

He pauses, running his hands through what remains of his greying hair. Another sigh.

Counselling 101: Don't let the patient dictate the conversation.

Dad changes tack. 'Lottie, where do you want to be in five years?'

I shrug. 'I'm only sixteen. I don't know.'

'Evelyn knows.'

I roll my eyes so hard I swear they turn back in my skull. Roll them so hard I'm looking back at the kitchen again. D'Angelo is still acting suspicious at the base of the fridge, turning in circles, big fluffy tail raised to the roof. I don't say anything, even though I can see what's happening.

'Lottie. *Lottie!*' Dad actually snaps his fingers at me. Like I'm a dog.

I glare at him.

'Evelyn already knows exactly what she's going to study at university,' he says. 'And you, you haven't spared a single thought for the future.'

My blood boils and I bite my lip. Hard. 'Evelyn's a complete *moron*, Dad. No one likes her at school!' Not strictly true, of course. But thinking of Grace and that goofy smile aimed directly at my mortal enemy makes me want to puke. Again. 'She's awful.'

'Charlotte!' The stepmum is on her feet, mouth tight. Leo is gumming at her bare foot, baby drool spreading across her skin. Disgusting.

'It's okay, hon,' my dad calls, using his calming counsellor voice. 'I've got this.' He smiles at Celeste and then leans in close and grasps my arm, hissing, 'I've had enough of this. All you do is sow discord and say smart things. You have such a bad opinion of Evelyn, but she's handling everything with maturity and integrity. Perhaps you should try to emulate her instead of being so defensive all the time.'

And there's that word again.

Emulate.

I wrench free of his arm, blood boiling, teeth grinding, fury bursting. I smile sweetly. 'The cat is pissing on the floor.'

'What? No, no, no!' Dad leaps across the room in a flash,

paper towels and spray bottle in hand. Celeste is there too, Leo wrapped in her arms as she directs Dad in the bestest, most correct way for him to clean the cat pee.

I sit quietly on the awful velvet counselling chair, seething. D'Angelo trots by and I watch her go. I'm more pissed off than I can remember being in ages.

He wants me to be more like Evelyn? Is he serious?

Counselling 101: Never, ever, ever compare your patient to their worst enemy.

Ever.

I get up and stalk to my room, slamming the door behind me so hard the walls shake. I throw myself onto my little single bed, not upgraded since I was ten, and the iron bedhead rattles against the windowsill, metal on wood, old paint chipping.

Be more like Evelyn.

I bet they'd all like that.

Grace.

My dad.

Celeste.

I roll over and violently kick my blankets so they fly to the floor. I'm filled with fury, my blood singing with it. Pissed. I flick my music on, a flurry of frantic guitar notes and tight staccato drum beats exploding across the room, a thick screaming voice, heavy and low. It fills me up. Fills every empty space with sound and rhythm and music. Dad pounds on the door and tells me to turn it down.

I ignore him.

I ignore Celeste when she knocks on the door too. And I stay curled on my bed as the afternoon wears on, sending more *sorry* messages to Grace who doesn't reply, until finally the door creaks open and standing in the entrance is my absolute worst nightmare.

Perfect hair, perfect teeth, perfect brain.

Perfect sneer.

She snaps off my music and the room swells with silence, my ears ringing. She's so proper, her school uniform buttoned tight and neat, her skirt reaching just below her knees, while the rest of us roll ours up to make them shorter. She's perfect in every way. And much prettier than me with her pointed dainty features and rosebud mouth.

'Hey, shithead,' Evelyn says as she throws her bag onto the floor below her desk, flopping onto the other single bed across from mine. The springs creak mercilessly. 'Great job today.' She holds up her hand and shows me the teeny tiny band aid stuck to her palm.

'Stay away from Grace,' I warn but my stepsister just laughs, shaking her head as she kicks off her shoes.

She's such a faker. She's got everyone fooled.

My dad. Our teachers.

Even Grace.

Be more like Evelyn, Dad says.

Sure, they'd all like that.

Every single one of them.

I stop. Pause. And slowly my mouth tugs into a grin.

Except Evelyn.

4

BEST-LAID PLANS OVER NOODLES

It's torture. Complete and utter. Stuck at home with the step-mum and Leo, whose one role in life is apparently to cry. Loudly. All the time.

Evelyn wakes early and is gone before I manage to turn the snooze off my alarm. Dad praises her 'dedication' and 'commitment' outside our room. It pisses me off no end because she's managed to hide all my shoes while I was sleeping. Seriously, *all* of them. No one ever notices *that* side of Evelyn.

And besides, I dedicate myself to stuff. I'm committed.

It's just some things are considered more impressive to be committed to. For instance, Evelyn wanted to learn the flute and be part of an orchestra. Everyone tripped over themselves to pay for her lessons, to buy her an instrument, to drive her to practice. But when I wanted to take guitar lessons from this great place in the city that teaches actual metal music, everyone decided it was a big joke. I got boring classical lessons at school and the use of the stupid sticky school guitar.

The things I care about don't seem to fit into our stupid new blended family. And after a whole year spent in the shadow of my evil stepsister, I'm about ready to make a change.

I leave our tiny shared room yawning, wearing the hugest, coolest metal t-shirt I can find. It hangs to my knees like an enormous nightie. I love it.

Celeste less so.

She wishes me good morning with a strained smile, her gaze wandering over the shirt design and back to my black hair and smudged makeup. It's a judgey look and immediately makes me defensive. I don't answer her morning greetings, instead shuffling to the fridge to pull out milk for cereal. I clatter around and watch Celeste carefully from beneath my lashes.

When she first moved in she was working in an office in the city part-time. Before Leo. Doing admin or whatever. I think people who work in offices are so bored their brains turn to mush, and that's why they spend their time gossiping about other people who work in offices or getting overly excited about really stupid things.

It reminds me of high school.

And I honestly cannot think of anything worse than graduating high school to move on to another organisation that's the same as high school.

Kill me now.

I glance at her as I scoff my breakfast, leaving my dirty bowl stacked in the sink. Back when she was still making an effort not to hate me, Celeste would spend like forty minutes every day telling me what happened to her at work. Like, once there was a full on medieval-style political coup where half the office were trying to edge out their manager and the other half were all whispering about it quietly behind their desks. Another time two people wore the *Exact. Same. Tie.* Like the *exact same* shade of blue or whatever. There was a riot.

Actually that last one was a joke I saw on the internet, but it's basically the same thing. That's what she used to subject me to, every single time she came home from work. Boring stories.

It was a living hell.

I wrinkle my nose as I finish clinking around in the kitchen sink, before mumbling something about going out to get some sunshine.

Celeste stiffens. She's on the floor now with Leo. 'But you're grounded, Lottie.'

I stop. 'No, I'm not. Dad never said.'

'You are. I told Donal to ... Never mind. You are. I'm telling you now.' She wobbles to her feet, brushing the frizz from her face, attempting to appear fierce and parental.

I frown, irritation flaring bright and hot, except then I calm myself, a slow grin spreading across my face. 'Sure, Celeste. No worries. Grounded. I'll just hang out in my room then.'

The stepmum seems stumped, which almost makes me laugh. She thought we'd be fighting all day.

Well, I have better things to do.

'Lottie ... did you ... do you want to maybe come with me to the grocery store this afternoon?' Her tone is hopeful. 'We could get a coffee together with Leo.' Tentative.

'I'm pretty sure Leo is too young to drink coffee.' I'm considering it though.

She smiles. 'It'll be better than sitting in that stuffy room all day. Just don't wear that t-shirt, okay? Everyone will think I'm a bad mother.'

Immediately I shut down, glaring at her as I tug my stretched shirt. 'You're not my mother.' I grit my teeth. 'I'll stay here. I've got stuff to do.'

With that I turn and march back into my room, slamming the door. In the mirror on Evelyn's side of the room I gaze at my shirt, swaying this way and that to get a better look. I got the t-shirt at an op shop, a real find. The band is from Norway and they've never toured here so it was the best luck. It was like a gift, especially for me, hidden behind this weird fur neck ruff at the back of the rack.

I found it the same day my mum left for Sydney.

The shirt isn't even offensive. Just black. Like wearing a black t-shirt is going to change me. Everyone should be more concerned with what kind of person I am and less with how I look. Isn't that what Dad always says during his father-daughter counselling sessions? He says it's all about who you are inside, yet he still gives me crap about my dyed hair and band shirts.

It almost gives me second thoughts about my plan.

Like I'd be giving my stupid blended family exactly what they want.

Two Evelyn Taits.

But honestly, the chance to mess with my stepsister is too good to pass up. Also, I do find my shoes. Eventually. She's shoved them inside the washing machine. Turned on the water and everything, soapy liquid floating like rainbows over grey.

I slam the lid and walk away huffing.

When Celeste is finally ready to leave the flat I'm crouched on the thin balcony mucking around with my tomato plants, the afternoon sun blazing and my t-shirt blowing in the wind like a black sail. My plants have seeded out of tomato tins, a funny irony to me, and are growing well, lush leaves furry and green. They smell fresh, too.

I glance at the flat next door. At the glass window. It's not facing our balcony exactly, more side by side, but I guess someone could see through if they really wanted to. If they angled themselves just right.

Moon eyes.

I frown and turn back to our flat as Celeste mumbles something to me through the screen, probably reminding me I'm grounded. I ignore her as the main door slams and then watch from above as she comes out with the stroller and walks off slowly along the cracked pavement, beating sun streaming between the tall old buildings.

The second she's gone I have one leg hitched over the balcony, bare toes reaching for the wrought iron of the next balcony over, hovering over the deep gap between. There's a word for that kind of gap but I can't remember what it is. Something I read on the net. For the space in-between things.

I catch hold of the railing and fling my body over the barrier, narrowly avoiding death and landing in a low crouch on the porch. And then I'm bobbing up and down at the window near the closed glass doors, trying to peer inside without being seen.

The glass doors slide open.

Jude stands there, freckles bright in the afternoon sun. 'You coming in?'

I assess him carefully for moon eyes but find none. Clearly his dad is confused. I'm not sure how that makes me feel, but my belly is churning in a way that reminds me of Ms Peters's floral shirt. Jude opens his mouth but I quickly wave my hand in front of his face. 'Shhhh, your dad might hear.'

Jude just stares at me. 'He's at work.'

'Your mum then.'

'She's in Italy.'

'Oh. Okay.' He already told me that but I forgot. I stand. 'Okay, let's go inside. Can you feed me?'

Jude rolls his eyes but steps back from the sliding door to let me into the house, air-conditioning wafting out, delicious and cool. I reach up to poke his cheek as I squeeze by and he bats my hand away as he says, 'I think we have some noodles left. Maybe. If you haven't eaten them all already.'

I sniff. 'I really don't know what you're talking about, Jude.' I step inside his flat, which has a similar layout to ours. As in absolutely no layout, just a huge open space. All this cool art is laid out on the walls. I don't bother inspecting it because I've seen it all before. Blueprints for this and that. Buildings. Vehicles. Spaceships? Weird stuff that Jude's mum is into.

The flat is dark and cool and I flop onto the couch. It's big and bouncy with cracked pale leather. Something upset and cold itches at the back of my mind as Jude steps behind the kitchen bench to rustle inside a cupboard. It takes a moment for me to figure out what's wrong.

Oh.

'Jude? Sorry I got you suspended.' I glance at him but he's already making the two-minute noodles. 'Seriously. I didn't mean to. It just sort of happened.'

'S'okay.'

I frown. 'It's not that great though. Like I said. Sorry.'

His head perks up over the kitchen counter, his eyes glowing. Bright blue. Like an alien. 'Was your dad mad?'

I drag my legs onto the couch, wrap my arms around my bare knees. 'Yeah. This is the first time old Jerry ever suspended me.'

His head disappears and clattering starts from behind the

counter again. 'How is that even possible? You've done so much crazy stuff at school.'

'Um, no. I haven't done any crazy stuff, ever. I'm offended that you think I have.'

He pops up again, this time with two bowls. Crazy blue eyes shining in the dark. He raises his brows. 'Liar.' He pours hot water from the kettle onto the noodles and closes the container lid. 'You vandalised Evelyn's locker.'

'No, I didn't.'

'You definitely did.'

I sigh. 'Okay, but that was ages ago.'

'It was four days ago.'

I blink. 'Well, I only did it because Evelyn threw my homework in the river and I had to get her back.'

'As if you'd done your homework anyway.'

I gasp. 'Maybe I *had* done it! You don't know.'

I huff and puff, offended, until finally Jude hands me a steaming bowl of noodles and I peer into their glistening mass. He throws himself onto the couch beside me, folding his long legs. We eat in silence for a few moments until he asks, 'Well, had you?'

My mouth is full. 'Had I what?

He shrugs. 'Done your homework.'

I glare at him and clunk my bowl on the coffee table. 'That's not the point, Jude. The point is Evelyn never got into trouble. Only I did.'

Jude stuffs noodles into his mouth. 'Well, that's her secret power, isn't it? She never gets caught.'

'It's ridiculous,' I mutter, reaching for my bowl again. I take a massive bite, noodles spilling down my chin. I slurp some more and then mumble through my mouthful, 'It was even worse yesterday. Did you know Sebastian was out there? He saw the whole thing.'

Jude grimaces, sinking low on the couch. He's finished his noodles and the bowl sits empty on the coffee table. He crosses his arms over his chest. 'So?'

I glare at him. 'So, Sebastian is too pretty to witness me doing crazy things. He's going to think *I'm* crazy now.'

'So you do admit what you did was crazy then?' This close Jude's eyes are less glowy, but still crazy blue, freckles crowding every inch of his skin right onto his eyelids. And right now his whole face is annoying me.

Even though I did get him suspended.

I wave my hand. 'Whatever. Look, I'm in a strange conundrum, okay? And I can't think of anyone else who can help me.'

'You mean you *have* a strange conundrum.'

'What?'

'You *have* one, you're not *in* one.'

I glare at him. 'I really don't care if I have it or I'm in it or if it's poured on top of my head. That's not the point of this unexpected visit.'

He smiles. 'Right. Go on.'

'The point is, I need your help. For an experiment.'

He brightens up. 'An experiment?'

'Yeah.' I place my bowl down again, empty now, and shift closer to Jude, lowering my voice. 'I've decided I'm going to beat Evelyn at her own game. I'm going to act like her and totally win everyone back. Grace and Sebastian. And I'm going to fool my dad and Celeste. And school too.'

Jude's face turns blank. 'Sebastian? Why?'

'What do you mean, why? Because Evelyn's been stealing my friends, and Dad thinks she's better than me. And frankly, because it will piss her off. She put all my shoes in the washing machine this morning, Jude. If I can do Evelyn better than Evelyn can do Evelyn ... Well.' I spread my hands and shrug, grinning happily.

Jude doesn't seem to share my enthusiasm. 'But that's stupid. Besides, Evelyn's my lab partner.'

'I'm not suggesting we kill her and dump her! I'm asking you to help me be good. What's the harm in that?'

He blinks. 'Kill her and dump her?'

I sigh. 'Are you even listening to me? Not that. The other thing.'

'You want to be good?'

I click my fingers at him. 'Yes! That's what I'm saying. How do I do that?'

He says nothing, just stares at me until it's almost uncomfortable, blue eyes shining and shimmering. Finally he mumbles a quiet, 'But why me?'

I huff, exasperated. 'Because you're *smart*, obviously.' I give him my most winning smile, trying to get him onside, our faces close.

He blinks. Says nothing.

I sigh. 'Honestly, I just need some direction. Because I'm not great at it. Being good, I mean. And if you could help me I'd be most grateful.'

Jude smiles, slow and smirky, and I get the distinct impression he's teasing me when he says, 'Yeah, the past can hurt, but the way I see it you can either run from it, or learn from it.'

It's my turn to stare. 'Umm ... okay.'

Weirdo.

Except ...

Except.

The more I think about it the more I realise he's right. So freaking right. I've just been fighting my stepmum and Evelyn all this time. My dad too. I haven't been *doing* anything. I haven't been learning or adapting to get on top of the situation. I've been an idiot!

I look Jude up and down. 'Wow, see? I knew you were smart.' I glance back through the glass sliding doors towards the balcony outside. 'Hey, what are those spaces called? You know, the gaps between things? There must be a name right? I'm sure I heard it somewhere.'

He's confused. 'Interstice?'

I'm in awe of him, repeating it slowly, letting the word roll off my tongue. 'In-ter-stice. Wow, thanks Jude.' I'm super impressed, and express it by slinging an arm around his neck and dragging him in close to ruffle his hair affectionately. His cheeks slowly turn pink beneath the freckles as he attempts to shove me off.

I ignore his struggles. In fact, recently I've discovered I adore embarrassing him. He's way too easy. I grin. 'There, see? So we're partners now?'

He untangles his body from mine and then removes my hand from his hair. 'Charlotte—'

'*Lottie.*'

'Right, Lottie.' He shakes his head. 'Is that your entire plan? You're gonna be good?'

I nod.

'That's stupid.'

I glare at him and he shrugs. 'You should just stop retaliating.'

I stop, stunned. 'So what you're saying is, I should stop trying to get Evelyn back ... and instead expose to everyone what she does to me! Then it'll be *her* getting in the shit with my dad for once.' I grin at him happily. 'You are so smart.'

He blinks. 'Well, that's not really what I ...'

I wave my hand. 'That's perfect. Seriously.' A grin spreads across my face. Some evil cackling is about to follow except Jude stands up.

'None of that is actually gonna work. You know that, right?' He picks up our empty bowls and takes them into the kitchen, stopping at the sink to run the water.

'Um, no. I don't know that.' I trail after him, standing in the kitchen to help dry up.

Jude shoves me lightly with his shoulder, biting his lip. 'If you really want this to work you have to do something big. Like beat Evelyn at something she actually cares about.'

My eyes widen. 'Like that dumb science scholarship.'

Jude snorts. 'Well, maybe something a bit more achievable. You're definitely flunking science, especially after yesterday.'

I don't bother to answer that. 'The dumb orchestra placement then.' I stop drying. Actually, the dumb orchestra placement is not so dumb at all. In fact, I've been thinking about it for a while anyway. The chance to get a scholarship for a two-week program in the city at the conservatorium, the chance to really learn classical guitar. Playing classical music is hard, and playing technical metal is hard, too, so a placement like that could only help me.

And even better? Evelyn and her awful flute went last year.

And the year before that. And everyone at school is certain they'll be sending her again this year.

I grin as I begin drying the bowl again. 'Genius,' I admit. 'It could work.'

Jude's cheeks flush a little as he finishes up. I'm silent as I trail behind him to his bedroom, thinking about how I can do this. I'd have to practise. Hard. But it's possible.

Jude pushes the door to his room open and heads to his desk like the nerd he is while I flop onto his bed, arms above my head, feet kicking. Everything in Jude's room is super clean and neat, with sunlit white sheets and dark blue walls, and shelves everywhere filled with carefully placed textbooks and planners. We couldn't be more different if we tried.

I roll over and then notice that I'm actually not wearing any shorts under my massive t-shirt. Which is not excellent. It does hang to my knees, but still. I sit up, folding my legs beneath me, bare skin now lost in swathes of black material.

I glance at Jude quickly, because sometimes I forget he's a boy. I forget to think about the things I should, because he's just Jude. The same as he's always been. Right now he's acting weird though. I frown. 'You alright?'

'Me? Oh yeah.' He blinks. 'Fine, fine.'

I pat the space beside me. 'How are we going to make this plan happen?'

He makes a face, but still joins me on the bed. 'It's not that hard. You just do it. You know, be nice. Don't screw up.'

My palms are sweaty already. 'Yeah, cool. Super easy.'

'Exactly.'

I don't think he's sensing my sarcasm. 'I'm just really easily …'

I trail off, attention snagged by this unbelievably strange object I've just spotted on one of his shelves.

'Easily distracted?' Jude grins, quick like lightning.

I ignore him, tottering on the side of the bed now, reaching high to grasp the *thing* off his shelf.

I collapse beside him. 'Um, Jude. What is this?' I wave the awful doll at him, horrified. The face is made of porcelain, the brows thin and spidery, the mouth a tiny painted rosebud. She's wearing old-school clothes, as if she lives in a Jane Austen drama. And her expression is really *really* mean. I turn to him with wide eyes. 'I think she's planning to kill you in your sleep.'

He groans, blush creeping up his throat as he flops back on the bed. 'Put it back.'

I nestle the doll on his chest instead. 'Where did you get that thing? It's terrifying.'

He flicks the doll off him. She ends up face down on his covers. 'My aunt bought it for me. It's a replica of, I dunno, some old English queen or something.' He shrugs helplessly. Which is awkward when he's lying down. 'My dad says I can't throw it out 'cos it was so expensive.'

I scoop the queen off the bed, sitting now with my kneecap shoved into Jude's rib cage. I look at her from every angle, biting my lip. 'You want to throw this away?' I rotate the doll slowly, gesturing like one of those television display women who sell cars. 'You're saying *you* didn't select this? This beautiful thing right here?' I turn the doll the other way, then plunge her towards Jude's face. '*This* doll? This one? This beautiful doll?'

Jude bats me away, mouth twitching. 'Stop it ... Lottie!'

That's when the knock sounds on his door. Loud and sharp. We both freeze.

'What are you doing in there, Jude?' His dad's voice. Booming and overly loud. 'I hope you're not watching anything weird, son. Grounded means no girls. On or off the screen.'

I shove my hand over my mouth to stop my burst of sudden laughter. Mainly directed at Jude's utterly horrified face.

'Daaaaad!'

'Well, can I come in?'

That wipes the smile off my face. Jude's dad already hates me. He doesn't need to find me on his son's bed. Jude seems to have the same idea because he's literally shoving me over the far side of mattress, hands all over me, freckly face blanched now.

'Just a minute, Dad!'

'Stop it,' I hiss. 'Jeez, you're such a scaredy-cat.' I'm not sure if there's a wire crossed in my brain, but I don't tend to get that worried in situations like this. Honestly, what's the worst his dad could do to me? Ground me?

Whatever.

Except Jude is obviously quite distressed so I decide to give him a break. 'Right, I'm out of here.' I tweak his nose, just 'cos I can, and then flash him a massive grin before jumping up and striding towards his window. It slides open easily, like it has a million times before. Open sesame. No flyscreen. All these old places are the same.

I slide through the open space and then duck low onto the balcony outside. Hot, hot, hot. The black painted metal of the railing burns my skin, sun beating heavily on my back. 'Ow, ow.' I scuttle around until my bare feet find a little shade.

From inside Jude's room voices ring out, him and his dad.

'What's with the doll, son? You into ugly girls now?' Booming laughter.

Jude: *mumble, mumble* ... something I can't hear.

They go on like that as I twist over to the railing and sling my leg over, reaching over the massive gap between our homes. The *interstice*. Hurriedly I climb back to where I'm meant to be. By the time I've reached my own balcony I am once again of the firm opinion that Jude's dad is a total dick.

Jude, on the other hand, is my saviour.

I grin as I slide open the glass doors and pad across our dark flat towards my bedroom and the sticky school guitar.

Step one in my new master plan to destroy Evelyn Tait?

Practice.

5

HOW TO SET YOUR WORLD DOMINATION PLAN INTO MOTION

As far back as I can remember Evelyn Tait and I have been trying to destroy each other. And when I say as far back as I remember, I mean since last year on the twenty-first of March when she and her mother both moved into my house. Or more accurately, last year on the twenty-second of March when I woke to find Evelyn had salted my tomato plants.

That was a fun morning.

My dad got a new wife and, seven months later, a fat baby boy. I got an evil stepsister who lives in my bedroom and hates my guts. And the most insidious thing about all of it?

No one believes me when I tell them what she's like.

Which is why it's so utterly gratifying to watch Evelyn's face right now from the corner of my eye. I'm standing in front of our science class, my hair brushed back neat into a long ponytail and my uniform buttoned tight and ironed flat. The ironing is courtesy of Jude, of course, because who honestly knows how to iron?

Anyway, warm feelings are blooming in my chest. Evelyn is gaping, and right now she doesn't seem so damn perfect at all, with her mouth wide open like a fish. It's kind of excellent. Grace is there too, of course, sitting right next to my literal worst enemy. And I'm enjoying her expression too, because Grace actually appears impressed. With me. Like she's remembering we're meant to be best friends. Double excellent. Ms Peters is clearly a little bemused, but she's still liking what's happening. I can tell.

Phase one of Jude's plan is working. I knew the boy was a genius.

I smile. Sweet as sugar. Sweeter. 'I wanted to apologise for my behaviour the other day, Ms Peters. To both you and Evelyn. I was out of line. I've been feeling so guilty the last few days and just had to apologise first thing this morning.' I make a sad face, my eyes wide and innocent, lips turned down and quivering. 'I'm so sorry, Ms Peters.'

I think I've done a pretty bang-up job of appearing contrite but I catch Jude's eye at the back of the class, and slowly he shakes his head.

Too much?

I cough. Tone it down. Hanging my head I mumble my final 'sorries' and then flee to my desk, right next to Grace's. I spend the whole class with my head down and my mouth shut, concentrating on being guilty or whatever. Ms Peters drones on and on with her lecture, but I notice how she smiles at me every now and then. Progress!

Grace clearly notices too. She leans close and hisses in my ear, 'Dude, what is going on?'

I frown. 'I'm trying to make amends. To you as well. I'm serious.' I lean over and pat her hand fondly, and Evelyn on her other side watches me suspiciously. I want to laugh because the whole thing is utterly glorious. Instead I keep my face nice and blank as I add, 'Things will be different from now on. I promise. I'm going to take things more seriously. No more getting in trouble.'

I smile and Grace's mouth slowly turns up at the edges, curling and pleased. 'Oh. Well, okay. I'm glad.' She hesitates. 'And ... what about me and Evelyn?'

This part is harder. I grit my teeth and my wide smile becomes strained. Out of all the freaking girls in this school my best friend had to choose my awful stepsister.

I take a deep breath and Evelyn leans forward, listening intently from across Grace, her eyes shining as she waits for me to make a mistake. If I do she'll go in for the kill. Like a wolf. Like a dingo. Like some other monstrous carnivorous animal who wants to murder me. Metaphorically, of course.

I nod carefully. 'I get it. Honestly. Or at least I'm trying to.' I take a deep breath, voice wavering. That's part of the act though. Jude reckons if I give in too easily or enthusiastically they'll both know I'm lying. A little bit of hesitation is needed to sell it. 'If Evelyn's someone you truly care about then I'll try my best to understand. You're my best friend, Grace. I don't want to stuff us up over something stupid like this.'

Grace beams.

Evelyn's face falls.

My stepsister can't call me out now without appearing like the bad guy, so she just grits her teeth and sits back in her chair. Grace turns to her work and I discreetly send Jude a thumbs up, my hand held behind Grace's back. He doesn't see. Too busy reading his textbook with his tongue sticking out. Like he doesn't even care about our master plan.

Idiot.

Ms Peters has her back to us, pointing out something on the board when Grace leans in close again. 'Lottie?'

'Yeah?'

Strands of her bright pink hair brush my cheek as she whispers near my ear, 'It's good if you're trying something new, you know? Change is a good thing. I'm glad for you.'

I look away, inexplicably hurt. 'Yeah, of course.'

She grins at me but I pretend I don't see.

What's so wrong with how I am that everyone wants me to change? My dad. Celeste and Jerry. Now Grace, too?

A bit of my triumph seeps away.

Class finishes and I split, avoiding Grace and Evelyn, avoiding Jude. I need a little space to think. I make it to my locker and that's when a voice says over my shoulder, 'Hey. Good to see you're back.'

I turn slowly.

It's Sebastian Lewis.

For real. Talking to *me*.

Shit.

'Umm,' I say helpfully.

Sebastian's right there, facing me. And he looks ... nervous?

He steps closer. 'It was pretty mad what happened the other day, but like ... sort of interesting, too?' He opens his mouth and then shuts it again, looking confused, like he doesn't know why he's saying what he's saying.

My expression mirrors his. 'Huh?'

Sebastian runs a hand through his tousled hair, pushing it away from his gleaming eyes. Which are green. Sea green. Like the ocean. 'What I meant to say ...' He coughs. 'To *ask*, I mean, was whether you got in a heap of trouble?'

I blink. Has Sebastian finally noticed I exist? Because he saw me fall off a table onto Evelyn Tait's head?

Weird.

I nod slowly. 'Right, yeah. Totally grounded. My dad's so mean.' I edge around him 'cos he's looming a bit close. He's a lot taller than me, and he's super pretty. Half the people in this school are mad into him. I drop my heavy bag onto the linoleum floor with a thump, cheeks flushed and heart racing. I have to set one thing straight. 'Look, I just … I want you to know I'm not *normally* like that. Like what you saw in the lab the other day. And I feel awful about it, because Jude and Grace both got suspended because of me.'

He shrugs. 'They didn't suspend Grace. She was here yesterday.' He smiles easily, the kind of smile that would normally make me a little weak in the knees. The boy is truly *very* pretty.

But right now I'm a little confused.

'What? Grace wasn't suspended?'

'Of course not.' He frowns. 'She didn't do anything.'

'But what about Jude?'

Sebastian smirks. Which is slightly less pretty. 'I dunno. He hasn't been here in days.'

Wow. That makes me feel bad.

I frown as I open my locker and muck around inside, shoving books between the crowded tomato tins I brought in this morning. Soft lush leaves sprout every which way and I slowly extricate the biggest tin with the most beautiful plant.

Sebastian's eyes bulge. 'What the hell is that?'

I recoil. 'A tomato plant.' Little green fruit swell between the leaves. I bite my lip. 'Obviously.'

Sebastian grins slowly at me. 'You really are pretty strange, Lottie.'

Huh.

It's nice that Sebastian is smiling at me. Like so *so* nice. Like dream-come-true nice. But I'm not sure how I feel about being called strange. I wrinkle my nose. 'Um, thanks?'

He smiles back at me, looking at me properly for the first time in all the years we've gone to the same school. And I have this terrible thought. Like maybe Sebastian only finds me interesting because he thinks I'm a troublemaker. Like maybe he's not interested in *me* at all.

And that sort of pisses me off. In fact, I'm irritated enough to lash out. Because that's what I do. And it's taken me all of five minutes to forget I'm supposed to be trying to be good. I flick my ponytail over my shoulder and straighten the buttons on my school blouse. 'Look, Sebastian, I'm not like ... some specimen or whatever. And I'm not a delinquent, okay? I'm trying something new.'

He blinks. 'Something new?'

I fumble over my words, trying to remember what Grace told me. 'And ... change is a good thing. Like, we can't always be the same.'

'Huh?'

'What I'm trying to say is ...' I pause, clutching my tomato plant against my chest. This is getting out of hand, but as much as it hurt to hear Grace say that me changing is a good thing, witnessing Sebastian's interest because of the old trouble-making me is somehow worse. I clear my throat, words bubbling from my lips.

'Okay, so the past can hurt, yeah? But we can run from it, or we can learn from it.' I'm quite proud I remembered Jude's little mantra. It rolls off the tongue just so. 'Change is a really good thing,' I finish.

Sebastian shakes his head. 'I have absolutely no idea what you're talking about.' Then his face morphs into a slow wide grin. 'Are you messing with me? I've heard that saying from somewhere ... what's it from? A movie?'

'It's not from anywhere,' I protest. I'm flustered now. And my face is burning hot because I just spouted a whole bunch of drivel at Sebastian Lewis. *Sebastian Lewis.* I avert my gaze, awkward and mortified. 'I gotta go.'

'Oh, okay.' He takes a shuffling step forward. Is it actually possible he's a little disappointed? 'Maybe I'll see you later then? At lunch?'

I do a non-committal embarrassed wave thing and run away down the hall. Classroom doors are open and the place is getting crowded. I pray no one was listening to the crap that was flying out of my mouth just now. I hunch over my heavy tomato tin and weave through the press, careful not to spill a trail of dirt across the shiny linoleum floor. Sort of succeeding.

Sun streams through the corridor and everything is lit up bright, too bright, and the heavy whir of overworked air-conditioners is loud and humming in my head. Students are everywhere. It's chaos.

Still feeling stupid, I stick my shoulder against the office door and press inside, cradling my peeling tin, the tomato label already fraying at the edges. It'll be prettier for sure when the branding fully comes off, but it'll also be a lot less ironic. A tomato plant growing inside a tomato tin and all that.

The office is nice and cool, and empty as anything. The

secretary must be on a bathroom break, which makes my life a lot easier. She doesn't like me all that much.

I stride past a line of cracked plastic orange chairs, meant for the bums of offending teenagers, and shove my foot against the set of inner doors that lead into the principal's office. I poke my head into the gap. 'Jerry?'

He's at his desk. Takes one look at me and drops his head into his hand. 'Yes, Charlotte? Just walked right in, did you?'

He doesn't even bother to correct me on the name thing. I smile weakly and step inside, the quiet of his office humming in my ears. 'Geraldine isn't at her desk. Maybe she's on a pee break?'

'Very nice. What can I do for you?'

I take a deep breath of the cool air and step forward, holding out my tomato tin, the plant bursting bright green and thick from the silver tub, the stalks twisted around little bamboo stakes to hold it upright. 'This is for you.' I place the tin carefully on the edge of his desk. 'I wanted to apologise, you know? You don't deserve to deal with what you do because of me. So I'm sorry. This is a sorry gift.'

Jerry blinks. 'Oh.'

'Do you like tomatoes?'

'Well ... I'm not ... I guess ...'

'Good.' I flop onto his threadbare couch with a sigh. Jerry doesn't try to stop me. He's still watching his new tomato plant like it might do something interesting.

I sigh. Loudly.

He doesn't notice so I do it again, even louder this time.

Old Jerry raises his brows at me. 'Yes, Charlotte? Something on your mind?'

I sit up quickly. 'I don't think it's very fair that Jude got suspended because of me.'

'No?'

'No. He was just there. He actually didn't do anything at all. Just watched from the corner doing this.' I make a face with my mouth gaping, eyes bulging, hands to my cheeks all shocked like. 'That's why I think it's a little unfair you punished him. Wrong place, wrong time, right?'

Jerry frowns. 'Well, I'll take that under consideration.'

I smile. 'Cheers, Jerry. He really did just stand there. Seriously. That's it.'

Jerry is poking at his new special tomato plant, so I gesture at it with my chin and grin. 'It's a tomato inside a tomato tin, get it?'

'I don't ... no. I don't get it.'

My face falls. 'No, I mean, that's it. What's there to get? It's ironic, isn't it?'

He scrunches his face like he's trying to solve a particularly difficult calculation, so I wave my hand in the air. 'It doesn't matter. Look, I was wondering if I could run through a problem with you?'

He sits a little straighter. 'You need help with something?'

I nod eagerly. 'Yeah. So you know Sebastian Lewis, right? He's another student here?'

'Yes. I know him.'

I bite my lip. 'Well, to be honest, I've been into him for a long time. And today he actually talked to me.'

Old Jerry does the face scrunching thing again, like he just ate a lemon, only this time it includes a soft snort. 'Do you mind if I continue working while we have this fascinating talk, Charlotte? Would that be okay with you?'

'Hmm? Yeah, of course.'

'Thank you.' He resumes his two finger typing, like he was introduced to a computer only a week ago. I want to go help him but I'm pretty sure it wouldn't be appropriate. So I just continue talking while he types agonisingly slowly.

Tap.

Tap.

Tap.

I sigh. 'Dunno what my issue is exactly, but everything is making me feel weird. Like Grace wants me to be different, and so does my dad. But then Sebastian was maybe only talking to me because he thinks I do crazy stuff. And that didn't make me feel great either. I mean, I *know* what people say about me.'

'What do people say about you, Charlotte?' Jerry says this a little absently, but I'm pleased he's listening.

'They call me stuff behind my back. You know, dumb jokes about this.' I point to my black hair and then to the makeup on my face. 'Just stupid stuff.'

'Uh huh.' *Tap. Tap.*

'Sebastian maybe doesn't mind it though.' I lean my head against the wall thoughtfully and peer at the ceiling.

Jerry stops with the tapping, like he just caught up. 'People call you names?'

I laugh. 'Obviously. Goth. Lesbo. Stuff like that.'

'Lesbo?'

'Oh, well the lesbian thing isn't so much aimed at me, more at Grace. You know Grace Singh? She's my best friend.' I don't wait for an answer. 'People are idiots, like no one can distinguish her pink-haired lesbian thing from my non-lesbian metal thing. But whatever.' I scuff my sneakers against the floor, kicking my heels against the boring grey carpet. It's the kind of carpet Celeste would love. Ugly carpet. Totally her thing.

'So what do you think?'

He's caught out, blinking a bit. 'About what?'

I throw my hands up. 'About Sebastian! Obviously.'

Tap. Tap. A heavy sigh. 'I don't think I'm really qualified to answer that, Charlotte. The school counsellor maybe ...'

'No that's fine. My dad's a counsellor so I get enough of that stuff at home.' I match his sigh with one of my own, a little deflated. Coming to see old Jerry for a nice chat usually makes me feel better, but not today. I shrug. 'Do you just sometimes feel like things are changing? Like, shifting or whatever?'

He stops the slow typing and assesses me over the tops of his glasses, brows raised. 'Do you?'

I lean forward. 'Yeah. Definitely.' I pause. 'I mean, the past can hurt, but the way I see it you can either run from it, or learn from it.'

Jerry cocks his head to the side suspiciously. Takes a breath as if to say something and then changes his mind. Instead he asks, 'Is that from *The Lion King*?'

I close my eyes. 'I ... would really like to say that it's not.'

Silence fills the room and then it seems like Jerry is about to say something else, except I've had enough humiliation for one day. I launch to my feet, sneakers catching on the carpet as I blurt, 'Gotta go, Jerry. Need some water. Great chat. Thanks.'

I fly to the door and slip outside, catching sight of his face as it swings shut.

I'm pretty sure he's trying not to laugh.

6

THE FOUR PILLARS OF IRREVERSIBLE FRIENDSHIP

Grace is at my place. Friends again. Everything good and back to normal. Excellent.

Except now when we sit on my bed, my attention is dragged towards the other half of the room where Evelyn's stuff sits. Her neat desk and her stupid orchestra posters. The little porcelain animal figurines lined up on the exact same window that used to be my best exit out of this house, now blocked by her piles of ugly stuff. And most of all, I can just feel it. Her presence, constant, like a shadow hanging over me.

Now when Grace comes over I won't know if it's 'cos she wants to hang around with me, her best friend, or if it's because she's hoping Evelyn will turn up.

The thought gets beneath my skin, like some bitter itch, crawling around and infecting everything. I sigh and clutch my pillow tighter. I want things to be how they were. I glance quickly at my best friend. Except maybe Grace was always secretly watching Evelyn whenever she came over. Maybe this whole thing happened a long time ago. Maybe she only just got up the guts to tell me now.

Maybe, maybe, maybe. I don't know.

'Are you even listening, Lottie?' Grace says.

I blink. 'Yeah of course.' We're talking about boring stuff. About school and that English assignment and this crazy festival thing out in the bush Grace has wanted to go to for ages that apparently we're actually doing this year. I sigh, paste on a smile. 'That sounds ... like fun.'

Pillar One of Friendship: White lies.

Grace flashes me a grin. She's aware I'm not into the whole dressing in costumes thing like she is, but I know she doesn't actually like metal music either, and she still listens with me when she comes over, a wash of technical riffs and muddy vocals blasting from my computer speakers. It's how our friendship works, I guess: a little compromise here, a bit more there. We share the things we like and meet in the middle.

I smile back, slow and self-conscious, trying to add a bit more genuine interest into my voice. 'I'm serious, it'll be fun. I can dress as a fair maiden or whatever.'

'I thought metal heads loved all that old medieval stuff,' she says. 'Like folktales and antler crowns and stuff.' She hauls herself back on my bed and props her feet against my bedside table, shock of pink hair pushed back nice and neat with a cute polka dot bow. I know how proud Grace is of that hair. It's naturally thick and black, so it wasn't easy for her to turn it so pink, a colour that looks like electric candy floss against her brown skin.

I snort. 'That's not *all* metal, just black metal. And anyway, it's more like pagan stuff and the occult, not medieval shit. Besides, I like other genres better.' I try to imagine myself walking around the school halls in a crown. 'I don't think medieval stuff is really my thing.'

Grace smiles. 'I promise you'll enjoy it. And I'll help with the costume.'

I sigh. 'Alright.' And I don't chuck a fuss like I normally would, because I'm trying to be good. 'Let's do it.'

Pillar Two of Friendship: Compromise.

'Awww.' She launches herself up and hugs me, nice and tight. 'Oh, and look what I got you.' She pulls a piece of rumpled paper from her pocket and holds it just out of my reach. She's tiny, Grace is, but the girl is fast, and she jerks the paper away every time I try to grab it. Soon we're laughing in that stupid uncontrollable way when it's not actually that funny at all, but you just can't stop. My ribs ache and my cheeks hurt from smiling too much. That's how it's always been with Grace. Silly. Since we first met.

Pillar Three of Friendship: Time.

The two of us against the world. Thick as thieves.

Or so my mother used to say.

That thoughts sobers me, and Grace uses my hesitation to take gasping breaths, still holding the paper beyond my reach. 'Stop, stop,' she laughs. 'I'll give it to you, okay? But first, *first* you've got to tell me what the hell is going on, Lottie.'

I widen my eyes. Innocent through and through. 'What do you mean?'

She cocks her head to the side and wrinkles her nose. 'Nah, you're up to something. I can tell. You were weird at school today. Really weird. And the tomato plants. I thought you loved those things. You gave them all away.'

I fling back onto my pillow, stuffing it behind my head, reaching to turn the music louder. I swear the windows rattle. I grin at Grace, shout over the rumbling song, 'It's an experiment.'

'What?'

'An experiment!'

Grace slides onto the carpet and travels on her knees to my computer, turns the volume way down. 'What did you say?'

I lean closer over the side of the bed. 'An experiment, Grace. I give up something precious to me, give the teachers a gift, be nice for a bit, what do I get in return?'

She makes a face. 'I dunno. Less detention hours?'

I laugh. 'Well, yeah. But a chance to start fresh, right? Everyone expects me to screw up all the time, but Jude reckons if I get them to start fresh, to believe I turned over a new leaf, they'll treat me different.'

'Jude?'

'Yeah. If I treat them nice, maybe they'll treat me nice.' I say it like it's a revelation, but Grace just frowns.

'Well, yeah, Lottie. That's the way the whole world works, isn't it? You reap what you sow.'

'What?'

She shrugs. 'You receive what you give. Treat people the way you want to be treated. All that jazz.'

I nod wisely. 'Right. An eye for an eye.'

Grace frowns. 'Uh, no. That one's different.'

I shrug. 'Whatever. It's working anyway. Did you see in homeroom? I was like five minutes late but Ms Breannie just looked at her tomato plant when I walked in and said nothing at all! I didn't even get in trouble.' It was pretty excellent.

'I don't know if she actually saw you.' Grace waves her hands in front of my face. 'Harvey just swallowed that chunk of glue after all.'

My eyes widen. 'He did?'

'Mmmhhmm. Didn't you see?'

I roll onto my back. 'Nah. That's sad.'

Grace grins. 'Yeah, super sad.' She pauses. 'Aren't you gonna ask what's on the paper?'

I sit faster than she expects and snatch it from her waggling fingers. 'Ha! Too slow.'

She fake pouts. 'I was gonna give it to you if you asked nicely.'

I raise my brows at her. 'No, you weren't.'

Her pout turns evil as she agrees, 'No, I wasn't.'

The paper is full-on scrunched now, pencil lines on the inside smeared. I sound out the word written in Grace's scrawly scrawl. 'Ang ... Anguilliform?'

'Yep. Word of the day.'

'Meaning?'

Grace leans forward, elbows on my bedspread. 'It's truly beautiful, Lottie. You're gonna love this one.'

Pillar Four of Friendship: Shared interests.

'Well, come on, don't keep me in suspense!'

'It means to resemble an *eel*! Like, to be in the form of an eel. Isn't that amazing?' She sinks back on her knees, face blissed out. 'I love it.'

I pause. 'As in, Evelyn's a bit of an anguilliform?'

Grace glares. 'No! But yes. Except not like that. Like, she has an anguilliform body ... or whatever. Stop that, Lottie.'

I roll away from her flailing hands, out of reach against the wall. 'Okay, okay. Sorry.' I peek at her from behind my pillow shield and say solemnly, 'It's an excellent word, Grace. Thank you.'

She grins. 'You're welcome.' She flicks her gaze meaningfully towards the corkboard above my overflowing desk.

Laughing, I launch to my feet. 'Alright, alright. Calm down. It's going up.' The creased paper is pinned into a place of honour and then I step back to admire my handiwork, *Anguilliform* pinned carefully right next to *Interstice* and Jude's awful *Lion King* bullshit. I frown. That one needs to come off.

From the floor comes Grace's voice, just as my music swells a little louder. She's returning the volume to where it's supposed to be, which makes me smile. Evelyn would never do that. There's not a compromise bone in her stupid mean body.

Grace shouts over the music, 'Honestly some words are just too good to be true. I never knew I needed to describe someone's eel-like body until today.'

I sit back on the bed, my attention still locked on my board. 'I know, right? Like how did we ever describe my stepmother before this moment?'

Grace giggles. 'Or Mr Virk?'

I frown. 'Nah, old Jerry's okay. Nothing eel-like about him.'

'What about Harvey then?'

'Harvey and his gluesticks,' I say absently.

'Or maybe Jude?'

That one I like a whole lot less. 'No, not Jude.' I think of his mass of freckles and crazy blue eyes. 'He's more like ... an alien. In a good way?' I really mean that. 'It's nice of him to help me.'

Grace snorts. 'What, the tomato plant thing?' She sits up. 'How many times have *I* told you to be nice?' She places her hand over her heart, wounded. 'How come you never listened to me?' Her hand moves to her forehead, her tone turning lamenting. The girl needs to join the school drama club. 'What power does this boy have over my best friend? Tell me, please,' she wails. 'Has he cursed you? What is this strange magic?'

'No magic,' I mumble. 'Like I said, I'm trying something new. A project. And he's helping. Besides, you're the one who said change is a good thing.'

Grace reaches over and turns my music dead off. The silence is deafening, the air humming with the sudden emptiness.

'Yeah, but don't change too much, Lottie.' She reaches up and pats me affectionately on my cheek. 'You know I love you just the way you are.'

That turns my heart warm, and a slow smile creeps onto my face, small and shy. So maybe Grace still is my best friend. Maybe things aren't changing quite as much as I thought they were. Maybe everything is going to be okay.

My bedroom door swings open and Dad is right there, hovering in the doorway. 'Don't encourage her, Grace. My girl's a troublemaker.' He grins his goofy dad-grin and I groan.

'Daaad. Don't listen at my door! How many times do I have to tell you?'

He shrugs, reaching to pick my school shirt off the carpet, folding it even though it's sweaty and gross, and placing it back into Evelyn's chest of drawers instead of mine. I don't say anything because I'm okay with it.

'I wasn't listening at the door, *daughter*,' he says, 'I was just coming to see if you and Miss Grace here want to come on a grocery trip with the family. Evelyn's home. We're all going.' He turns to Grace now. 'It's late night shopping on Thursdays, you know.'

I roll my eyes. 'Of course she knows, Dad.'

Man, this being good thing is hard! I clear my throat, lose the sarcastic edge to my voice. Evelyn will not win this battle before it's begun.

I glance across at Grace and can already tell she's dying to go, has been since Dad mentioned Evelyn's stupid name. I force my mouth into a sugared smile, saying sweetly, 'Sure, Dad. That sounds lovely. We'd be delighted.'

He frowns. 'I am ... frightened by that response. But okay. If you're coming you better hurry. We're leaving right now.'

Celeste calls from behind him, something about dirty nappies and dinner. Not my favourite words to be found in the same sentence. Grace turns to me and stage whispers, 'We're not eating dirty nappies for dinner are we?'

Dad snorts. 'Delicious. Lovely. Alright, let's go, girls. Evelyn and Leo are already waiting in the car.'

He pats my head as I trail out of my room after Grace, who nearly trips over the cat as she gallops across the room for no other reason except to jump beneath our feet. I don't bother getting changed. I'm wearing denim cut-offs hidden beneath a massive band t-shirt hanging to my knees – what my dad likes to affectionately call my 'death dress'. Charming. Hilarious. I slide into my thongs and, laden with a pile of empty shopping bags, follow Grace downstairs into the car park under the block, and slip behind her into the van.

And yes, we have a van because our ridiculous family got so freaking huge since Dad married Celeste. She keeps trying to get him to sell his old classic car. He keeps saying he will, but the months pass and it's still here, sitting in our garage.

I ignore the way Grace winks at Evelyn as we all cram together around the baby seat, my brother gurgling happily. Grace makes goo goo eyes at him and Evelyn watches my best friend in a way that makes me want to puke on her.

Like, go get your own best friend. And leave mine alone.

I pretend not to notice the way their fingertips brush together over Leo's fat pudgy baby legs.

Suddenly I feel kind of alone.

Which is sorted out extremely quickly, because when we get to the grocery store we run into Jude and his dad. I'm bent beneath the most massive stack of toilet paper ever seen, so big it won't fit in our trolley and so instead is perched precariously on my shoulder. Grace is laughing at me but I don't care. If it was Sebastian Lewis I might have been embarrassed. But it's just Jude and I've known him forever. I poke my tongue out at him from behind the toilet paper stack as the adults all shake hands.

'Ed,' my dad greets the other man warmly.

'Right, er, hello, Donal. Celeste.' Ed's response is slightly less aggressive than the last time we saw him outside the apartment block. 'So, listen, I think I owe you an apology. The school principal called me and told me what Charlotte did.'

Everyone turns to stare at me.

Dad's jaw clenches. 'What did she do?'

My heart beats faster. Yeah, what did I do?

Ed clears his throat. 'He said she pleaded on Jude's behalf, managed to get his suspension struck from his school record, confirmed he had nothing to do with the whole ... laboratory smashing thing.'

Oh. Right. I guess I did do that.

Dad beams at me. Celeste does too but I ignore her, only returning Dad's smile. Evelyn looks irritated. She loves it when I get in trouble. This must be killing her. I bat my lashes at her and smother a laugh, because I've become the golden child simply because when I screwed up, I didn't drag Jude down with me.

Go figure that one out.

Dad ruffles my hair. 'Good girl,' he says fondly.

Well, whatever, I'll take it. I wink at Jude and shift my massive toilet paper roll onto my other shoulder. Grace raises her brows at me, hovering close to Evelyn.

And then we all go for milkshakes together.

No, seriously. We do.

7

SIPPING MILKSHAKES AND LYING

The evening is balmy as hell, thick and hot in the height of summer. These days the evenings stretch bright and sunny forever and the dark only arrives late at night.

It's Celeste's idea, of course. She is the queen of truly awful ideas, and there's this dingy pub just around the corner from the shopping centre, nestled within one of those old heritage buildings. On either side sit empty shopfronts, the glass gathering dust and the awnings drooping beneath thick vines, summer leaves lush and purple. The pub has serious family vibes and is packed out with Thursday night punters drinking beer and cider, kids sipping lemonades, tables spilling out from the building onto the cracked pavement outside.

And that's how I find myself crushed beside Jude, squished on a table eating hotdogs and drinking milkshakes with Dad, Ed and Celeste, as well as Grace and Evelyn. Oh, and Leo, of course. All of us playing nice happy families.

I lean close to Jude, shoulder to shoulder, and hiss in his ear, 'The Lion King, huh? Seriously?'

He steadfastly ignores me, saying something about how much he loves hotdogs to Celeste. A riveting conversation, I'm sure. I glare at her and open my mouth to say something snipey when Jude's hand squeezes my knee beneath the table. That's shocking enough to make the words die on my lips.

'Well, isn't this just a nice family trip out,' I say lamely instead, losing the nasty sarcasm. Without it my words sound almost ... sincere.

Celeste blinks at me, glass of beer halfway to her mouth, hovering. Then she smiles, eyes crinkling at the corners. 'Yes. Isn't it just?'

That's when Leo spews on himself and she laughs like she doesn't have a disgusting baby inside a pub where people are actually trying to eat, and slips away to take care of it. Ed and Dad have drifted off to the bar, and Grace and Evelyn are just wrapped in each other, Grace gently pushing Evelyn's cascade of hair behind her ear.

I lean across to Jude and sigh. 'Thanks. It's hard to be nice.'

Jude frowns. 'Not really.'

'So you two are bosom buddies? You and Jude?' Evelyn's stupid head is poking out from behind Jude, her brows raised. 'Are you into each other now, Charlotte?'

Grace giggles like she can't hear the poison dripping off the words. 'Don't be an idiot, they've always been like this. Besides Lottie's not into *him*.'

I gape at her and Jude sort of blushes. He opens his mouth, obviously to protest, but I get in first.

'Hush, Jude,' I say, squishing my hand into his face to shut him up. 'Let me handle this.' I shift closer, leaning across him to get at Evelyn, my head practically shoved under his chin.

'Well, Evelyn,' I say, my voice sharp and nasty, 'I think you'll find—ow!'

I glare at Jude who just shrugs, all innocent like, as if he hasn't just jabbed his finger into my spinal cord.

Right. *Right.*

I'm meant to be good.

I sort out my face, the sneer turning into a sweet smile. I lean my elbow on the table, chin resting in my hand, my body still shoved across Jude, who is turning out to be surprisingly useful in keeping me on track. Clearly a good investment. I glance at Grace, wide-eyed and sweet. 'Hey, here's a thought. Why doesn't Evelyn come with us to that country dress-up thing, Grace?'

Surprise flowers across Grace's face. 'Really? Would that be okay?'

'Of course. I mean, do you even have to ask? I can't wait to spend the day all together.' I smile at my stepsister. 'Won't that be lovely?'

Evelyn's mouth is tight. 'I don't want to go anywhere with you,' she hisses.

And I retort … nothing.

At all.

Because Jude's poking me in the ribs again. It takes a little effort but instead of lashing out I slap a wounded expression onto my face, peer back at my stepsister all shocked and hurt.

Sudden silence falls across the table.

Grace's expression turns pained and Jude just frowns, both of them staring at Evelyn as she coughs awkwardly. 'I meant to say … I'm pretty sure Charlotte doesn't really want me to come.'

'She invited you, didn't she?' points out Grace.

I suppress my grin. This is going brilliantly. Grace will see how mean my evil stepsister is to me, and then she'll dump her and stuff will return to normal and everything will be great forever.

I sigh, contented.

Except I've underestimated Evelyn.

Her expression changes. 'Well, in that case, sure. I'd *love* to come.' She shoots daggers at me as she bellows loudly towards the bar, 'Hey, Mum, can you drive us to a thing? Me and Charlotte want to spend some quality time together.'

I cringe as Celeste's head pokes up, Leo strapped against her chest all nice and vomit-free. She's clearly delighted, and immediately yells back, 'Sure, honey. I'd love to! Where am I taking you?'

Evelyn turns to me, but I have no idea so I look at Grace. She sighs and then shouts to the bar, 'It's a medieval festival in the countryside. Next month.' She lowers her voice, speaking to Evelyn. 'But you have to get dressed up.'

Celeste sure seems pretty happy by the bar. She wraps her arms around my dad, heads together and both of them glancing back our way with enormous smiles, so glad all their blended family issues have suddenly been resolved.

Evelyn stole my thunder.

Grace is happy. Dad is happy. Even freaking Evelyn looks happy.

She is truly a worthy opponent.

Grace reaches across the table for Evelyn's hand and they murmur all low about costumes, heads bent together. I frown, crinkling my brow as I lean closer to Jude to whisper beneath my breath. 'See? She's evil.'

Jude just wheezes in response. 'Can you ... get off ...?'

I'm still all over him, my elbow sunk in his belly. 'Oh, sorry.'

I sit back straight and Jude gasps and coughs. 'Thanks.'

'That's quite all right.'

Evelyn's stupid head pokes out from behind him again. 'So, you might wanna think about bringing someone, Lottie.' She grins at me and I think she's implying I'm gonna end up a third wheel. 'What about Sebastian Lewis?'

I glance at Grace in surprise. There's no way she'd tell Evelyn about my years-long crush, right? She wouldn't. Yet she doesn't meet my eye.

She did.

Hurt blooms in my chest, sharp and tangy.

'No, I'm bringing Jude,' I blurt, slinging my arm around his shoulders, dragging him in close. 'Right, Jude?'

'Uh ... right?'

I nod furiously at Evelyn with a big smile pasted on my face. She stares back at me with the exact same expression, both of us filled with tension.

Until Celeste and baby Leo make their way over to talk logistics about the trip.

I watch as Celeste touches her hand to the back of my stepsister's neck, softly brushing hair from Evelyn's collar, filled with quiet affection. Evelyn smiles at her mum and my heart clenches.

I don't think my mother would ever touch my hair in that way. I can't picture it, no matter how hard I try.

My mother isn't the affectionate type.

'Come on, Jude,' I mumble, pulling at his t-shirt. 'Let's go.'

I slide off my stool and ignore Celeste, saying goodbye to Grace before winding through the thick crowd to find Dad and Ed at the bar, and inform them we're leaving. We're only a short walk from home so Dad's cool with it, and Ed seems pretty pleased he doesn't have to move from his position at the bar.

Excellent dad that he is. I firmly drag Jude away by his elbow.

Outside, the noise of the pub follows us down the quiet laneway, windows flung wide open. Light spills out too, a warm orange glow to fight the blue twilight creeping between the old buildings. Buses roar by on the road and traffic lights wink in the gathering dark.

'Ugh. That was terrible,' I announce, though in truth I'm feeling much better now, out here with Jude in the dark where I don't have to pretend.

Jude says nothing, just smiles as we walk.

Further back from the main road, the car park near the shopping centre is dark and nearly empty, the only light seeping from streetlamps nestled beside an abandoned construction site. Rusted metal pipes prop up walls, reaching towards the sky with no purpose.

The wind picks up and I grasp the cool metal of a stray shopping trolley, climbing inside and calling for Jude. 'Push me, please.'

He does.

Grace says he does anything I ask him to.

I glance behind me. A glimpse of bright blue eyes as the trolley wheels over the shadowed bitumen, the cart scaring a bunch of screeching seagulls. They take flight, soaring into the deep blue-lit sky.

The moon is creeping up now, silver and curling. I lift my arms above my head, hair streaming in the wind as I close my eyes. Sometimes I think heaven might be an empty car park in the summer with Jude Carillo. I don't feel so bad about being me when we're hanging out like this.

Suddenly I open my eyes, fingers grasping the edges of the

trolley as it careens wildly over white lines. 'Jude,' I call, getting dizzy. 'Do *you* want things to change?'

Jude stops the trolley from spinning, his sneakers scraping hard against the bitumen as he attempts to hold me still. 'Why are you asking that?'

The trolley steadily winds to a stop. My cue to climb out.

I sigh. 'I dunno. Just that Grace says she loves me like I am, but still, she seems pretty happy for me to patch things up with Evelyn and do better at school or whatever. Same as Dad. But none of those things are exactly who I am, are they?'

Jude laughs and I glare at him. 'I'm being serious, Jude.'

He muffles his grin with his hand. 'You can still be you without getting in trouble every two minutes, Lottie. It's not that hard.'

'And there you go again. It *is* hard. For me it's hard.'

We walk side by side behind the centre, beneath the train tracks. The roller doors lining the building are locked tight and big painted skips sit against the back walls, overflowing with cardboard boxes and empty packaging. I kick at a sheet of plastic with my thong. 'You never answered my question though,' I say, glancing across at him.

Jude is already staring at me. He says quietly, 'Sometimes I think I don't want anything to ever change.'

This time I laugh. 'Whatever. You were pretty pleased when I got your suspension lifted!'

'My *dad* was pretty pleased.'

I grin and nudge him with my shoulder. 'So does that mean your dad loves me now? Can I use the front door instead of your window?'

'I never asked you to use the window.'

'Yeah, but it's pretty fun. I'm like, the best climber ever now.'

Jude shakes his head, but I know he doesn't care. I've been visiting him that way since we were eleven. Mainly because his dad yelled at me for an hour after I broke Jude's arm, which was obviously an accident and barely even my fault, but I was a little scared of Ed after that. For a short while at least. And when I got over that, it still just seemed easier. Like, my parents thought I was in my room, so they'd have these hushed fights in the living room for hours, and Jude's dad thought he was studying, and no one would ever check on us. Really we were just sprawled across his bed playing video games.

I sigh.

'And you?' I say. 'How is it with your mum away? Like, with your dad, I mean?' I ask the question lightly, not sure if it's awkward.

'Oh, well, you know ... fine.' Jude's cheeks colour but I pretend not to notice.

I nudge his shoulder gently. 'You can say it. He's acting like a douche. Am I right?'

Jude blinks. 'You're talking about my dad.'

I grin. 'Oh, I get it. There's a word for this. You wanna hear it?'

'No.'

I ignore him. 'It's *tacenda*. It means things better left unsaid. Stuff to be passed over in silence, right?' I nudge him again. 'Like your dad being a douche.'

'No. I mean, yeah ... but *you* can't say it.' He looks upset. Which is something I am supremely good at. Upsetting Jude. He frowns. 'Only *I'm* allowed to say it, Lottie. Because he's *my* dad. Not yours.'

'Well, say it then. Tell me.'

He shakes his head. 'Nah, I'm not going to say it.'

'But you're thinking it, right? Right?' I elbow him but he grabs my arm. I squeal and twist from his grasp and lose a thong in the process. 'See what you made me do? These are my favourite shoes.'

Jude snorts. 'They cost you like, two dollars.'

'Two dollars fifty, thank you very much.'

Jude sighs and picks my thong off the bitumen to hand it back. 'Well there you go then.'

I hop around on one foot for a bit and then slide the thong on, my hand clutching his shoulder for balance. 'Cheers, love. Much obliged.' Jude flicks my hair in response, making a face at my fake English accent.

I scuff along the gravelly pathway for a bit in silence and then twist until my back is to my friend, face turned to the wide open sky, enjoying the salt in the air and the cool wind against my skin. My band t-shirt flaps around.

Jude mumbles something real quiet behind me.

I turn. 'What?'

He bites his lip. 'What was Evelyn saying before? About Sebastian Lewis?'

Heat rises in my cheeks. 'Yeah, right? What was that about? I can't believe Grace told Evelyn that stuff. It was totally private.'

Grace is gonna get a talking to later. Secrets are secrets. I don't care if Evelyn *is* her girlfriend. I'm still her best friend.

I'm seething but Jude's voice brings me back to earth. 'No, I mean, what stuff did Grace tell her about him?'

I wave a dismissive hand. 'Just that Sebastian talked to me in the hall. I don't know, nothing.'

Jude stops walking. 'He talked to you? Why?'

I spin around to face him, walking backwards now. 'I don't know. For serious. It was really weird.' I turn around again and Jude jogs to catch up as I say, 'I'll tell you one thing though.'

Jude's voice is weird and strained. 'What?'

I shrug. 'Sebastian is even prettier close up.'

Jude scowls. 'Gross.'

I turn to him with wide eyes. 'Excuse me?'

He leans close. 'You heard me.'

I make a face, wrinkling my nose and frowning.

'Here's a game,' Jude says suddenly. He takes a deep shaking breath. 'Me and my mum used to play it. If something's hard to say, you say the opposite of it. Easy, right?'

I shrug, bemused. 'Okay. Whatever. You first.'

He stops walking again, face serious and blue eyes glowing in the dark. The freckles covering his skin meld into the shadows. 'I really hate you, Lottie. I mean it. Seriously.'

I blink, taken aback, because it's weird to hear anything that harsh come out of his mouth. Then a slow grin creeps across my face. I pounce on him, flinging an arm around his neck and dragging him forward with me. 'Oh my gosh, I'm so glad you said so. I totally hate you too!' I'm laughing but Jude drags my arms off without cracking a smile, mouth tight and brows angry.

'Fine. My turn again,' he says. 'My dad thinks I'm super cool. And I think he's super cool too.'

My face falls. Well, that's just sad.

'This game sucks, Jude.' I don't know what's wrong with him. Why he's being so weird. I hate seeing this expression on his face. Except then I get an idea. 'What about your mum? She think you're super cool too?'

Jude's expression slowly shifts, and his mouth is twitching. 'Nah, she really hates me.' He grins real wide, quick like lightning, wind tumbling his hair real wild, and I grin back at him.

'Okay, okay,' I say. 'Me next. Yes. Sebastian is totally in love with me. He just came straight up to me at a cool party I went to and asked me to be his girlfriend. Exclusively.'

Jude's shoulders stiffen and he falls a step behind but I keep talking. 'Evelyn isn't better than me at everything and my stepmum totally loves metal. She thinks it's a beautiful art form. And she loves me too.'

I peer at the sky, blinking rapidly. I'm feeling pretty sorry for myself until Jude's quiet voice asks, 'And your dad?'

His question makes me stop, the hollowness in my chest filling with warmth. A slow grin breaks across my face and I swing back to face him, my hair flying in the wind. 'Oh, my dad really hates me. He thinks I'm the worst.'

Jude's crooked smile returns, shy and small. But pleased too. I like it better when he's smiling.

I continue. 'My dad just gives up on me whenever he gets calls from the principal. He thinks I'm a giant waste of space.'

Jude laughs. 'He sounds awful.'

We walk in silence the rest of the way back to our block. It's quiet here. Only cobbled roads and no cars. Light spilling from streetlights. The sky dark and big overhead. When we reach the top of the stairs I grasp Jude's elbow before he can slip inside his empty flat, whispering, 'Your mum will be home soon, right?'

Jude shrugs, eyes glittering in the darkness. His strained expression makes me wonder if maybe I didn't ask him the right questions earlier, when we were playing the game of opposites. I should have asked him how he feels, what he thinks will happen when she comes home. If she *is* coming home.

But I don't know how to ask him now.

Instead I squeeze his arm and lean close, voice low and serious. 'Jude, I think maybe I should warn you, but you know that queen doll your aunt gave you?'

He nods, his breath warm against my cheek and his body stiff.

'Well, I saw an article on the net, and she's ... well, I don't know how to tell you this, but she's from a cursed batch of dolls.' I lift my hand over my mouth and make a shocked face at him. 'And you have to be careful because I heard those cursed dolls, they just love to murder boys with blue eyes and freckles more than anything else in the world.'

He blinks at me.

I poke my tongue out at him and drag open our door as quick as I can, shouting a loud, 'Sweet dreams,' over my shoulder as I disappear into our home.

But not before I catch the smile on Jude's face.

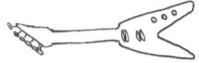

My family is already home and it's late, Grace long since gone. But before bed I approach Dad in his 'study' carrying one of my most prized tomato plants. This one is tall and strong, the leaves lush and fuzzy. And it's covered in hard green cherry tomatoes, the stalk staked against their heavy weight. I push the tin onto the corner of his desk. 'Here, Dad.'

He raises his eyebrows, neck deep in paperwork. 'What's this?'

Celeste is watching from the kitchen, cleaning yet another round of misplaced cat pee, but I roll my eyes anyway. 'It's a tomato plant. Obviously.' And I'm certainly not giving one to Celeste.

He laughs, a rumble deep in his gut. 'Obviously.' Pause. 'Are you giving it to me?'

Suddenly I'm shy. Which is the weirdest thing. This is my dad. I don't need to feel shy. 'It's a present. To say thanks. I know I'm ... difficult sometimes. Like with the whole suspension thing.'

My dad beams. Beams and beams. Like, I don't know if I've seen him so happy in ages. Or maybe he does feel that way, but never around me.

He clears his throat and drags the tin closer across his desk to inspect his new prize. 'Beautiful! Tomatoes!' He smacks his lips, like he's trying hard not to say 'Mamma mia' in a fake Italian accent. I'm glad he doesn't.

He does hug me though. I squirm and pretend I'm much too old, but I can't remember the last time he hugged me and the contact reminds me of better times. Of family. Of what we had and lost. I blink back tears until I remember that maybe our family never had what I thought we did anyway. And then I'm thinking of Jude and his dad. Of how super cool they both think each other is.

'Dad?'

'Yeah, kiddo?'

I hesitate, then say it quickly. A rush of breath. 'I'm glad you're my dad, Dad.'

He blinks down at me. Then grins. 'You're glad I'm your dad-dad?'

'Ugh!' I push him off and he laughs loud and rumbling as I stalk away.

'I'm going to bed,' I shout. 'You're stupid.'

But his laughter still rumbles through the house long after I've changed and am sliding between my sheets. A creeping smile has taken root across my face, even in the darkness of my shared room.

Evelyn is already in bed, her back squarely to me. Her shoulders rise and fall weird, kind of staccato, and for a moment I wonder if she's crying.

She isn't though, because her next words are acid.

'You and your dad make me sick. You're gross with all that lovey-dovey shit. You're so fake.'

I flinch, trying my best to think about Jude and all the lessons he's been drumming into me.

If you did something wrong, admit it and apologise.

If someone did something good, admit it and congratulate them.

Be kind.

And be brave.

He says that's what his mum tells him all the time.

Be kind and be brave.

Well, I don't know how to do either of those things in this situation, so I just mutter a dumb, 'Shut up, Evelyn,' into the darkness and then lie there seething and feeling stupid.

But it doesn't matter. Evelyn's breathing changes, turns to sleep. And slowly the creeping smile returns to my face.

8

USHERING IN THE NEW AGE
WITH TCHAIKOVSKY

In the music room at school I sit and practise until my fingers hurt. The school guitar is a classical one, the wood cheap and the sound dull. But it's better than nothing.

I get in early to practise before classes start and then I practise again during lunch, the sun hot and heavy outside, heat glaring against the glass windows and seeping across the empty room.

I've been learning at school for a while now, practising at home too, so although I'm not brilliant, every day things seem to come together just a little more. Like my fingers get less sore and I can play for longer, and when I read the notes on the page they don't seem quite as indecipherable as they did the week before.

At school I play endless scales and classical scores, but at home I crouch on my bed and try to pick out the riffs in the metal songs I like, playing along even though a classical guitar is the exact wrong guitar for the sound I want. For that I'd need an electric, to play heavy and deep. And an amp. And a bunch of effects pedals.

Which all sounds super expensive.

I'm starting to think I need to get a job.

I stop playing the Tchaikovsky piece and sigh, a bitter taste flooding my mouth when I think of Evelyn's expensive flute, which was practically handed to her on a silver platter. Or, at least, inside a custom-made wooden box.

I stick out my tongue in disgust, though there's no one in the empty school music room to see it. But it works out supremely well because the next thing I know, Evelyn herself has slammed open the door and stomped inside, glaring at me.

I pull my tongue back in my mouth. She's breathing heavily, clearly pissed as hell. I can only hope it was me who irritated her this way.

I sit straight and shift the light wooden body of the guitar on my knee. 'Yes?'

She's straight out with it. 'Why are you doing this?'

I bat my lashes. 'Doing what?'

She groans. 'You applied for my scholarship. Mr Virk just told me.'

'I don't think that scholarship is *yours*, Evelyn.' I grin and she presses her hands over her face, more stressed than I've seen her in ages. It's quite wonderful. 'The whole point of a music scholarship is that it's a *scholarship*. It's for anyone who can make the cut. Like me. I'm going to make the cut.'

'Shut up,' she snaps. 'Just shut *up*! I know what you're doing and it won't work. Right now everyone thinks you're wonderful just because you haven't got into trouble for, like, three days, but next week? It'll wear off. They won't care anymore. They'll stop noticing. No one else gets praise for doing nothing, *Charlotte*. It won't last.'

I smile, rather enjoying seeing my evil stepsister's cheeks

flushed and her forehead slick with stress sweat. 'Well, *Evelyn*, I don't actually agree with any of that, but thanks for the warning. I *will* keep it up. And I *will* win your stupid scholarship. What do you care, anyway? You went last year. And the year before that. Maybe it's time to give someone else a turn.'

She scowls, her mouth tight and pinched. 'You don't have any idea who you're messing with.'

I laugh easily. 'Yeah, I do. You. I'm messing with you.'

Evelyn stomps to the door and flings it back open. 'You better watch out, Charlotte. You better give up on this scholarship thing. I'm warning you.'

I stand, guitar in hand, chair screeching backward. Suddenly I'm feeling a whole lot less friendly. 'Warning me? *I'm* warning *you*. You better leave Grace out of this. Stop messing with my best friend. Then we'll talk about me pulling out of the scholarship.'

Evelyn's body goes rigid, and for a moment I think maybe I've surprised her. But then her fingers clench white and bloodless and her shoulders straighten. She stomps out the door and slams it shut behind her with such a loud bang it sets the windows rattling. A music stand slides over onto the linoleum floor, music sheets flying all over the place.

I leave the mess where it is and sit back down, settling the sticky guitar back on my knee and smiling to myself with satisfaction.

Well, I got under her skin.

I feel all warm and good inside. Turns out it's easy to mess with Evelyn.

Easier than I thought.

Why didn't I do this from the start? Life would have been a lot more pleasant. I grin and tinker with the guitar again, plucking and twanging strings and running my calloused fingers over the ridged neck.

But my heart is no longer in it. In the end I place the guitar back on the stand and pull out my massive headphones from my backpack, connecting them to my phone and flicking through the options. I select a favourite, one of those albums that's just start-to-finish perfect, like listening to each song alone could never measure up to the utter perfection that is listening to the album as a whole.

I press play and lean back in the chair, hands behind my head and eyes fluttering shut, enjoying the cool whirring air-conditioner and the emptiness of the room. The music slides over my skin, spurs my heart to beat fast, and has my toes and fingers tapping along with the riffs. I stay like that until the end of break when the clanging bell goes off in the hallway.

Obviously I don't hear it because the sound is turned up way too loud, but I'm trying to be a good student now, so I've actually set an alarm on my phone so I won't miss it. Last week I wouldn't have bothered. I'd have still been in here listening to music for another hour and then snuck into the back of class when I hoped Ms Breannie wasn't paying attention. But this week I'm a changed woman.

Just as I've finished packing up, the door opens and this time it's Jude's head that pokes in. He has dark shadows across his cheeks, like he hasn't slept, with bleary eyes and bed hair.

'Whoa, what's wrong with you?'

He shakes his head. 'Nothing. I was coming to see if you'd heard the bell.'

I grin and hold up my phone. 'I set an alarm.'

He throws me a sleepy smile. 'Nice. Very smart.' He steps inside the room and pulls loose sheets of paper from his bag. Heaps of them. 'So here are notes for science. For maths. And for English. What else do you have again?'

'Um, art? With Ms Kang?'

'Right.' Jude frowns. 'I don't have notes for that.'

I juggle the hailstorm of loose papers he's handing me, all of them covered in tight neat script. 'Um ... what's all this for again?'

'If you want to impress everyone then you have to make an effort in class.'

An effort? In class?

I shudder and Jude rolls his eyes.

'Did you ask me for help or not?'

I sigh. 'Yes, I did.'

'Well, this is the way to go then.' Suddenly he grins, wide and wicked and quick as lightning. He grabs me by my shoulders, bright blue eyes blazing among the freckles. 'Lottie. You are more than you have become.'

I narrow my eyes suspiciously. 'Is that another quote from *The Lion King*? It is, isn't it?'

'What? No!' Except he's unable to keep a straight face this time. 'I'd never do that to you, Lottie. Imagine if you, like, repeated it to someone not knowing where the quote came from. For instance, Mr Virk, maybe. How embarrassing would that be?' He snorts with laughter and I fling his hands off my shoulders. I'm going to kill Grace for telling him.

'You can't fool me anymore, Jude. I watched it on the weekend.' I waggle my finger in his face. 'I know all your tricks now.'

He coughs. 'Oh. Second bell. We're gonna be late for class.'

I shake my head, and because I have too much stuff I shove some of my music books at Jude to carry. He smiles and takes them without a word as I heft the rest of my crap onto my back and clutch the school guitar in its soft case against my chest.

He's still chuckling when we enter the stream of students out in the hall, laughter only broken by a yawn as Grace joins us, all sharing our next history class. My attention flicks across the students milling around the corridor, because Sebastian shares this class too. I can't see him though.

I'm nervous after our weird conversation the other day. Like I want to talk to him again, but I also dread it. My belly is all churned up inside.

'Did you hear about him?' Grace flicks her chin towards Jude, who's rubbing at his face again. He frowns at her.

'Grace!'

She blinks innocently. 'What?'

I turn between them both. 'What? What's going on? Tell me.'

And right then Sebastian looms from the lockers and smiles at me, falling into step at my side. 'Yeah, what?'

I gape at him, Grace gapes at him and Jude just scowls.

'Nothing,' Jude says tightly, but Grace nudges him hard with her elbow.

'Actually it's a good story.' She grins and then draws in a massive breath before launching off into a tirade, her words all running into one. 'Jude said he couldn't sleep for hours because his dad never came home from the pub and he was by himself and there's some creepy doll his aunt made him keep and she was watching him from the shelf and in the end he had to go and put her in the fridge, just so he could rest!' She guffaws loudly into her hand.

Jude groans like he's in actual physical pain as I repeat in wonder, 'The fridge?'

Sebastian raises his brows, still walking with us for some reason. I don't mind it, obviously.

'Well, yeah.' Grace shrugs. 'How would she crawl out from there? She couldn't. It was a great idea. It trapped her forever.'

'It was a *terrible* idea,' interjects Jude, his voice resigned. 'The face cracked 'cos it froze. My dad was completely pissed at me this morning.'

I burst into loud laughter, unable to hold myself back. 'That's an amazing story,' I choke out.

Sebastian laughs too, more of a quiet low rumble, and a part of me wishes I could control myself and laugh with a little more finesse as well, but it's too hard, and in the end I just give in to the urge. It's too funny.

When we get to class, Jude drops my music books heavily onto my chair, stomping between the desks to his seat near the back of the room. He keeps throwing angry looks back my way but I can't help the giggles, which keep on coming. Grace flops into the desk next to mine, and Sebastian hovers weirdly beside us, hesitating, until the crush of arriving students pushes him back to his own desk near Jude.

Disappointment surges through my stomach at the lost opportunity to speak with him, but I'm sort of relieved, too. What are we going to say to each other? *Hi, my name's Lottie and I've been secretly in love with you for almost two years? Or, Sebastian, your face is just too pretty? I'd like to kiss it please?'*

I've got nothing.

I sigh, my laughter drying up as I drag my history textbook from my bag. We're on the World Wars this term and it's pretty awful stuff. Enough to keep my mind off Sebastian, who normally draws my attention like a beacon at the back of class. I refuse to turn around to peek at him, and instead just stay focused on Mr Jenner and his lecture.

Which gets more difficult a half-hour later when Jamie Gorecki and his friend Finn throw balled paper at each other across the room. Projectiles soar over our heads as Mr Jenner shouts at them to stop. I twist in my seat, my gaze leaping up, up, up over Grace's head, over Jamie Gorecki's head too, to land on Sebastian's face at the back of class.

I stop. And stare.

Because I'm pretty sure he was already looking at me, his eyes locked on mine. He doesn't appear embarrassed to be caught out, his mouth twisting in one corner, half grin, half smirk.

I blink.

Slowly I turn back to the front, tingling all over, like there's electricity in my blood.

9

JELLYFISH AND
CARS FILLED WITH BOYS

Saturday night and I'm at home. I've done nothing but sit in my cramped shared bedroom, studying and practising guitar all day. Jude's notes came in handy, too. The boy really is quite smart.

Despite how hard my brain is working, I can't get Sebastian's smile out of my mind. Every time I think I've managed to quash the feeling of it, the tightness in my chest and shivers across my skin return harder. I can't get away from it.

I sigh, pushing my books away and flicking on my music instead, the wash of sound filling the room like water, seeping into every corner and hidden space. I lie back on the floor and close my eyes, letting the thunderous riffs beat through my heart instead of memories of Sebastian's ocean gaze in class.

Pining for Sebastian is bad. It's only going to end up hurting, because there's no scenario I can see where Sebastian and me is ever going to happen.

And I've always known that, obviously, but now it's different. Worse.

He's talking to me and smiling at me. And all my defences are cracking and peeling away. Like in the beginning. Back then

I used to know when all his classes were and I used to adjust my own schedule to be walking the same halls as him, at the same time, just in the hopes we'd somehow collide. And I never even told Grace how if he was in the same room as me I'd know it, like he was a shining, glowing lighthouse, beaming out his location so loudly I couldn't ignore it. Or how I'd feel the spaces between us like a solid sizzling thing if we happened to draw near, my shoulders tense as I tried my best to appear normal, casual, and not completely and utterly obsessed with him.

I don't do any of that stuff anymore, because I clawed my pride back. But the truth is it's all still there, scraping at the back of my mind. My full-blown crush, caged and hidden, desperately waiting to spill out again.

I groan and slap my hands to my face, rolling onto my side. This sucks. I hate it.

Except just for a moment, just for the length of one single song, I let myself sink into it, into the feeling, into Sebastian's ocean eyes and curling mouth when he smiled at me in class.

And I disappear.

Until someone flicks my music off and Evelyn is towering over me, a sneer twisting her pointy face.

I flinch. 'How long have you been there?'

'Long enough to be shouting at you. Why do you have the volume so loud? You'll wreck your ears.'

I drag myself up until I'm sitting, my spine pressed against my bedframe. Now it's my turn to sneer. 'Because that's how I like to listen to it, Evelyn. What do you want?'

She plops on the bed opposite mine and gives me the side eye, silent for a long moment. She sighs, and bites her lip. Finally she says, 'Grace wants me to tell you about some stupid metal gig in the city. She thinks we should all go together.' She turns away, not looking at me.

'A metal gig?' I breathe. Then I get suspicious. 'Why are you telling me this?'

My stepsister scowls. 'Because Grace asked me to. Because if you agree to go, she wants to go too, and if she goes then I'm going with her.'

'Why, though?'

Evelyn blinks. 'Because she's my girlfriend.'

'No, I mean, why Grace? Why *her*?'

Evelyn doesn't say anything and I mutter, 'I didn't even think you were into girls.'

'Well, I am,' snaps Evelyn. Then she hesitates. 'I mean, now I am. Since Grace.'

'What about Jamie Gorecki? Weren't you and him together at that orchestra thing last year?'

Her mouth tightens. 'So? We're not together now.'

'But I thought you liked him.'

She stands up, towering over me. 'Well, I don't anymore. Now I like Grace.'

I don't enjoy her tone. Slowly I pull myself to my feet until I'm taller than her again, glaring right into her face. 'I don't believe you,' I hiss. 'Is this about Jamie Gorecki? Are you trying to make him jealous?'

Evelyn barks a disbelieving laugh.

'Then it's about me,' I snap. 'You're using Grace to mess with me, right?'

Evelyn shouts, 'Not everything is about you, Lottie.' Then she laughs, loud and bitter. 'Maybe everything in this stupid house revolves around you, but not this. Me liking Grace has *nothing* to do with you.'

She thinks our house revolves around me? When it's *her* trophies lined on the shelf over the fridge and *her* awards stuck with magnets where my kiddie drawings used to sit?

I shout right back at her, 'It has *everything* to do with me! She's my best friend, Evelyn. And you need to back off her right now.'

Our door slams open and both of us fall silent. Celeste stands in the open space clutching a wailing Leo against her chest. Her gaze flicks between us.

'What's going on?'

Her frizzy hair is out of control and I swear there are extra lines crowding the corners of her tight mouth. 'I heard shouting.'

I glance at Evelyn stiffly, and then gape when she smiles and says, 'Nothing's going on, Mum. Me and Lottie were just talking about an all-ages gig in the city we want to go to with Grace. Do you mind if we go together on the train?'

Celeste sags with relief, cuddling Leo against her shirt. His wailing is dying down and he's grabbing at her frizzy hair with a chunky baby fist. It must be painful but Celeste doesn't even flinch. 'A gig? That sounds lovely, Evie. But I get worried about you out at night in the city by yourselves. I can drive you. When is it?'

Evelyn shrugs. 'In, like, a few weeks, I think.'

Celeste nods. 'Okay, but I think your dad better go with you.'

Evelyn stiffens, her words tight. 'Donal is not my dad.'

I glance at her, thinking we may have something in common after all.

I cut in before things get out of hand, because Celeste's eyes are flashing as she draws in breath to respond.

'I'll ask Jude,' I blurt. 'Jude'll come.'

Celeste agrees absentmindedly because Leo is screaming again. She drifts from the doorway with one final frustrated glance towards her daughter, which I watch with interest, and then she's gone, leaving me and Evelyn alone again.

I flop onto my bed. 'Is it really all-ages?'

Evelyn doesn't move from the centre of the room, doesn't answer me either, her shoulders tense. 'Thank you,' she says stiffly. 'This'll make Grace really happy.'

I scowl. 'Like you care what she feels.'

Evelyn sucks in her breath sharply, then just grunts, turning on her heel and following her mum. I poke my tongue out at her and then flick my music back on, hoping the sound of it will scrape this conversation from the inside of my brain.

It doesn't.

But five minutes later my phone pings. A text. I think it's gonna be Grace except it's an unknown number.

I'm downstairs. Wanna go for a walk?

I stare at the words as a second message pings through.

It's Sebastian by the way.

It couldn't be. No way. But I still fly out of my room, and then back in to check my reflection in the mirror. I push my long hair this way and that before giving up. I look okay. Band t-shirt and jean cut-offs, hair messy, but that's kind of my style. I still have thick eyeliner on from this afternoon.

I look like me. And that will have to do.

I feel sort of stupid telling Celeste I'm going out for a walk, even more stupid when I'm spat out from the house laden with heavy baby bags and a buggy, my gross brother gurgling happily in his stroller in front of me, his wailing finally stopped. I was too embarrassed to tell Celeste I was maybe meeting a boy, at least not in front of Evelyn, and definitely not when it might not even be true.

The stairwell doors swing shut behind me and the noise of the apartment block is swallowed by the buzzing street, the windows from the Afghan restaurant spilling light onto the cobblestones and the scent of sweetness and tang mixed with coriander filling the warm air. It's getting dark out here, deep shadows clinging to the buildings, setting sun glowing orange as traffic hums languidly by, cars sporadic and slow.

And no sign of Sebastian anywhere.

I'm such an idiot. I drag my phone from my back pocket and am just about to text the mysterious number when a figure emerges from across the quiet street.

I stare.

'Hey,' says Sebastian, like it's the most natural thing in the world that he's here beside me in the swelling darkness. Then he notices the buggy.

He blinks at Leo in surprise. Leo gurgles back.

Then my brother wails again.

Sebastian wrings his hands, clearly stressed out. 'Do you know what to do with him?'

I grin and jostle the buggy until the movement calms my brother back down. 'Yeah, of course. I've lived with him for ages.'

'Oh. Right.'

We stand for a few more awkward seconds and then I laugh nervously. 'Why are you here, Sebastian?'

'Grace didn't tell you?'

I shake my head.

'Oh, I just needed someone to show me around the Port.' He smiles his warm smile, his ocean eyes sparkling in the dark. 'And she suggested maybe you'd have some time. She gave me your number.'

I bite my lip and say nothing, just push the buggy along the cobblestones. 'I guess I've got some time.' When I glance across at Sebastian he's smiling again, falling into step beside me.

We stroll together between the peeling buildings, beneath heritage banks and government offices from the old days, me pushing the buggy and Leo's focus rolling to the sky where the clouds turn dark. We turn towards the river, walking in silence as the wind picks up, a relief as the sticky day turns cooler, night truly setting in.

And it's like in the beginning, the distance between us crackling with electricity and humming like a solid thing. There's no escaping it now, everything blooming anew in my chest, in my belly, back to where I was almost two years ago. Like no progress was made at all.

I don't mind it.

This feeling.

Sebastian is watching me. Keeps glancing across. Staring. I frown at him and he pretends he wasn't. 'Here,' I say. 'You push this.'

He doesn't complain, taking the stroller from me and making aeroplane noises for Leo.

'Are you an only child?'

Sebastian is startled, turning back. 'Yeah. Just me.'

'You live with your mum and dad?'

He shrugs. 'Yeah.' He pokes Leo again and my brother giggles. 'Where's your mum?'

I freeze a little. 'My actual mum, you mean?'

He shrugs again, nods. We've reached the river, concrete pavement right to the wharf, the pathway dropping off into nothing. Black inky water. Choppy from the wind and filled with ghostly white jellyfish, bobbing silently beneath the waves. Their bodies curl slow and languid, floating beneath the surface. Flying.

'My mother lives in Sydney,' I say.

He's awkward suddenly, as if sensing something in my tone. 'Oh. Sorry. I shouldn't have asked.'

I take a deep breath. Taste salt in the air. The wind picks up, cool and sharp, and the lights on the overpass bridge flicker on, one by one, orange electric glow spilling out across choppy waves as cars rumble over the cracked bitumen. Leo keeps wriggling so I heave him out of the stroller and flop onto a bench, propping him in my lap. He kicks like crazy. A happy pudgy thing.

'I don't mind talking about it,' I say quietly. Which is interesting because it's true. Yet no one in our house ever talks about my mother. It's like she's just gone, wiped from the face of the earth. Except for those occasions when she calls me, and then she only does that on the home landline, so she can talk to Dad as well. She never just texts me. Never calls my mobile. It's almost a relief to let the thoughts of her spill over now.

'You know that word, *saudade*?'

Sebastian shakes his head.

'It means to, like, nostalgically long to be near someone again, someone distant. Someone gone. But when I think about it, it probably wasn't all that great when she was here anyway. Rose-tinted glasses and all that, right?' I sigh. 'I think she was cheating on him. With someone from her work.' I reposition Leo in my lap as Sebastian slides onto the bench beside us, elbow to elbow now. 'They never actually told me. But I figured it out.' I throw a crooked smile at Sebastian. 'You know, creeping around and listening at doors and stuff. And then she was just gone. They got divorced and I heard my dad on the phone saying she's living with some dude in Sydney, but she never told me that directly. And then like, two minutes later, Celeste and my evil stepsister moved into our house. And apparently now my mother is marrying her new boyfriend in Sydney too. They just haven't set a date.'

'That sucks. I didn't know any of that stuff.'

I hesitate. He's staring at me again and suddenly I'm super awkward, as if I've just spilled my guts to a stranger. Which I have. 'Well, it's okay. I'm dealing.' I frown. Normally I don't talk about this stuff with anyone except Grace. And Jude. But it's different with them. They're my friends. Everything with them is different.

Sebastian hesitates too, the air between us heavy, and I wonder if I've ruined this thing before it's begun with my over-sharing. Gulls freewheel overhead, the sky turning inky black over the river but still tinged with blue above the bridge. His eyes shine with river water light as he says, 'Is that why you're like ...'

I frown. 'Like what?'

He shrugs. 'I dunno. Like, you keep acting out. You know, getting into trouble and stuff.'

I bark out a laugh. 'Oh no. I've always been like this.' I grin at him. 'Seriously. Always. When I was seven I poked holes in my teacher's car tyres.'

Sebastian is clearly shocked, which is fun. Maybe that's why I can never find the line. I like that look on his face a bit too much. I sigh. A habit to break.

'Why?' he says.

I shrug. 'I dunno. I saw it on television, I think. I can't remember. It's actually really hard to do, though. I had to get inventive.' I grin at him. 'And you?'

He looks confused.

My hands turn sweaty, throat dry and heart leaping inside my chest, but I ask it anyway. 'Why are you suddenly hanging out with me?'

I want to know. It's all too strange otherwise, and I have this fear we'll go back to school on Monday and he'll ignore me like he always has and it'll be like it never happened.

Sebastian coughs, glances my way and then at his hands. 'Honestly? I'm not really sure.'

'Huh,' I say. 'That's not exactly what I was hoping for.'

He bites his lip. 'I guess I just find you ... interesting. You're different from other people.'

Something defensive crackles beneath my skin. Like I can't quite put my finger on it but something about those words doesn't make me feel as good as it should. I can't think of a response though, so I stand and drop my happily gurgling brother into his arms, stretching my hands above my head as Sebastian juggles my gummy sibling, Leo's chubby legs in the air and fists flying.

I sit back down, and eventually say, 'I'm not though. Different, I mean.'

Sebastian's attention is trained on Leo, playing with my brother's flailing hand. He glances at me with ocean eyes. 'Yes, you are,' he says.

I frown. 'What about Jonathon Lee? He's into metal music. And he always causes trouble.' I wrinkle my nose, because although we have a lot in common, I can't stand Jonathon Lee, who's in the year above us. Although maybe that's why I hate him. I found out we have *too* much in common. My voice turns sharp. 'He's just as different as me. Are you interested in *him*, too?'

Sebastian muffles a laugh. 'I'm gonna be completely honest here and say that you're much prettier than he is.'

'Oh.'

That's the kind of smooth-talking that should most definitely not be taken to heart. My mother always said so. But I can't help it. My cheeks grow warm and my fingers tingle.

But still. I don't want him to be interested in me for those reasons. I'm more than just metal and trouble.

I watch him suspiciously as he clears his throat, bouncing Leo on his knee. 'I saw you playing guitar in the practice room at school.'

I'm taken aback at the abrupt change in subject. Also ... he saw me? I cough. 'Oh, yeah. I take classical lessons at school. And I muck around with other music at home. I'm not that great.' Then I add with determination, 'Yet.'

Sebastian uses his chin to gesture at my flapping band t-shirt. 'That kind of music?'

'Yeah, but it's harder at home because Celeste says it's noise. She says that's why the cat keeps peeing on the floor.'

Sebastian blinks. 'The cat pees on the floor?'

I nod absently. 'Yeah. But my dad deals with my music. He knows I like it. It's Celeste who hates it. I'm pretty sure she wishes I'd go live with my mum.'

I can't believe I said it out loud.

And now the words are out I can't ignore how true they feel, all that tiptoeing around Celeste in the house, the tension and the silence. I push my hair from my face. The wind is stronger now, thick and warm.

'So, tell me,' Sebastian says quietly, hefting Leo against his chest. He must be getting tired because Leo is heavy if you aren't used to it, but he doesn't say anything. My brother is grabbing chunks of his hair now but Sebastian holds on anyway, patiently untangling the chubby fingers. 'Tell me why it isn't noise.'

'Oh,' I say. No one's actually asked me that before. 'Well … um, I guess … what do you want to know?'

Suddenly I'm lost for words. I don't know where to begin.

Sebastian shrugs, glances at me. 'How about the lyrics? You can't understand what they sing about, right? Doesn't that annoy you?'

I laugh, warming to the subject. 'Nah. It's never about the lyrics. It's better if the voice sounds like an instrument, like it's just part of it all. I don't care about lyrics.'

Sebastian smiles at me, crooked in the darkness. 'Then what *do* you like?'

I'm pretty sure he's just humouring me, but I take my opportunities when they're given. Grace never asks me about my music. She listens to it when she comes over, and that's enough. Jude never asks. But I don't care, I tell him anyway. The thought of him makes me feel weird, but I push it from my mind.

'It's the feeling,' I say. 'The more intense the music the better the feeling.'

'Like ... an angry feeling?'

'No. See that? I hate that. I'm not angry. Everyone always thinks I'm angry, and that's why I listen to it. But it's not like that at all. Not even close. I love it. It's a good feeling. Like a happy feeling. It just ... lifts me up.'

'This does?' Sebastian's peering at my band t-shirt, which has some skeleton things on it. He grins at me, teeth glittering in the darkness. 'It's a very nice t-shirt.'

I giggle because he's teasing but not making fun of me. It's nice that he listened. That I don't feel stupid now for trying to explain something that's impossible to put into words. I grin back.

And that's when one of the buzzing cars rumbling over the bridge pulls to the sidewalk and Jamie Gorecki hangs out of the passenger window, long hair tousled by the wind. 'Hey,' he calls. 'Sebastian. Sebastian!'

Me and Sebastian both stand up, him going stiff as he heaves Leo against his chest, baby-brother legs and hands going everywhere. Leo grabs some of my hair and tugs.

'Ow!' I try uncurling his tight fist but it doesn't work. Sebastian tries awkwardly to help but Leo just gurgles and reaches for some of his hair too, yanking hard. Sebastian grunts sharply.

So both of us are standing tangled together in my brother as Jamie Gorecki and Obi Okocha gape from their car across the pavement. Excellent. I think the other two boys in the car are from school, too. Some of Sebastian's friends that I never talk with.

'What are you guys doing?' Sebastian yells loud enough that anyone walking the riverside would hear him. Obviously they don't because the Port isn't exactly a hotbed of activity, but still. He's loud.

'Nothing,' Jamie shouts back. 'Just cruising.' Then his voice changes, filled with innuendo. 'What are *you* doing, man?'

Finally I manage to get Leo's stocky fingers out of my hair. I yank away but that causes me to knock heads hard with Sebastian, my forehead against his chin, and that sends me reeling, rubbing my fingers against my skin. I'm about to ask Sebastian if he's okay, except Jamie and Obi and their car full of buddies pulls away from the curb. Which might have something to do with them being parked illegally.

I lift my hand to wave as they drive off, but Sebastian's gone all stiff and quiet beside me, very definitely not watching the retreating car and instead concentrating on Leo's grabby fingers. So I drop my hand back to my side and frown after the car as it tears away, tyres screeching.

I glance at Sebastian and a sick feeling blooms in my stomach, the night turning sour and grey.

Was he embarrassed by me?

Did he wish his friends hadn't seen us together outside school?

Sebastian walks me home after that but nothing is the same. I'm super aware of how my body moves and what I say and every flicker of expression that passes across his face. But I can't figure him out. What he's thinking. How he feels.

The night is dark, the moon dull. Leo begins to cry, his wails rising with the wind and shrieking gulls.

Sebastian says goodbye real fast next to the apartment

stairwell and just like that he melts into the dark night. I watch the space where he was and wonder if I sunk into a dream. Either way, I'm fully awake now. Like cold water to the face.

I sigh, and push open the stairwell door, squeezing Leo and the buggy through into the dark flickering space.

'Where did you go? I was looking for you.'

Jude is sitting on the bottom step beneath the flickering lights, elbows on knees and hair falling across his eyes. He's not looking directly at me, gaze dancing over Leo in his stroller instead, and I wonder if his dad is out at the pub again, his flat empty like it always is these days.

'Nowhere,' I say. 'I just went with ... I went walking.' I trail off awkwardly. I don't know why I don't mention Sebastian. But I don't. It's on the tip of my tongue but I swallow it back.

Jude sits all stiff and weird and doesn't look at me and finally I ask, 'Can you help with the buggy?'

Jude snorts, but still drags himself to his feet. I lift Leo into his arms, both of us standing pressed together for a moment until I manage to get Leo free from his harness. We drag the stroller upstairs, Jude at the top with Leo clutched against his chest and me at the bottom, taking the full weight. It's sort of mayhem. We're awful caretakers but we do make it.

I drop a kiss on little Leo's head as Jude carefully hands my brother back to me. Leo does a wet baby smile, like I'm his favourite thing in the world and I laugh, some of the sourness in my belly that Sebastian left behind lifting.

Jude raises his brows, flickering fluorescent light playing across his crowded freckled face. 'You and Leo seem to be getting along better these days.'

I giggle. 'Nah, I totally hate him.'

It takes a moment for Jude to catch on, to remember our game of opposites, but when he does he grins lightning quick, his eyes glimmering in the dark.

Back to the old Jude.

I grin back, thinking that maybe it doesn't matter if Sebastian is embarrassed of me. What do I care? I've got other friends who like me just the way I am. Like Grace.

Like Jude.

And then the door to my flat slams open and Celeste sticks her head out and yells at me for kidnapping Leo. It turns out I have five missed calls on my mobile so Jude goes home to an empty flat and I endure ten minutes of being lectured about responsibility while the whole time Evelyn lurks in the kitchen and throws evil smirks my way. Grace was here with her apparently, without telling me, but she's long since gone home.

Afterwards I go to my room and lie on my bed with my headphones on, music cranked as loud as I can handle. I don't think about Sebastian.

Not even once.

10

IDENTIFYING PATHWAYS TOWARDS IMPROVED SELF-ESTEEM

I flop next to Grace, the plastic chair scraping against the concrete. She's bought a pie from the tuckshop and is stuffing it into her face, seated alone at a long table. The rest of the room is filled with screeching, wailing students, the scent of food hanging thick in the air, a mix of savoury and too-sweet.

I wrinkle my nose. 'You didn't want to sit outside?'

'Too hot,' garbles Grace through a mouthful of pie.

I nod. The outside world is truly blazing today, the sun high and bright and the sky blue, blue, blue. Even inside it's muggy and thick with the heat of a million students, the air-conditioners trying their best to keep up. I look at my wilted sandwich and sigh, peeling back a corner to reveal greens long since gone soft and limp. Celeste packed it for me.

I stand up, announcing, 'I'm gonna get some chips,' just as Jude turns up. I throw my sandwich at him. 'It's special Celeste brand, wet lettuce and vegemite.'

'Sweet.' He grins and collapses onto his chair, the sandwich unwrapped in one second, and deep in the innards of Jude within the next. I roll my eyes and head to the canteen, my attention flickering over the faces I pass, across the tables and the other students sitting there. I don't see Sebastian. Haven't seen him all day. But I'm waiting for it. The inevitable moment he crosses my path and I raise my hand to wave and he just breezes right by, ignoring me. Everything returning to how it used to be. Sebastian living his nice life with his nice friends. And me watching from afar.

I sigh, irritated with myself. It shouldn't matter if he's embarrassed. It shouldn't. Because I'm fine with who I am. It's only him who isn't.

And yet it hurts.

Except when I return to our table carrying a greasy box of steaming chips, I freeze, heart beating just a little faster against my rib cage.

Sebastian is sitting there.

Next to Grace. Across from Jude.

At our table.

It takes me a moment to collect myself, but finally I slide into my chair beside Jude and manage a casual nod to Sebastian. Jude is hunched all stiff with his elbows on the table and fingers dancing across the white plastic surface. Me, I can't peel my attention away from Sebastian, soaking up his ocean eyes and tousled hair, the way he smiles at me sheepishly and shrugs.

'Hope you don't mind,' he says. 'Thought I'd hang with you guys today.'

'I don't mind,' I choke out, and both Grace and Jude snort loudly. I glare daggers at them, before glancing across the lunch room towards Sebastian's usual table.

His friends are still there. Jamie. Finn. Lucas. Obi. All those guys.

But Sebastian's *here*. Sitting across from me.

I peek at him from beneath my lashes. He's watching me. Smiling widely, white teeth and sparkling eyes. So I guess he's not embarrassed at all. Warmth steals back into my belly, the final trace of sourness from Saturday night melting away.

A slow smile creeps across my face and I reach for a chip.

Jude gets there first, snatching it from beneath my fingertips. I watch in horror as it sails towards his mouth and disappears into the abyss. I slap him upside the head.

'Ow!'

I huff. 'You deserved it. These are *my* chips. Mine. Go get your own.'

He smiles at me sweetly, nudging my shoulder with his. 'Yours are better though.'

I roll my eyes. 'And why is that exactly?'

He bats his lashes. 'Because you already paid for them. Obviously.'

'Ugh. You already ate my sandwich. Now you're eating my chips! What's next? Leo?'

Jude barks a laugh. And then steals another chip. 'I don't want to eat your baby brother, Charlotte.' He goes for another but I slap his hand away.

Grace sighs loudly across the table, well used to our antics. She's texting on her phone and I glare at her. It's probably my gross stepsister. She's probably inviting Evelyn to lunch, to sit with us.

I open my mouth to protest, but Jude gets there first, greasy salt covered fingertips pinching my cheek and tugging me close to his face. 'Be nice,' he whispers through his grin. 'Remember?'

I shove him off. But he's right.

Be nice.

About Evelyn.

Right.

I slap a cheesy smile on my face and lean across Jude to address Grace. 'You can invite Evelyn to sit with us if you want.' I grin at my best friend and she blinks back at me.

'Oh, I already did.'

My grin stretches wider. 'Good.'

Jude elbows me and I sit straight again, shoving two chips into my mouth. Grace is smiling now, focused on her phone again. I pull a disgusted face just as Sebastian clears his throat.

'So,' he says, 'you two seem close.'

He's glancing between me and Jude, watching Jude like he's seeing the other boy for the first time. Which maybe he is. I mean, we all share a lot of classes, but Sebastian doesn't seem particularly observant of the people beyond his friend group.

I would know.

I shove another chip into my mouth. 'We're not that close,' I say, just as Jude says, 'Yeah. We're really close.'

Grace waves her hand, not even peering up from her mobile as she interjects, 'They're best friends. For like ten years.' She glances at Jude. 'Right?'

'Right.' He smiles at Sebastian, slow and wide. Which makes me frown.

And also, what did Grace say?

I turn to her, hurt. '*We're* best friends,' I say, pointing between her and me.

She ignores me and leans close to Sebastian. 'They've lived next door to each other since they were kids. But honestly, I don't know how they make it work. Jude is way too good for Lottie.'

Jude laughs and my mouth drops open. 'Excuse me? He's too good for me?'

Grace pulls a face, slipping her phone away. 'Obviously. He's perfect and you're awful. I don't know why he puts up with you.' She uses her fingers to count as she says, 'He gets good marks, everyone likes him, he's good-looking and nice ...' She leans across the table and points at me. 'And all you do is get him into trouble.'

'When did I ever?' I'm scandalised. I shake my head at Sebastian so he knows my friends are exaggerating.

'Last week,' says Jude. He's eating my chips again and not even looking at me. 'You got me suspended.'

'Yeah, but I fixed it! And besides, Jude does bad stuff too.'

Jude stares at me blankly and Grace laughs. Loudly. 'No, he doesn't,' she says. And I find I don't quite have an answer to that, except I'm feeling put out, all my friends ganging up on me in front of Sebastian. I grimace and then notice Sebastian is scowling too, mainly aimed at Jude who is smiling pleasantly back at him. And I don't like that at all. I'm supposed to be making a good impression. I elbow Jude in the ribs but he only smiles wider, barely breaking eye contact with Sebastian as he rubs his side.

That's when Evelyn joins us, dropping down next to Grace.

I groan. Inwardly, silently, because I don't want Jude grabbing my cheek again. But, seriously, all this conversation needs is another voice to join in with the Charlotte-bashing. And I happen to know that Charlotte-bashing is Evelyn's absolute favourite activity.

'What are we talking about?' Evelyn says, leaning across to give Grace a quick kiss on the lips.

Sebastian gapes at them and I catch Jude rolling his eyes,

arms crossed over his chest. He certainly seems defensive. I poke him in the ribs and make a *what's wrong with you?* face, but he just shakes his head and ignores me.

'Nothing interesting,' answers Grace. 'You still okay to come over?'

Now my stepsister is hanging at Grace's house? I haven't been over there in ages. A stab of jealousy flits inside my chest. 'What are you guys doing?'

Grace grins. 'Working on Evelyn's costume. I've already finished mine. Then I'll get onto yours.'

I blink. 'What costume?' I say it at the exact same time as Sebastian, who is very confused, almost as confused as me.

Grace scowls. 'I knew you wouldn't remember! The festival, Lottie. The medieval fair.'

Oh. Right.

'Of course I remember,' I say, attempting to backtrack. 'I'm majorly looking forward to it.'

Grace pokes out her tongue. 'Whatever. Anyway, you should come over on Thursday. I've already got a cool idea.'

'What about *my* costume?' interjects Jude, but Grace just shakes her head.

'You have to do your own. What do you think I am, a machine?'

I grin. 'A sewing machine.'

'Ha ha, Charlotte. Very funny.' But Grace *is* laughing, so I guess she does think it's funny.

'Hey, Lottie,' interjects Sebastian suddenly. 'I hope you got back home okay on Saturday?'

I freeze, everyone's gaze falling on me. Grace smothers a grin and I remind myself to kill her later.

'Oh. Yeah. Totally, thanks,' I mumble. But he's smiling at me so I smile back. I can't help it.

Jude shifts on his seat, the chair scraping against the concrete loudly, breaking the moment. That's when I notice Sebastian glancing across the room towards his usual table. Evelyn notices too, unfortunately, and after Sebastian has cleared his lunch stuff and given me a soft smile in farewell, she says beneath her breath, 'Wow, that Sebastian guy sure seemed uncomfortable sitting here with us. Don't you think?'

I scowl at her but say nothing, refusing to feel hurt.

Maybe Sebastian is still a teeny bit embarrassed, but he sat here anyway. With us rejects. I glance around our table. He sat here with the lesbo and the goth and the quiet nerd. Even Evelyn who everyone says is super pretty is still considered a teacher's pet. Despite all that he still sat with us. And I think that means something.

No matter what Evelyn says.

I stand and shove my empty chip box at Jude. 'I've gotta go see old Jerry.'

Grace perks her head up. 'Why? What'd you do?'

I give them a mysterious smile, purposely vague, before skipping from the lunch room and back into the school halls. I don't actually know why Jerry asked to see me, but I have a reputation to uphold. Upstairs I slip past the secretary and bang on the door to Jerry's office.

'You wanted to see me, Mr Virk?' I ask when I'm standing in front of his desk. He peers at me over his glasses, flinching at my formal words. I flash an innocent smile

'Is everything going well with you, Charlotte?'

'Whatever do you mean, Mr Virk?'

He sits back. 'You're studying now? Outside class hours?'

'Why, yes, I am. Did Ms Breannie tell you?' I'm pleased.

He sits in silence, eyes narrowed. 'And you didn't get in trouble at all this week?'

I sway on my feet. 'Yup.'

He nods. 'Fine. Good. That's nice. Keep it up, Charlotte.'

I stand there waiting until he raises his brows again. 'That's it. Go away now.'

'Oh! Right, great chat, Mr Virk.' I grin at him, and skip towards the door. He stops me though, calling my name just as I'm about to slip outside.

'Charlotte?'

'Yes, Mr Virk?'

He purses his lips, hesitating. 'I'm glad to hear you applied for the music scholarship. And I'll give your parents a quick call today. Let them know about your progress.'

My smile grows wider. 'Ha! Thanks, Jerry ... uh, I mean, Mr Virk.'

He snorts and shoos me from his office.

11

ON THE TRAIN, BETWEEN SCHOOL AND YOUR HOUSE

Inspired by my talk with Jerry, I sit through another late afternoon study session with Jude in the school library and then get the train home with him and Grace. Evelyn is already long gone. She has her flute lesson after school and I couldn't be happier, considering it means she's somewhere else, anywhere else, instead of here beside Grace.

The three of us crowd together in one of the booths on the train, Jude squished between me and the window, thigh to thigh, Grace across from us. We're hemmed in by a bunch of retiree tourists off one of the massive cruise ships at the end of the peninsula. People are squished everywhere, the train chockers because there's only two carriages, barely enough for a normal day, let alone a cruise ship day.

I groan as the woman next to me presses in, her industrial-sized handbag poking into my rib cage. Grace is basically in the exact same position next to some old dude and his big backpack. I grimace and sidle closer to Jude, who is steadfastly gazing out the window, his body stiff.

I ask, 'So, guess what.'

Grace peers dreamily at her phone and I have to snap my fingers to get her attention. 'Guess what. Guess what.'

'Ugh. What!?'

I grin. 'Jerry said he's gonna call my parents to congratulate me on my outstanding behaviour.'

Grace scoffs, unimpressed. 'It's only been two weeks, Lottie. You'll be mucking everything up again by next Friday. Bet you.'

I'm insulted. 'No way. I'm a changed woman.'

I elbow Jude in the ribs for backup but he just shrugs and mutters against the glass, 'Deeds will not be less valiant because they are unpraised.'

'What?' I turn to Grace. 'What did he say?'

My best friend shrugs. 'I dunno. Some weird thing.' She returns to her dreamy phone gazing. Thinking about my gross stepsister probably.

I poke him. 'What did you say?'

Jude won't meet my eyes so I sling an arm across his shoulders and drag him closer. 'That's not from *The Lion King*, Jude. It isn't. I know. I watched it, remember?'

He grins, real close in my face, trying to extricate himself from my arm. 'I never said it was from *The Lion King*. It's wisdom. It means you have to want to do the right thing for *yourself*, even if no one ever finds out you did it.' He keeps struggling to get away but I'm having none of it. Our temples are almost touching.

'You're saying I have to be good but not tell anyone about it?' I make a face and hiss so Grace can't hear, 'Um, Jude, that basically goes against everything this plan stands for.'

He shrugs. Difficult when I'm still wrapped around his shoulders. 'Maybe you should re-think the plan, Lottie. Maybe changing is dumb.' His mouth grows tight and his eyes hard. 'Maybe you're fine the way you are.'

'Psshhh. Whatever. The plan is working.'

Jude scowls and shrugs me off, but I'm not letting him get away with it. 'What's it from then? The quote, what movie? Go on, tell me.'

He attempts to slink away but I poke him in the ribs, in the cheek, smile sweetly as he squirms. 'Come on, Jude. What movie? What movie?'

He pushes me off. 'Alright, alright. Fine.'

I extricate myself and sit back primly. I say nothing at all, just wait with my brows raised.

He sighs. Loudly. '*Lord of the Rings.*'

'Ha! I knew it.' I turn to Grace who steadfastly ignores me. 'Didn't I say I knew it?'

'I don't think so,' she answers. She's still on her phone. Texting now. My mouth turns down. Honestly. It could have been anyone. Anyone at all. Why does it have to be my stepsister?

I sigh.

Finally it's our stop and I wave goodbye to Grace and pull Jude out of the carriage just as the doors slide shut, my hand clutching his. The train rumbles away, shaking and grinding along the overpass bridge as I stand waving on the cracked pavement, unsure if Grace sees, so intent on her stupid phone and my stupid stepsister.

I sigh and turn around, almost slamming into Jude who's standing directly behind me. His cheeks are flushed beneath his mass of freckles and his eyes shine blue, as bright as the sky above. I drop his hand and glance upwards as I sidestep him.

It's cloudless and vast. Beautiful. I glance over my shoulder and raise my brows. 'You coming or what?'

He nods, silent as we walk down the train ramp to the street, where iron archways tower overhead and the traffic streams by in a rush-hour onslaught, buses roaring and cars beeping. It's nice walking with Jude through the Port. I'm always a little calmer with him, like my mind stops racing. I think it's because he's always been kind of quiet. I mean, he talks – he talks heaps – and he's irritating as hell, but still, he's quieter than most people. I glance at him and he smiles, small and quiet.

We walk slow, past the fast-food restaurants on the outskirts of the Port, alongside the billion old ramshackle pubs perched on every street corner. We slip along a thin winding cobbled lane between two old warehouses, stone walls and leaning staircases folded into overgrown backyards and hidden behind peeling tin fences. And the whole time Jude says nothing at all and just follows with his bright blue eyes and smile.

I perch on the very edge of Jude's bed. It's late and he's supposed to be helping me study but I can't concentrate. I slide onto the floor. 'I don't like it,' I whine.

Jude turns from his desk. Squints in the harsh light of the desk lamp. 'You don't like chemistry?'

'No. I mean, yes, that too. But you know how you bite your cheek, and then you keep biting that same spot accidentally over and over?'

'Uh, yeah?'

'I don't like how there isn't a word for that. Why wouldn't there be? It's a truly universal emotion.'

Jude frowns. 'I don't think biting your cheek is an emotion, Lottie.'

I kick my bare foot against his bed frame, rubbing my aching cheek and groaning.

Jude turns back to his work and for a while there is silence, only the tapping of keys and scratching of pen on paper. I can't take the quiet and the boredom so crawl up to kneel beside his computer chair, pressing my elbow into his and pushing him aside, my fingers dancing across his keyboard, searching the net for a song.

'What are you playing?' Jude murmurs. He doesn't stop me though.

I find it and click play, reaching across him to turn up his speakers as the music begins, quiet and atmospheric at first; deep mountain sounds. I imagine fjords and ice, dark lakes and misty forests. The song starts for real now, wiping the wisps away, filling Jude's bedroom with rasping raw vocals, high and wavering, and muddy messy guitar. I close my eyes and move my head, getting into it, letting the sounds crawl beneath my skin, beat inside my blood.

When I open them again Jude is smiling at me, one corner of his mouth curling up. 'What is this again? Doom metal?'

I sigh dramatically because I've explained the genres so many times before. He listens but he never really listens. A secret part of me doesn't mind, though. I'll just explain it all again. I like talking about it, anyway, especially with Jude because he sits quiet and still and smiles while I talk. 'No! This is *black* metal, doom is slow and melodic. Well, usually. But stuff like this is different. Listen.'

We do. But mostly Jude just keeps glancing across at me, a smile curling his mouth, as if he finds me amusing. I ignore him.

'It's more muddy, hear that? And the vocals are like, shrieking.' I turn it down a little, so we can hear each other better, my elbow pressing into his. 'I really like this song.'

'Is this the stuff you'd like to play? On guitar I mean.'

I shake my head. 'I'd love to play the more technical stuff. Like death metal. But it's harder.' I flick off the song to show him an example, finding a different video featuring a guy and a girl from a death metal band filming a playthrough. It's just them sitting in a room and performing only the guitar sections of a song, displaying their skills in perfect tandem, perfect harmony, fingers flying across the fretboards. I stare, mesmerised, until Jude says thoughtfully, 'What about *cheekobitus*?'

'Huh?'

'For the word. You know, the word for when you keep biting your cheek.'

I laugh, delighted. 'I like it. But it should be more, I dunno, beautiful and inspiring sounding.' I think for a bit. Try to come up with the silliest nonsense word I can. 'What about *larbostrome*?'

'Sounds like a throat lozenge,' Jude murmurs. 'Or pasta.'

I giggle.

We go back to silence, me watching my playthrough videos and Jude scratching at his homework beside me, elbows pressed together. Eventually my attention wanders, bored once more, glancing across his carpet, across the walls and ceiling. His horrible royal doll is on the shelf again. Staring at me with her newly cracked face. I shiver. Creepy.

I chew on my lip, formulating this brilliant idea for a prank, which involves stealing the horrible doll and leaving it in disturbing places to freak Evelyn out. I laugh beneath my breath before remembering I'm playing the long con now, and being good is my new endgame. Which means getting better at my schoolwork is also my new endgame. Which means actual old-fashioned work.

Which is boring.

I collapse onto the carpet and roll onto my stomach, my massive metal t-shirt getting tangled. Basically I roll around inside the material, like I'm living inside it instead of wearing it. I bat at Jude's ankle with my hand. 'I've got a larbostrome, Jude. It aches. Help me.'

I exhale sharply and roll around some more as Jude leans back over his chair to frown at me.

'Do you want a drink to help with your larbostrome?'

'A drink of alcohol?'

Jude's mouth twists into a grin. 'I meant of juice.'

I nod pitifully and he shuffles off. His dad is out so their flat is empty. I'm pretty sure Eddie doesn't hate me anymore, but it's hard to forget my conversation with Jude in the parking lot and the game of opposites we played. I'm feeling quite protective of him right now and not so sure how I feel about his dad.

No, that's a lie.

Eddie pisses me off.

But yelling at Eddie definitely doesn't fit into my new life plan.

I roll off the floor and scuttle onto the bed as Jude comes in with two glasses. I settle next to him and sniff at mine, taking experimental gulps. Tangy and sharp.

I bite my lip. 'So where did you say your mum went again?'

He stiffens. 'Overseas. Visiting family.'

'Yeah but where?'

'Croatia. But like, her family is Italian. Was Italian. But after her folks came out here the borders moved.'

'That sounds … complicated.'

He shrugs, carefully casual. But I know him well and so I see the way his blue eyes dim, the way his mouth grows hard and tight. I plop my glass on his bedside table and lie back, so I'm no longer facing him, giving him some space. I don't want him to feel like I'm interrogating him. But I still want to ask.

'When's she coming back?'

He hesitates, the muscles in his back tight with tension, stiffening beneath the thin material of his t-shirt. 'I dunno.'

I'm silent for a moment, and then I ask carefully, 'Have you been speaking to her?'

'Yeah. She calls my mobile.' He turns to face me suddenly, eyes on mine. 'I could've gone with her. She asked me to. But I had school and … stuff here. And I didn't want to give it up.' He turns back around, his body stiff. He seems small suddenly, though he's not really, not since our second year of high school when he grew nearly as tall as me and his shoulders got wide and his body stocky.

I hesitate. 'Are you okay?'

'Yeah, of course. Are you hungry? I'm hungry. Come on, I'll make us something.' He stands abruptly and I pretend not to see when he flicks his palm across his eyes real fast, as if wiping away tears.

If it'd been Grace I'd have launched myself at her then, hugged her until she cried for real, until she got it out of her system.

But it's different with Jude. I don't know why.

It didn't used to be. When my mum walked out the first thing I did was climb over our balconies and crawl through his window, collapsing on his bed in tears. It's hard to remember fully but I'm sure Jude must have hugged me back then. Pretty sure I fell asleep like that, beside him here in his bedroom.

But that was nearly two years ago and something has changed between us.

Though I don't know what.

So I say nothing and don't touch him as I trail behind him into the main area of the flat, and I sit on the couch as he fusses around in the kitchen and cooks pasta for us to share. And I pretend not to see the stacked empty vodka bottles next to the bin.

I muck around with my phone for a bit, playing games because it seems easier than talking, and then finally fling my mobile onto the coffee table and leave to use the bathroom.

When I come back the water in the pot is boiling over and the sauce is sizzling in the pan and Jude is nowhere to be seen. And that's when I catch the glimmer of my mobile. Three missed calls from Sebastian.

I call him back straight away, my heart beating fast, but Sebastian doesn't pick up. I call Jude's name and drift to the window, and that's when I see them both downstairs on the empty street, a streetlight seeping yellow sickly light across the cobblestones.

I take just enough time to flick off the stove before heading downstairs. Voices swell through the stairwell, both of them talking, yet when I emerge into the warm night they break off. Sebastian is smirking and Jude is seething.

I snap, 'What the hell is going on?'

They both flinch at that. I didn't mean it to sound so harsh but, honestly, I'm a bit freaked out. 'What are you guys doing out here?'

Sebastian smiles easily, relaxed. 'I'm here because of you.'

A humming surges in my ears, and I try to remind myself that he was uncomfortable sitting with us at lunch, but then another part of me shouts that he did it anyway. I smile slowly in the dark. 'Yeah?'

Sebastian grins back. 'Yeah. Jude was telling me more about that festival thing you're all going to and I was saying I might tag along.' He smirks at Jude. There is no other way to describe the expression on his face, and it makes me feel strange, yet his next words send me soaring again, my two-year crush hitting like a floodgate opening. 'I mean, if you'll have me, Lottie.'

I nod numbly. 'Uh, yeah. That sounds good.' I glance at my flat. 'I mean, my stepmum is driving us, apparently, but I don't reckon she'll mind.'

Sebastian is pretty pleased with himself. 'Cool. Well, you can text me the details.' He smiles wide at Jude. 'And I guess I'll leave you both to it, then.'

I wave as he walks down the street. A car revs to life and he hops into the back seat, and when it drives by I'm pretty sure I see Jamie's face in the driver's seat and some other boys from school. I'm pretty sure they're laughing, too, and I don't know what that means.

Jude turns and stalks back inside without waiting for me,

the stairwell door practically slamming in my face. I scrabble against it and slide into the dimly lit darkness within, calling for Jude up the stairs. He's taking them two at a time, his sneakers scuffing against the concrete, almost out of sight. 'Hey,' I yell. 'Hey! What about my pasta?'

He turns at the top of the stairs and peers down, breathing heavily. It's too dark to see his expression, but his eyes glitter with the dim fluorescent lights lining the stairs, his silhouette blue.

For a moment I think he's going to say something, see him drawing breath, but then the stairwell door slams open again and Jude's dad comes in behind me. I lurch out of his way as he stomps past, the sharp tang of liquor clinging to his clothes, as if they're soaked in it. Eddie clomps up the stairs, hesitating in front of Jude, who refuses to move out of his way, electricity and tension thick between them. In the end Eddie says nothing to his son at all, simply sliding past, his head down so he doesn't have to meet Jude's gaze.

We stand there when he's gone. Jude staring at me in the dim blue light and me frozen in place at the bottom of the staircase, unable to say all the things that sit heavy on my tongue. None of them seems good enough. And so for once I don't say a word.

Finally Jude steps back, eyes still on mine. 'Goodnight, Lottie.'

'Goodnight,' I whisper as he melts into the darkness. I hear him walking long after he's disappeared, his footsteps echoing on the concrete.

I feel strange and light-headed when I get home, yet it turns out Jude is wrong about doing good for internal reasons. Jerry, it seems, is a man of his word.

The whole family gathers together in our kitchen to praise me. Leo makes pudgy baby noises of approval and Celeste touches my chin softly, and even her eyes are smiling. Dad envelops me in a massive bear hug. And all the while Evelyn watches with crossed arms, mouth tight and pinched.

I'm such a good daughter. So different now, so studious and trouble-free.

My parents love me. My teachers love me. And best of all?

Evelyn is absolutely seething.

I smile at her sweetly as Celeste kisses my cheek.

But I still feel sick.

12

OLD MEN WITH POWDERED FACES AND CURLY WHITE WIGS

The buildings at school are big and squat, nestled in the middle of a wide parched oval, all yellow summer grass and lined-up monstrous pine trees. If I stand at the right angle I can catch a glimpse of the ocean over the fence and across the road. Waves lapping and blue water calling on hot days, when heat bakes the footpath and the school hallways are cool in comparison. Inside the buildings I can't see the water. But I always know it's there. It's in the way the air smells, in the humidity. Rust and salt.

I love the smell of the ocean.

Grace spots me in the crush of students. We haven't talked yet this morning, have different first classes, but she does this very dramatic thing where she acts as if the crowd is dragging her away from me, desperately grabbing for my hand and sliding a piece of paper into my palm before she is swept screaming my name in the opposite direction, the tide of people ripping her away.

Freaking hilarious, Grace is.

I stop and open the note, reading the word scrawled across the page.

Tarantism.

I whip out my phone and search for the meaning. Grace is never useful enough to handfeed me the definitions.

Tarantism – the uncontrollable urge to dance.

I giggle and text her a picture of the last horrendous district dance we attended. The photo is blurred and the dance was meant to be a dry zone but, let me tell you, it wasn't. The picture clearly shows a bunch of blurry teens all dancing madly to some awful rubbish music. We got there, took a few quick snaps, and then we had the uncontrollable urge to leave again. So we did. We took our own bottle of contraband to the river and watched the stars and the jellyfish. Stayed until curfew and then ambled back home.

Which would have worked out great if Evelyn hadn't ratted us out.

I can't believe Grace has forgotten about that.

I scowl and slide my phone away, prowling through the rush of morning students again.

Sebastian is waiting for me at my locker. At first I think that's a good thing, except then I remember how weird last night was between him and Jude and feel nervous. And he looks strange, too, uniform wrinkled, tie askew. He's still super pretty, even all dishevelled. Maybe more so because of it.

I sigh.

I don't know what's wrong with me when it comes to Sebastian. I think my longing for him set in so deep over the years that now I'm basically useless around him. But he's popular in a way that makes him unattainable, untouchable. And yet ...

'Hey Lottie.'

I stop right in front of him and heave my bag from my shoulders, letting it drop heavily at our feet. 'Hey.' I feel shy.

He's got his head to the side, assessing me. 'What's up with you hanging around that Jude kid? You were at his house last night?'

Well, he's straight out with it. 'Our parents are friends,' I say carefully, which is sort of the truth. 'I go over there for dinner a lot. Like Grace said, we grew up together.'

I don't know why I'm being so careful with my words. I don't know why any of this matters.

Except Sebastian bites his lip, clearly suspicious, which throws me.

Is he jealous? Is that what's happening here?

Jealous of Jude?

I'm shocked. Too shocked to ask the question I've been dying to ask since Sebastian first began talking to me out of the blue.

Does he like me? Is he playing with me? Is he serious?

I don't ask and Sebastian doesn't answer.

Instead he awkwardly shrugs and then a slow smile spreads across his face. 'Okay,' he says finally. 'I just don't want to be stepping on anyone's toes.'

I have no idea what that means. Jude's toes? I nod wisely. 'Right,' I say.

That's when I notice the tide of students in the hallway are giving us a wide berth. People are watching us, interested. Sebastian doesn't seem to notice. He lifts my books into my locker and then says, 'But seriously, you know what that Jude dude said in class today about Mr Virk?' He suddenly snorts with laughter. 'Huh. *Jude dude.*'

'It rhymes,' I point out.

'Yeah. Anyway, he said he's a great principal.' He raises his eyebrows at me like it explains everything.

'Jerry? But he is. He's an excellent principal.'

Sebastian frowns. 'Come on, Lottie. We're talking about Mr Virk!'

I shrug. 'I like him.'

'Maybe there's something wrong with you, too.' He smiles when he says it, though, teasing. I don't think he means anything by it, but it does remind me that we're different, that I don't exactly fit into his group of friends. For some reason he's making an exception for me. For my music. My clothes. My capacity to get everyone around me in trouble every two minutes.

And I don't get it.

But I'm not complaining. I'm still not sure how he feels, if he likes me or if this is some sort of game. But I think maybe he does like me.

And he's just so pretty.

I smile back. 'Maybe there is.'

Grace emerges then from the crowd of students, stopping at my elbow and totally ruining my moment, oblivious. She has a stack of papers pressed against her chest, frowning in concentration. She says something about notes from Jude and schoolwork and then looks up and sees Sebastian. 'Oh. Hello.'

Sebastian smiles warmly. 'What's up, Grace?'

'Oh, nothing. Just ... being at school.'

Sebastian blinks at her. 'Right.'

I clamp my hand over Grace's shoulder. Firmly. 'Excellent. Sebastian? We got stuff to do. See you later?'

He doesn't appear that excited about it. 'Sure, whatever. Go.' For a moment I get worried, like he thinks I'm trying to blow him off or something, except then he grins, adding, 'I'm looking forward to the festival, Lottie.' And with that he melts into the crowd, still smiling at me over his shoulder, joining the fray to head off to his next class.

I stand grinning after him. A little goofy.

Grace disengages my hand from her shoulder, stiffening as she glances down the hallway after Sebastian. 'Are you sure about this, Lottie? I can't figure out if I like him or not.'

'You're the one who gave him my number!'

She shrugs. 'Yeah, only because I knew you wanted me to. But seriously, sometimes he's nice, but sometimes ... I dunno. I'm just not sure.'

'Is this because he laughed at your hair?'

She pouts. 'No. Like I said. I'm just not sure.'

'Of course you're not sure. You don't like anyone.' Mainly I just say that to irritate her. And sure enough ...

'What? But I like *everyone*!' She's gaping at me. 'I get along with everyone!'

I giggle. She's almost as easy to tease as Jude. Who was actually meant to be meeting me for a study session right about now.

I frown. 'Where's Jude?'

Grace shrugs. 'I dunno. He said he was busy. But he gave me all this stuff.' She shoves the papers at me, leaving me scrambling. Notes. Study materials. Boring stuff.

I sigh. There's no way I'm going to be able to concentrate on this stuff if he's not around to help me.

'Do you want to help me study?' I ask Grace hopefully.

She just snorts and turns around without a word, disappearing into the rush of students.

I guess that's a no then.

Slowly I make my way to my next class, a study period. Jude is nowhere in sight. I spread my things across a desk and ignore the general hum in the room, other students talking and laughing, trying to block them out and concentrate on my work.

Studying is hard without Jude. Within ten minutes my mind has wandered and I'm thinking about Sebastian again, how it might actually be possible he likes me, judging from the fact he wants to go to the festival. Because why else would he want to go?

I let myself daydream until thoughts of Jude break in, thoughts of his dad and the weirdness hanging over their house. And the irritating tension between him and Sebastian. And also I think about Evelyn. And Celeste and my dad. All my problems come pouring back in.

I grit my teeth and forcibly focus on the work in front of me, on my books and Jude's notes, on his scrawl spread across the pages. Except without him here to help me decipher the words and text, nothing ends up feeling like it should.

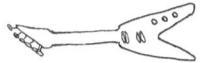

The next couple of days pass in a blur of study and guitar practice. Of quiet smiles across classrooms from Sebastian and some very strategic avoidance of Evelyn, both at home and at school. Grace ditches school on Friday to work on my costume and suddenly I'm the responsible one, because when she asks me to join her I say no.

Instead I'm sitting in the music room at school with Mr Smith in the late afternoon, and he's watching me play the piece he's chosen for the audition video, some old-timey classical guitar thing that requires a lot of fiddly fingers and picking. My fingernails ache from tugging at the strings and my hands are growing thick callouses from pressing hard against the fretboard. The whole thing is super painful and the song must be about a thousand years old, the kind of thing some old dude with a powdered face and a white curly wig would've played.

And yet ...

I guess it's growing on me.

The music.

It's so different to metal and yet every day I find new correlations, new commonalities, and when I go home and listen to my favourite albums I wonder about those guitar players. Were they classically trained? Do they understand the theory behind the riffs they play? Are the technical melodies directly influenced by some old crusty song like the one Mr Smith has me playing over and over again?

He sits now in the thick afternoon sunlight at the piano, an upright thing that creaks when he opens the wooden lid. He's bathed in a cloud of dust motes floating in the air-conditioning and his fingers play scales across the black and white keys. He asks me to imitate, using only my ears and no written music to copy the sounds, to pick the notes of the scales on my guitar strings and follow what he does, just a few beats after. And I can do it. If I concentrate hard enough. Little by little, I can do it.

He's a strict teacher and rarely smiles through his enormous bushy beard. I'm pretty sure he misses the old days, when he would've been allowed to rap me on the knuckles with a ruler every time I bunged up a note, but still ... I'd never admit it to anyone, not even Jude, but I kind of like the music we play in that room. And I like the way Mr Smith's mouth twitches at the corner, almost imperceptible through his wiry beard, whenever I copy the scales correctly, or play the old-timey song just a little bit better than I played it the day before.

When the scheduled hour is over, Mr Smith offers to stay with me a little longer if I want, to run through some more pieces. He doesn't face me when he asks, but I know what it means.

Evelyn always stays back after music class, her and this other random dude who plays drums. And what do they have in common?

They're both really good.

I stare at Mr Smith's back as I stumble over my words, agreeing to stay. I know what the offer means.

It means my hard work is paying off.

It means he sees potential in my playing.

In me.

No teacher has offered to spend more time on me before, or believed in me enough to offer me anything except detention slips and complaints. I sit still in the orange sunlit room and listen as Mr Smith explains theory to me, using his ruler to point to the music notation on the page. And though they're sore, my fingers follow his instructions and dance across the guitar strings.

And I think that maybe, just maybe, I never gave any of my teachers a real chance to offer me anything before. I slide my hand along the neck of the guitar, skin against polished wood, and think of home. Of Dad telling me to meet people halfway, to offer something before I expect to get something in return.

Mr Smith's voice grows sharp, and I shake my head to clear it, music and theory and sound filling every inch of my mind for just one hour more.

13

IF I WAS LONELY I'D PROBABLY CALL YOU. WOULD YOU CALL ME?

'And then he, like, totally praised me. And said I've got a chance to actually get the scholarship.' I'm so happy I'm dancing, skipping beside Jude and clutching his arm. He seems distracted but I'm too excited to care.

'Great,' is all he says.

'It's more than great! It's *ineffable!*'

Jude pulls his bag from his locker as I bounce beside him, guitar bobbing against my shoulderblades and the straps digging into my skin. 'Jude,' I press. 'Jude?'

'Uh huh.'

'Do you know what that word means? *Ineffable*?' I don't wait for him to answer. 'It's a word you use for describing something that's too vast to be put into words. Grace gave it to me.'

Jude slams his locker shut and shoulders his bag, glancing at me. 'You've missed the train.'

I shrug. 'I know that. You brought your bike. I'll come home with you.' I continue to follow him as he strides out of the halls into the heat of the sunshine outside. The pine trees that line the oval shimmer in the sun, a heavy wind pushing their tips back and forth and the green sea frothing just beyond the dunes. The thick air is filled with salt.

I breathe deep and follow Jude towards the bike rack. He says nothing as he unlocks his chain and pulls the bike away from the stack, ignoring me for some unfathomable Jude reason. He climbs on and looks like he's actually about to pedal away and leave me behind without another word when he stops very suddenly.

'Lottie. What are you doing?'

I've stopped hovering and instead have climbed onto the back of his bike, right where his bag holder sits, balanced with my sneakers out at the side and my guitar perched upon my back. 'What?' I ask innocently, grasping at his backpack.

Jude stands up, almost sending me flying. 'Girl, I'm not a chauffeur!'

I gape. 'What's wrong with you?'

'Nothing.' He slowly sits back down and then dutifully begins pedalling. I smile. Jude's too easy. He always does what I want.

I spot Sebastian, waiting by the gate, but only have a second to wave at him before we've passed him by, rounding the corner where a massive bougainvillea bush hangs off a fence blocking our view. I have this sudden terror that maybe Sebastian was waiting for me, and now I've missed him, missed the opportunity to spend time with him, just the two of us. I glance back over my shoulder as the fences whiz by, lost in my regrets until the bike swerves onto the street and I'm brought back to reality.

I tug on Jude's backpack as we turn onto the road leading to the beach. 'So, Jude. Why are you mad at me?'

'I never said I was mad at you.'

'Yeah, but I can tell. You've been weird the last couple days. You're avoiding me.' I sigh and rest my head against his backpack, fingers holding onto the straps to keep my balance as Jude pedals over the bitumen, taking the backstreets through the winding suburbs where the houses are old and run-down, overgrown gardens encroaching on wide empty streets.

I know something's up with Jude because he's literally only been properly mad at me three times in all our years as friends. Once when we were eight, when he found out it was me who burned all his Phantom comics, another time during the first week of high school when I met Grace and began to hang out with her more often than I did with him, and then again when we were fourteen and I started going out with Jonathon Lee.

Looking back, I guess most of those were my fault.

I can't remember why I burned the comics, except maybe I just wanted to set something on fire and Jude's comics happened to be closest. And it turned out Jonathon Lee, though into a lot of the same things I am, was a stuck-up prick who was really mean about me behind my back. And, in hindsight, I could definitely have handled the Grace friendship thing better, instead of leaving Jude all alone for his first two weeks of high school. He made friends eventually, of course, but even now, me and Grace are still his best friends, so it was my fault that he felt left out at school.

I still feel bad about that.

But these past few days of silent treatment from Jude?

I have no idea what that's about.

I prod him again. 'You're mad at me. Admit it.'

He sighs. 'I'm not mad at you. Not everything is about you, Lottie.'

I stiffen, because Jude doesn't normally say stuff like that, though I've certainly heard it from others. Dad. Celeste. Even Grace.

But never Jude.

I bite my lip and remain silent, and Jude glances quickly over his shoulder at me, cheeks flushed from pedalling. He sighs again. 'I just have lots going on right now. That's all.'

I brighten immediately. 'Aaah, so you're *distracted*! Not mad.' That makes me feel better.

Or at least it does, for a moment.

Then my head quickly sifts through all the things that might be bothering him, turning and twisting and assessing.

We ride in silence for a few streets, cruising in the middle of the road because there are no cars in sight. I clutch at Jude's backpack and think about the stuff that's surely inside his head. I clear my throat.

'Jude?'

'Yeah?'

'You know it's sort of the same, right?'

He swings his head to check for cars and then stands up on the pedals, winging past a train station just as the bells peal and clang and the gates lower. 'What is?'

'The stuff going on with you. Your folks. It's sort of the same as mine.' I hesitate. 'You know, like what happened when Mum left.'

The more I think about it the more certain I am of the similarity. Jude isn't close with his dad, and I guess these days I'm not close with my mum. His family is breaking apart just like mine did.

I gaze at the ocean as the bike turns from the suburbs onto

the seafront, towering pines lining the wildflower-laden dunes, heavy heat and salt blowing in off the water. The bitumen here is even hotter, baking in the sun, clouds stretching above, streaked with orange and gold.

Jude stops the bike and my sneakers hit the ground. Neither of us get off, though. We just look out over the water, sun burning my skin. I lift my hand to wipe sweat from my forehead, shading my face.

'The worst thing,' I say, 'is when no one talks to you about it.'

Jude glances at me sharply. Then slowly his gaze returns to the horizon. 'Yeah. I guess.' He takes a deep breath and slowly lets it out again.

'You can talk to me,' I press. 'If you want to.'

At first I think he won't. We stare out over the beach, quiet, listening to the waves in the distance. Then Jude clears his throat. 'I think all this stuff with my dad's been going on for ages. But they were working together to, like, hide it or something.' He turns to me, peering over his shoulder as I clutch at his backpack, still perched on the bike. 'Like your mum and the affair, I guess.'

I nod. 'Yeah.'

Jude's still watching me. 'So what happens now?' His voice is barely a murmur. 'You tell me, Lottie.'

I shrug, my heart racing. 'I guess, nothing. Even though you're at the centre of it, you're not really part of it. So it's up to them. You just wait. If they divorce or not, you can't do a single thing to change it.'

He says nothing, still watching me, sun lighting his skin, crowded freckles bright and glaring.

'I guess I keep wondering ...' He stops and shakes his head, a smile flitting across his face and then disappearing just as quick.

I wait.

He looks back over the water, not meeting my eyes. 'It feels like my fault,' he says eventually. 'Because of my dad. Sometimes I think I didn't turn out ... how he wanted.'

'Your dad's a dick.'

'Lottie!'

'It's *true*. You're perfect, Jude. *He's* the one who didn't turn out how he wanted. And I reckon he's just taking it out on you.'

Jude's cheeks flush beneath the hot sun, staring at me.

I bite my lip. 'I guess when my parents got divorced I realised they were really just people.' I pause, embarrassed. 'Does that make any sense?'

Jude says nothing, only frowns, so I blow out a breath and attempt to explain.

'Before that they were only my parents, right? Like I had assumed they knew what they were doing. And if they ever told me something, I just assumed it was true. But maybe it's not true. Maybe they made it up. Or, even worse, maybe they think it's true but actually it's not. Like how they never told me about the cheating thing. They probably thought they were protecting me.' I shrug. 'Or like how your dad is wrong about you. Maybe no one is really who you think they are.'

Jude looks away, at the cracked pavement, heat wavering off the sidewalk. 'You mean, maybe my parents have absolutely no idea what's going to happen either.'

I nod. 'Probably.'

Jude's sweating from the heat and the bike ride, and my skin is prickling from the sun. I nudge him, skin against skin. 'So I get it,' I say. 'And you can talk to me about it. Whenever you want to.'

Jude raises his eyebrows. 'You're gonna listen to me spill my guts? You? Listen?' He scoffs. 'You can't sit still long enough to watch a movie.'

I'm offended. 'I'm sitting still right now, aren't I?'

Jude grins and shakes his head, gaze travelling from my sneakers, which are scuffing against the cracked curb, to my fingers, which are picking out guitar riffs against my school skirt.

I get off the bike, embarrassed. I hadn't realised I was being so fidgety. I cough and then mumble awkwardly, 'I can sit still, Jude. I can listen for you.' I make a point to say it because it feels important. And I want him to know.

He doesn't answer, and when I glance up he's grinning at me. 'Perfect, huh?'

I blink. 'What?'

'You said I was perfect.'

I frown. 'I'm pretty sure I never said that.'

But Jude just grins, ditching the bike against a pine tree. He slings a sweaty arm around my neck and drags me close. 'Wanna go for a swim?'

He pulls me towards the beach walkway as I glance back at his bike. 'You didn't lock it though. What if someone steals it?'

'I don't care. It's my dad's bike.'

I raise my brows at him as we step down the wooden stairs, planks gone grey from years under the hot sun, sand spilling into the cracks in the grain. Summer wildflowers, yellow and pink, sweep in fields of colour on either side of the winding pathway. 'I never knew you were so vindictive, Jude. It's like a whole new side of you.'

Gulls circle above, soaring with their wings glowing from the sun, and Jude grins, freckles so crowded across his skin they even stain his mouth. I've never noticed that before. I realise I'm staring and turn towards the ocean instead, suddenly hyper aware of his body pressed against mine, his school shirt slick with sweat.

'Maybe I've got a good teacher,' he says and I frown. I don't want to teach Jude to be vindictive. He's different to me. Good. I wouldn't want him to change.

I murmur, 'Yeah, but how will I get home if someone steals your bike?'

'I'll walk you.'

I stare at him again, because there's something in his voice, our faces close. He's not taller than me, maybe even a whisper shorter. But he's different these days. The way he carries himself is different.

I shove his arm off me, strangely unbalanced, like the ground is tilting. 'Race you to the water,' I yell and tear away across the sand, stopping only to kick my sneakers off. My guitar gets better treatment. Jude, when he catches up, and I spend ages trying to decide where it will be safest, our race forgotten. Eventually we use the heaped seaweed, dried and crackling from the hot sun, to build a barrier of shade. And then we pile up our books to protect it even more.

In the old days I would have gone swimming in my undies. I wouldn't have thought twice about whipping off my skirt and school blouse and plunging in. But this time when Jude pulls his shirt over his head and kicks off his sneakers, I'm left feeling inexplicably shy. At the beginning of summer I hadn't cared about stuff like that – me, Grace and Jude dropping by the ocean all the time on our way home, our hair stiff with salt and our hands smeared with sand, skin flashing everywhere.

But now it's different. I try not to notice what Jude looks like without his shirt as he beckons me to follow into the waves. I peer at the sky instead, at the dunes and frothing water, anywhere but at him, trailing after until my bare feet sink into the wet sand and the sea swells around my ankles.

I go in fully clothed, in my school skirt and blouse. And Jude doesn't say anything about it.

By the time we re-emerge from the waves I feel better, my throat hoarse from screaming and laughing, my hair hanging in salt ropes down my back and my uniform blouse sticking to my skin. Jude keeps sending glances my way as we walk barefoot up the sand until I finally mouth *what?* He won't tell me though, just shaking his head, cheeks flushed pink from the hot sun.

My guitar is exactly where we left it, but Jude's bike isn't.

Just like I said, someone stole it, and I spend the long walk home giving him hell about it, until he threatens to throw me in the river. The daylight turns to twilight, the shadows growing long and winding, the highway buzzes and the factories hum as we reach the bridge, walking over the black salt water swelling underneath.

And everything is centred again. Steady. Me and Jude. Jude and me. Friends. Like we've always been.

And I dismiss the feeling of change humming in the air.

14

SPIRITUAL ENLIGHTENMENT, MEDIEVAL-STYLE

I lean forward. 'And are you looking forward to starting work again, Celeste?' I smile sweetly, meeting her gaze in the rear-view mirror.

She blinks. 'Oh. Well, yes. But it won't be for a few more weeks yet, Lottie. I've still got maternity leave.'

Evelyn gives me the evil eye from her place in the van's front passenger seat, her mouth tight. I bat my lashes at her innocently and keep talking to her mother. 'Tell us that funny story about your work, Celeste. It's a good one.'

Grace is distracted by my baby brother, cooing at him as he kicks his fat legs and smiles gummily at her.

'Which one do you mean, Lottie?' Celeste smiles into the mirror. 'There's a few.' She gives a low throaty laugh as my mind draws a big blank.

'Um ...' I search desperately. She's always spouting the most awful stories about her office days but generally I scrape them from my brain the second she's done. I never expected it might be essential to my new nice persona to have memorised any. I open and shut my mouth dumbly.

'Yeah, Lottie,' interjects Evelyn with a smirk. '*Which* funny story did you mean?'

Oh.

Oh!

'The earthquake one,' I practically shout. Celeste jumps in fright and I shoot Evelyn a triumphant glare. Sucker.

Someone kicks the back of my car seat. Ouch.

I turn to scowl at Jude who peers at me from beneath his hair, freckly nose wrinkled, a large plastic viking helmet perched lopsided on his head. It has curling horns that graze the car roof. Sebastian is sitting right beside him, squashed in the van looking incredibly uncomfortable.

'*What?*' I mouth at Jude, and he glances quickly at Grace, who has narrowed eyes, gaze flicking suspiciously from me to Evelyn beneath heavy lashes.

Right. More subtlety is the way to go.

Celeste clears her throat. She's delighted to talk about her boring office stuff. 'Oh, that's a good one. I guess I could tell you if you want to hear it.'

I sigh. I did this to myself. Still, it's worth it to get on her good side. Worth it to see Evelyn's scrunched sour face.

'Well, one day we were all in the office,' Celeste begins and I can barely contain my eye rolls already. Not a good sign. 'We were working in our separate offices. Because we were all in different offices, see? It's not open plan.'

Cool story, Celeste.

That's what I want to say.

I don't though. Obviously.

I don't want to undo weeks of solid work. I am officially a good daughter now. Which means stage one of my plan is working. It's stage two that I'm still waiting for.

Which of course is the part where Evelyn officially screws up and I take her position as the rightful best daughter in the house. It's going to happen. I can feel it. Her revenge plans lately have been getting more sloppy. She's been snipping my tomato plants on the balcony, cutting holes in my school uniform. Dumb stuff. Obvious stuff. Stuff that's making even Celeste suspicious.

Finally, *finally*, I think Celeste is catching on that Evelyn is actually the devil.

And that is not a development I want to ruin.

So I grit my teeth and smile and listen avidly to Celeste's excellent office story. Because she's loving the chance to tell it.

'Suddenly at lunchtime the office floor just started shaking.' She turns over her shoulder to glance at my friends with wide eyes, Grace, Jude and Sebastian the only three who haven't heard this story before. 'And so we all rushed out of our offices into the corridor, and our manager was freaking out – like, really freaking out. He kept saying, "It's an earthquake. We're having an earthquake." And then everyone was really nervous because it was an earthquake.'

She stops talking to frown at the road. We're way out of the city, ploughing down some empty highway with rolling yellow fields on either side, but these little brown birds keep hopping on the bitumen. 'Shoo,' says Celeste. 'Shoo.'

'And?' I lean forward to tap her shoulder, my wide maiden-style sleeves dragging across Leo's face and making him kick with shock as his world turns dark. 'What happened next?'

'Oh. Right.' She glances at Jude and Sebastian in the rear-view mirror, eyes sparkling, punchline on the tip of her tongue. 'Well then we googled it and it wasn't an earthquake at all! There was just some construction going on in the empty block next door.'

I snort, giggling for all the wrong reasons, and it takes me a moment to realise the barking laughter filling the car is Sebastian's. I make an *unbelievable* face at Jude over the car seat. He won't meet my eyes, though, squished in the littlest seat at the very back. Sebastian doesn't notice my disdain either, much too busy snorting with weird dog laughter at the single most boring and sad story I ever heard in my life.

Heard twice in my life.

I turn to Grace for support but she's giggling away too, one hand wrapped around Leo's pudgy foot and the other holding tight to her veil thing, which is perched precariously on her head and fastened with bobby pins.

'Shame on you both,' I hiss but she just shrugs helplessly, still giggling.

'It's really funny, Mrs Tait,' Sebastian calls breathlessly to the front.

Celeste blushes. Actually blushes. Like, cheeks pink and stuff. Gross.

'Oh, it's Mrs *Murphy* now, but thank you, Sebastian.'

Evelyn seems as disgusted as I am but Celeste doesn't notice. My stepmum glances at me in the mirror again and nods wisely, as if to say, *What a nice boy.* She turns to Sebastian. 'You can call me Celeste, though. I much prefer it.'

Sebastian grins. 'Okay, Mrs ... I mean, Celeste.'

She beams.

The whole thing is gross.

Sebastian flicks the back of my head, grinning as if he knows exactly what I'm thinking. I wonder if he's just playing a game, the same as me. That makes my heart soften a bit, and I allow him a quick smile. Sebastian isn't wearing a costume, which annoyed Grace, but I don't mind. He's very pretty in his white t-shirt. Though when I told Grace that, she pretended to puke. Behind me Jude is resolutely staring out the window, his body stiff and tight, hands clenched on his knees.

I switch off and gaze out the window too. But I do catch Celeste glancing at me every few moments when the road birds aren't taking every bit of her attention. And she looks happy. At me.

So I guess the earthquake thing wasn't a total waste of time.

A slow grin spreads across my face. 'Hey, Evelyn. What mark did you get on your English test this week?'

Evelyn stiffens as another kick lands on the back of my chair. This time I ignore Jude, my face turned innocently to the window, attention on the country farmlands and little crumbling pioneer cottages flashing by.

Evelyn doesn't answer until pressed by Celeste. And then it turns out Miss Perfect's mark wasn't all that perfect after all. In fact, she received a big fat fail on her test.

Which is obviously why I brought it up.

I, on the other hand, did quite well. Which I may have already mentioned casually at home, a statement that made my dad so happy he taped my results to the fridge.

Celeste's brows furrow. 'You didn't tell me you failed,' she says quietly.

'I don't tell you everything, Mum.' Evelyn's shoulders stiffen as soon as the words leave her mouth, like she knows she's just made a mistake. But the cracks in her perfect facade are showing.

'We'll talk about this more later,' hisses Celeste under her breath.

And that's the end of it. Frosty silence fills the car and more than once I catch Evelyn watching me with pure hatred in the side-view mirror.

Well, whatever. When I failed a major maths exam last year everyone thought I was going to be kept back. I remember the glee on Evelyn's face when she blurted it out to my dad. She told him I hadn't even been trying.

It was all sorted out in the end. Dad stepped in and made promises to the school. He stayed up late tutoring me over the holidays and I did a make-up exam and just scraped through by the skin of my teeth.

But the truth was, I *had* been trying. I'd been putting in extra hours of study in the library at school because I didn't want to fail. And Evelyn knew that. Because I'd sucked up all my pride and asked her to be my tutor.

In hindsight, I should have asked Jude instead, but it was during one of the three times in our life we were fighting, because I'd started going out with Jonathon Lee. Right then me and Jude weren't talking because I'd yelled at him about his attitude and possibly said some things to him I really didn't mean.

So I'd asked Evelyn instead.

She agreed, but apparently everything she taught me was bullshit, because I flunked my exam so hard it was almost hilarious. But when I tried to explain all that to Dad, did he believe me?

Nope.

Did he believe perfect good-girl Evelyn?

Yep.

And so the war between us kicked up a notch.

Which is why I am not remotely guilty about outing Evelyn in front of her mum. The girl deserves a dose of her own medicine.

Except then Grace leans across Leo's baby seat and frowns at me. 'Go easy on her, Lottie,' she whispers. 'She's got a lot going on right now.'

I arch my brows. 'Really?'

Grace pokes me in the cheek. 'Yes, really. I'm asking as your friend, okay?'

I sigh. And then finally nod.

Anything for Grace.

I smile at her, leaning across to hand her my mobile. I have my notes page open and one word sits there.

Kalon.

She googles it.

Ideal, perfect beauty, both physical and moral.

Or in some cases:

Beauty that is more than skin deep.

She grins at me, hand to heart, pretending to be super touched. Then she sticks her finger in her mouth and fake pukes. That has me exploding with laughter, wiping the tears from my cheeks. I'm so filled with hilarity I only slightly notice how Evelyn is watching us, all twisted around in the front seat.

Like she wants to murder me.

The rest of the drive is fairly uneventful. Sebastian keeps asking Celeste a million more office questions, which I'm pretty sure he's doing on purpose to irritate me, and by the time we reach the tiny town where the festival is being held I'm about ready to strangle him. He keeps grinning with his perfect teeth and his ocean eyes, confident and relaxed in the back seat, while Jude is the opposite, like he wants to be anywhere else in the world instead of right here with all of us. Grace is playing some boring game on her phone and Evelyn is sitting straight forward, pissed as hell. Leo, on the other hand, has begun to smell really, really bad.

The town is small and regional. Rolling yellow farmland and tiny dotted houses give way to wide flat streets, little box suburbs and the biggest pub you've ever seen. Seriously. It's enormous. And old. With winding verandas and chipped paint, barstools and scummy pool tables visible in the TAB bar through the window. Across the road is the soldiers' memorial garden, a staple of every small town, with a white statue nestled in a grove of dry grass and blooming roses.

And a toilet block.

That's where Celeste sends me with Leo. And because Sebastian is absolutely bonkers he comes along for the ride.

'I've always wanted to know how to change a baby,' he says.

My expression turns blank. 'Um ... why, dude? That's weird.'

He ignores me and watches the magic happen. And then splits from the baby change room decidedly greener than when he walked in. Honestly, I don't know what he expected.

I can't help but smile. Sebastian is quite excellent company. Even with all the teasing in the car. I sigh dreamily and think I'll keep him forever. When I return to the van, my gaze lingers on his face over the back seat. He grins back.

When Leo is all strapped in we roll the last ten minutes to the parkland. All of us press our noses against the glass.

The place is mental. Absolutely mental.

People with full metal breastplates and leather tunics stroll by, fur cloaks strung across shoulders. Huge iron swords are strapped to hips and long hair flows majestically in the wind. These people have gone all out with the re-enactments. They look ...

Fantastic.

We line up in a row beside the car to stare, all of us slightly less excited about our costumes now. I mean, Jude's wearing a plastic Viking hat with a t-shirt and sneakers. Sebastian isn't dressed up at all. The other dudes here have iron helmets and manly man hair that flows to their bums. It's all pretty epic.

I kind of love it.

The place is set up like a village. The smell of roast meat wafts from open fires and there are small glowing taverns, with stalls selling handwoven shawls and twisted silver jewellery. Other little sheds are full of people at work doing trades. Like old trades. Hammering and leatherwork and stuff.

Celeste straps Leo to her chest and shades her face against the boiling sun. 'I can't believe they're wearing that metal shit in this heat,' she murmurs.

Slowly we all turn to stare at her. Then Grace breaks into giggles.

Huh.

I didn't know Celeste could swear.

My stepmum claps her hands. 'Right,' she announces. 'I'm taking Leo to that kiddy pen thing. The rest of you ... spread out. Have fun. And I'll meet you back here in two hours. We'll get lunch.' She gazes doubtfully at all the spitting, sizzling meat. 'Do you think they cater for vegetarians?'

Grace nods. 'I reckon so,' she says doubtfully.

Then Celeste does something that shocks the pants off me. She turns to Evelyn and points a finger in her face. 'And you! Stay out of trouble.'

Evelyn scowls.

I gape, leaning across Sebastian to tug on Celeste's sleeve. She's not dressed up either. I lift a finger and gesture to my face. 'What about me?'

She blinks. 'Oh, well, yes. You too. Stay out of trouble, Lottie.'

I grin. All is right with the world again. 'Of course I will! You don't need to ask.'

'But you just … oh never mind. Go on then. All of you.'

She shoos us away like the birds on the highway.

Grace and Evelyn have drawn together, my best friend patting my stepsister's shoulder softly as if they're already sharing secrets. Gross.

They're both dressed as medieval maidens, courtesy of Grace, who did a great job with our outfits. The pink hair ruins the illusion for Grace a bit, though. Evelyn, on the other hand, is absolutely perfect, with her thick braid hanging down her back and flyaway strands hanging artfully around her face. She looks almost lovely, though it pains me to acknowledge it. The dress Grace created for her makes my stepsister glow, the bodice a deep dark green, all flowing satin skirts and ribbons.

I grasp Sebastian's arm with a scowl in their direction. 'Come on.' I drag him into the fray, and Jude follows slowly, his hand on his massive plastic helmet to stop it flying away. He doesn't look like he's having a very good time.

The little village streets are exciting, buzzing with costumed people and thick savoury food smells, with flowing dresses and shining iron armour and weapons. Behind the mass of stalls and taverns lies an open field, towering eucalyptus trees and modern barbed wire fencing ruining the perfect image of medieval jousting. Real horses thunder by with riders lancing watermelons in explosions of pink.

Sebastian turns in circles, attention being dragged every which way. 'This is awesome,' he whispers.

Beyond the oval a group dressed in black tunics with blue war paint are doing some warrior dance with mallet things, majestic hair flying in the hot wind. Behind them is an archery demonstration, the archers using long bows and hitting targets from a million miles away.

'It's like another world,' I say as I drag Sebastian onwards down a little dry bush trail towards the river. A marquee has been put up beside the water, bright red streamers flying in the summer heat. The sun beats on the cream canvas tent and inside a small feast is underway, a man and woman at the head of the table with circlets of gold and silver perched on their heads.

'It's the king,' says Sebastian. He throws me a lazy grin.

'And the queen,' I add. 'Oh, and look.' I point at the river, reeds sprouting from the rippling water and wavering in the wind. A huge wooden boat floats alongside the bank. A Viking longboat, carved and everything, a strange wooden creature curling from end to end. A dragon? A horse? I can't be certain. But it's beautiful.

It's like a scene from Camelot. Well, except for the huge gums with their spreading branches and silver green leaves. Other than the very obvious bush setting, it's picture perfect, like a folk tale.

That's when I realise we've lost Jude. I turn around and

around, trying to find him in the gathering crowds, but he's nowhere in sight.

Sebastian takes my hand in his, which sets my skin tingling. He shrugs and says, 'Leave him. He obviously has better things to do.'

Better things to do than hang with me?

I frown and smooth my dress against my hips. I'm dressed much better than Jude because Grace made me a velvet dress, black how I like, embracing the full metal look, and she wove a crown of sticks for me, too. My dark hair is out, long and straight, and my thorn crown circles my brow. I'm not going to lie: it's an awfully uncomfortable hat, and my slinky velvet dress is quite unlike all the hyper realistic woven dresses on display here, which seem like they were sewn by hand back in the Middle Ages. But still, I'm a fan. I spread my fingers over the velvet, swishing the hemline around my sneakers.

It makes me feel pretty.

And Sebastian's ocean eyes are confirming my feeling as fact, which is making me nervous. Is this really happening? Sebastian's followed me to this crazy festival because he's into me? More and more that's what it seems like.

He's into me.

I bite my lip.

And obviously I'm into him. Because I have been. Always. For the last nearly two years I've been dreaming about a situation exactly like this. Right here. Right now. Just the two of us together.

So it's only natural that I feel thoroughly sick right now. All that anticipation, all that hoping. It's a lot of pressure.

Sebastian clears his throat. 'Lottie?'

'Mmmh?'

'You're staring.'

'Oh. Right. Sorry.' I cough and my cheeks burn hot. 'I mean ... no, I wasn't.' I shake my head. I'm acting pitiful.

Embarrassed, I try to turn away but Sebastian catches my hand again, grins, and this time it's him leading me around. Although at first I'm still awkward as hell, things slowly click and soon I'm having fun again, mainly because Sebastian is easy to talk to. He jokes a lot and keeps touching my arm and asking me questions, his head bent close to mine. Soon I forget to be nervous and start acting like myself again. And he seems to like that even better.

I smile and follow Sebastian from this stall to the next, watching the blacksmith making a sword, or peering over his shoulder at a woman weaving a shawl. Sebastian buys me an icy cup thing, covered in strawberry cordial, and I slurp it happily under the burning sun, smiling at him and soaking in the ambience of a hundred Viking warriors storming past.

It's turning into a pretty fun day.

15

I WANT YOU, BUT I'LL WAIT
UNTIL YOU NOTICE

After I get tired of exploring, I send Sebastian to buy us sizzling taco things that are apparently well Middle Ages. While I'm waiting I drift back to the river where the trees sprawl over the water and it's a degree cooler. I collapse in the shade of a stretching eucalypt, kicking my sneakers against the grass and folding my legs beneath my dress. It's nice and quiet here, the crowds a distant hum, water trickling by and the wind rustling the eucalypt branches above. Crickets buzz and the grass is green and lush.

That's when Jude turns up, throwing himself onto the ground beside me. I frown. 'Where have you been?'

He grins, hazy, as he holds up a large ceramic bottle of honest-to-goodness spiced mead, the medieval alcoholic drink of choice.

I smile and untwist the cork with a satisfying pop. 'How did you get this?'

The bottle is nearly empty. I take a swig and the liquid is tart and sweet on my tongue. Like cordial except richer, more tangy. And with an aftertaste of spice.

'Apparently I look eighteen.' Jude wiggles his brows at me, slapping on a fake deep voice. 'Oh no, I think I left my ID in my other medieval hat.' He bats his lashes and I laugh.

'You don't look eighteen,' I murmur, taking another sip.

Jude's smile turns a little harder, a little sharper, but he says nothing, taking the bottle back from me. I'm surprised he's so keen on drinking, considering everything that's going on with his dad, but I guess that's why they call it drowning your sorrows. He takes another deep swig of the mead and something about him makes me snatch it back before he drinks the whole damn thing.

I frown. 'Did you drink all of this by yourself?'

That's not like Jude.

I take a few swigs, just to stop him reaching for the bottle again, heat tingling in my belly and toes, fire down my throat. Jude's blue eyes are a little more glazed than normal.

'Um, Jude, how're you feeling?'

He grins and leans in real close. So close. Dreamy. Glazed. 'Good. Thank you.'

I stick my finger on his forehead and push him back. And he lets me.

He's drunk. Very drunk.

Which would be the very definition of 'not staying out of trouble' according to my stepmother. Whom we have to meet again quite soon.

Jude's skin is flushed; not just his freckly cheeks but his sprinkled nose and forehead, too. Even his neck. There are no freckles there, though. The mass never crosses the ridge of his jaw, like an invisible line drawn around his face. His throat is clear, from the lines of his jaw down to his collarbone.

I realise I'm staring, like I was at the beach. I glance away, taking a huge gulping breath, eyes to the deep blue sky. It's hot. Thick. Dry heat crackles through the branches overhead. I wipe sweat from under my thorn crown.

Jude smiles slow and blurred, white teeth shining. Then he touches his head, swaying. 'Man, what was in that drink? I feel ... weird.'

I raise my eyebrows. 'Alcohol.'

He grins. 'Well, obviously.' He grabs the bottle to examine it, reading the label, his words a little slurred, fingers a little slow.

I bite my lip and watch him. He's making me worried. I know he didn't do this because things are all good with him. His cheeks are flushed bright and he's swaying all over the place, clearly stressed out, like he can't quite handle the way the world's spinning.

I know I need to calm him down before he draws attention to himself, so I reach out and grab his red face. Except because I am a bad person I say, 'You have consumed *So. Much. Alcohol. Jude.* Like, so much. You are going to be rip-roaring drunk for at least ten hours. You might never be sober again. Old alcohol is so strong. It messes with your mind.'

His eyes go wide. 'No way,' he whispers.

I nod, hands still clasping his cheeks. 'Yes way.'

I don't know what's wrong with me. Honestly. It's like if I see a little knitted thing with a loose thread, I just have to go and pull it. I do it even though I know everything will unravel. And then I will have totally destroyed the little knitted thing. Completely and utterly.

I know this. I really do.

And yet I can't help myself.

I sigh. Force myself to stop playing with him. Like, physically restrain myself. It's really hard work.

If only he knew what I'm willing to sacrifice for him.

I wrinkle my nose. 'Okay, business,' I announce. 'Tell me what we need to do about your dad. Do you want me to talk to him? Or talk to *my* dad?'

'No!'

I recoil. 'No? What do you mean, no?'

'No. I mean, I don't want to talk about it with you. I'm going to handle it.'

'Yeah, except that's clearly not working, so let me help you. Or at least tell me what's going on. You talked to me when we went to the beach.'

He scrambles to his feet, holding his plastic helmet in place as he wobbles over the grass, sneakers getting caught on nothing. 'Well, I changed my mind. I'm not telling you anymore.'

Uh oh. Not good.

I don't like it when Jude doesn't talk to me. We don't normally keep stuff from each other.

But there's no time to get upset because Jude is staggering towards the river. 'Oh, shit. Jude!' I scream, which has a nice picnicking family nearby scowling and covering their kids' ears. I scowl right back at them.

Jude, meanwhile, has slumped about a metre away from the water's edge. The grass is long and yellow, waving wildly around his shoulders. I stomp after him, sliding to my knees, thoroughly tangled in my velvet dress, the brittle river reeds and Jude's plastic Viking helmet. 'Are you okay?'

He swings his head towards me. 'Oh, sure. I'm grand. Thank you.'

'What are you doing over here?'

'Oh? Just ... resting. Do you want to rest with me, Lottie?'

I make a face. 'Well, not particularly, but ...'

His eyes do a weird puppy dog thing. So sad. So lost.

I sigh. 'Sure. Let's just sit here in this weird reedy place together and do nothing for a while. Sounds lovely.'

The puppy dog eyes disappear. He looks extremely pleased with himself. And he even smirks.

Jude.

Smirking.

It's entirely too strange on his freckly face, transforming him from the boy I know into someone with a secret.

I wrinkle my nose.

'Stop it,' I say. 'I don't like it.'

'Stop what?' He grins slow, reaching out to nudge my chin with his fingers.

I bat him away. 'No, stop it! You are acting crazy. Stop it.'

He drags the helmet from his head, which ruffles his hair over his eyes. Still grinning the knowing smile, he moves his fingers from my chin into my hair, his other hand pressing against my jaw, skin on skin. He's so close that I blink, confused.

'Jude, what are you—'

The rest of my words are lost against his mouth. My brain turns blank, his hands in my hair, fingers against my skin, mouth pressed hard against mine, the taste of liquor tart on his tongue. He presses me backwards, and I grab onto his shirt for balance because we're about to topple into the thick reeds, my fists curled around his t-shirt. Jude makes a soft sound low in his throat and I'm pretty sure I'm not kissing him back. I'm pretty sure but actually not so sure, because something is going wrong inside my head, emptiness and blankness beating hard against my skull and veins sizzling beneath my skin. My mind is wiped clean of anything rational or normal.

Jude pulls back, our noses still pressed together, mouths close and breath ragged, his wild eyes searching mine. I still haven't shoved him away yet, both of us breathing heavy, confusion flooding my body.

'What exactly are you guys doing?'

I whip around. It's Grace, standing gaping from the edges of the river reed mess we've crawled into.

I flinch away from Jude, extricating myself from his fingers and his mouth, breathing heavy, my face flaming. I stand quickly, staring at him then back to Grace.

Jude's staring too. At me. Expressionless, blue eyes locked on mine.

I clear my throat, blink at Grace. 'Um, we're doing ... nothing?'

Grace plants her hands on her hips and raises an eyebrow at me. Evelyn appears behind her, gaping a little. This is the last thing I want Evelyn to see. It's excruciating. Mortifying. I shuffle my feet, adding, 'We were ... just waiting for Sebastian.'

Sebastian. Yes. Where did he go again? Somewhere. I can't think straight.

Jude starts making odd noises, and I turn back to him in alarm.

'Are you okay?' I think he's dying.

'Ugh ... eeew.' His face screws up. He looks utterly repulsed, like he wants to spit something disgusting in the grass. He seems pissed, too, brows drawn tight and mouth hard, his words slurred. '*Sebastian.* You can't be serious, Lottie. You're ... he's ... *Yuck!*' He suddenly keels over in the long grass. Sleeping? Unconscious?

I'm insulted. 'Grace,' I scream over my shoulder, suddenly furious. 'Come and ... I don't know. Do something!' I'm so pissed off. What is Jude doing? Getting drunk and kissing me and then insulting me. Confusing me then humiliating me.

I kind of hate him right now.

It's way easier to focus on that than the hard beating of my heart or the tingling running across my skin. Or the fact that Jude just kissed me.

Once again my mind goes completely blank.

Grace makes her way into our patch of reeds, the picnicking family all watching solemnly while they eat, like we're a television show. My best friend sinks into the tall grass, so short that for a second only her shock of bright pink hair is visible bobbing through the yellow reeds. Then she reappears, pouting. 'What did you do to him, Lottie?' She sighs. 'You're the worst.'

'Me? Are you serious? It's him! *He* did this. This is *his* fault.' I stab my finger in her face and hiss, 'And if you breathe a single word of this, to anyone, I will murder you while you sleep!'

She nods solemnly. 'Jude kissed you.'

I flinch. 'He's just ... He's very drunk. And confused.'

She grins. 'Alright, alright, I'll help you. Heave him up. No, I said *up*, Lottie.'

'I'm trying!' I grunt. Jude's a hell of a lot heavier and more solid than he looks, and now he's gone full comatose, which is just excellent.

I groan, trying to ignore the fact that my hands are pressing into his chest, that I'm heaving his arm over my shoulder. That our faces are very close again. Though I seriously doubt he's going to remember any of this when he sobers up.

How could he do this to me?

'Evelyn,' yells Grace. 'Come help us!'

To my surprise, my evil stepsister does. She comes skipping right into the reeds like she's happy about it, too. I raise my eyebrow at her but she just shrugs. This worries me a great deal, but I don't have time to dwell on it.

'So,' I grunt while we all drag Jude out of the tangle of river reeds, pretending like everything is totally fine and normal, 'what have you two been up to?'

Please don't say making out with my disgusting stepsister. Please don't say making out with my disgusting stepsister.

Instead, Grace says something entirely unexpected.

'We have a surprise for you, actually.'

She slings Jude's arm over her shoulder as he mumbles pitifully.

'A ... surprise?'

I grab him around the waist and drag his other arm tighter over me, heaving him upright. His sneakers practically drag along behind us. 'Dude!' I poke him sharp in the ribs. 'Walk, will you?'

Jude stands immediately. Easily. 'Oh. Right,' he says. He straightens his plastic helmet and then strides off ahead of us up the riverbank towards the cluster of stalls. Totally upright and not at all stumbly.

'What is he ...?' Grace breathes, shading her face. She glances at me and then points after him. 'Well, go get him!'

I blink. And then do as she says, tearing off up the hill after

Jude, grasping hold of the back of his t-shirt and choking him a little in the process.

'Urg.' He turns around, rubbing his throat and frowning. 'You choked me.'

'I did not!'

'You did.'

'Children, children, come on. Stop fighting,' Grace says, arriving at my elbow. I notice her hand is clasped tightly around my stepsister's. I roll my eyes as she continues speaking, her voice hushed. 'Look, Evelyn has a surprise for you, okay? So please stop fighting and come with us. Come on!' She grins and drags at my dress, pulling the fabric and stretching it. I attempt to bat her off but she easily draws me along behind her. I lean back and grasp Jude's hand before he can wander off again, which has him raising his eyebrows at me.

I frown. 'Where's Sebastian? I'm supposed to wait for him back under the trees.'

Jude drops my hand, marching ahead.

My gaze follows him as Evelyn sidles up beside me and leans close to whisper, 'Do you think Sebastian saw you making out with Jude in the bushes? Maybe that's why he disappeared.'

I glance at her sharply. She's bluffing. He didn't see.

'I didn't make out with him,' I snap. Then I add, 'You won't tell Sebastian, though, right?' I'm pleading with her. 'Please don't, Evelyn.'

She laughs. 'If you come with us now then I'll think about it.' She skips off towards Grace, leaving me with no choice but to follow, peering into the crowds for Sebastian as I trail behind the group. She's definitely going to tell him. I sink my hands into my hair.

Why did Jude do this to me?

How could he?

I stop walking suddenly, remembering what Jude's dad said that time in front of our block when I got Jude suspended from school.

Moon eyes.

He said Jude had been giving me moon eyes over the balcony.

I glance ahead where Jude's walking with Grace, and when he turns around there's definitely no moon eyes. Mainly he's just got that smirk from earlier.

Ugh.

Drunk Jude is the worst.

I keep my distance from him as Grace drags us through a bunch of food stalls, past a woman who is braiding hair and another who is offering pretty henna tattoos. I'm a little sad at that, because in his current state I could easily talk Jude into getting henna done on his face. It seems like such a wasted opportunity, but I follow the others past the stall and don't ask to stop.

And then it turns out the day actually can get worse. Because my stepsister's idea of a nice surprise is her taking us out for a leisurely trip on the river.

In a Viking longboat.

16

GETTING RICH QUICK. NEVER ACTUALLY WORKS

'I don't think this is a good idea.' I say this in a nice way.

Grace is having none of it. 'Lottie! You sister did this for *you*. She's paid for the ride. She's trying to extend a proverbial olive branch.'

I make a face. Those are definitely not Grace's words. She's been handfed those directly. Evelyn blinks innocently over Grace's shoulder and I scowl at her. Which is a bad idea because Grace sees my nasty expression.

'There! You're doing it again, Lottie. I thought you asked Evelyn to come on this trip because you wanted to spend time with us.'

I'm flustered. 'I did. I did!'

'Seriously?' Grace raises an eyebrow.

I nod. 'Yeah.'

She grins. 'Then that's settled. Get in.'

I sigh. Grace is impossible to argue with. A lot of people like to say that about me, but clearly they've never tried a confrontation with my best friend.

Jude shuffles beside me and I scowl at him, and then say loudly, 'Where's Sebastian?'

Everyone turns to each other and shrugs. Apparently the boy is lost forever, never to return. This place isn't even all that big!

Or maybe he's waiting under the trees downstream, wondering where I am. The idea of it makes me feel unwell. Mainly because it's located awfully close to that patch of river reeds where Jude …

I grimace at the Viking longboat. It sits there at the edge of the river, floating innocently in the rippling water, alongside grasses that waver in the hot summer breeze. I should be spending today by Sebastian's side, getting to know him better, hanging out. Instead I have to sit in a boat with stupid drunk Jude and my evil stepsister.

I lift my hands in surrender.

Fine.

This whole thing is suspicious, but if I want to continue playing this game, I have to remain nice.

Ugh.

'Okay,' I say with a smile pasted onto my face. 'Let's do it. Let's go for a ride in … that thing.'

'Yay,' says Jude. I can't tell if he's being sarcastic or not. I glance at him suspiciously. He smiles serenely back at me.

I would have expected him to be acting a little more awkward, considering he just kiss-attacked me and all. Evelyn and Grace are getting excited, clasping hands and giggling like a young couple in love.

Puke.

I follow them and watch as they both gingerly step from the bank onto the bobbing boat, Evelyn's fingers wrapped tight around Grace's hand to help her in. I hold my big fake grin and step in after them. No one bothers to help me. And then it takes all of us to help Jude. We get him inside with only one of his sneakers being plunged beneath the water. He settles on the wooden bench next to me, relaxed and comfortable. I think he's already forgotten about the kiss.

Which pisses me off more.

I keep glancing at the river bank, hoping Sebastian might turn up, but the grassy hill and the shady trees remain still and quiet. I think about telling the others I'm going back for him, but then I realise I've got bigger things to worry about.

Like why there are four teenagers sitting in a hand-carved Viking longboat with no chaperone in sight. By now I'm fairly suspicious. 'Um, guys?'

Grace and Evelyn are whispering at the head of the boat, Evelyn waving her hands, being weird and agitated. Grace smiles, a little tightly, like she's disappointed, but then nods. 'You guys wait here. The guy must've got the time wrong.'

She steps lightly from the longboat back onto the shore, the craft bobbing beneath her shifting weight. Jude's face turns slightly paler beneath his explosion of freckles, despite the heavy sun. He did drink quite a lot and the boat is rocking heavily.

I'm concentrating on Jude, trying to decide if he's about to spew or not, while still watching Grace disappearing out of sight along the winding bush track. Evelyn reaches for the woven red rope that secures us to the shore and unties it, dropping it into the water. It floats like a long curling streamer across the surface before sinking out of sight into the brown depths.

'Um, Evelyn? What's going on?'

Evelyn smiles, cold and sharp. No pretending now. 'We're going for a ride.'

I flinch.

One, Evelyn clearly has a plan.

And two, what a totally evil movie villain thing to say. So clichéd!

I tell her so and she's none too pleased. That's when Jude leans real close and practically presses his face against my neck to whisper, 'I think Evelyn is going to drown us.'

I shove him away and turn back to Evelyn, glowering. 'You're hijacking this ship.'

She nods. 'Yeah.' We're already floating away from the shore, the languid current drifting the longboat into deeper water. The bank remains quiet and still. Empty. The gums waver, over-hanging the water, and wind rustles through the dry reeds. The river isn't all that big but we won't be going back without getting wet. Evelyn grins. 'I'm stealing it. But guess who's going to get in trouble for it?'

I sigh. 'Me?'

She laughs. Like literally throws her head back and does an evil cackle. And Jude chooses that moment to stick his face against my throat again to hiss, 'I feel sick.' He's clutching my arm with bloodless fingers as I try to bat him off.

I raise my free hand at Evelyn, like I'm trying to calm a wild animal. 'Evelyn. Let's be reasonable. Your evil plan isn't going to work. You told Grace you paid for a trip.'

She narrows her eyes. 'So?'

We're floating right in the middle of the river now. The main fairground is hidden beyond a huge tangle of towering eucalypts and scrappy twisted wattle-myrtle trees downstream, drawing slowly closer. Jude presses his sweaty forehead against my shoulder. I shake him off, continuing, 'If you paid for this, why wasn't there a driver?'

She snorts. 'They're not called drivers, Lottie! This is a boat.'

'Whatever! You think you know everything!' I glare at her. 'What are they called then? Go on. Tell me.'

She opens her mouth and then hesitates. Blinks.

I point at her. 'Ha! You don't even know! As if you're going to get away with this. Your evil plan has failed.' I grin. I think I'm enjoying myself.

Until a smile creeps over my stepsister's lips. 'It hasn't failed.' My belly sinks. 'Grace went to get the boat driver guy. Whatever! And when they come back they'll see that you recklessly stole the boat and kidnapped me and were an absolute pain in the arse. And you're going to get in so much trouble.' She stands up, the entire boat rocking wildly from side to side. Actually, she's doing that on purpose, one foot on the keel (the port? Aft? The side!).

'No way,' I say. 'You know how I know you're going to fail?'

'Charlotte,' Jude whispers. 'I feel really sick right now.'

'Jude, get off me! Do you know how I know, Evelyn?'

She scoffs. 'Tell me.'

'Because everyone knows if the evil villain reveals her entire plan to the hero while waiting to enact said plan then it's immediately doomed for failure.'

'That's true,' chimes Jude.

I smile at him. 'Thanks, Jude.'

He grins back. Moon eyes.

I'm shocked enough that I do a double take, his bright eyes shining like the blue sky above, clear and cloudless, staring at me filled with ... with ...

I shake it off. He's drunk.

I clear my throat. 'And anyway, Evelyn, you forgot something important.'

Evelyn's foot kicks hard at the side of the boat, making it dip harder. Jude moans.

'What's that?' she asks.

I'm triumphant. 'I have a witness.' I wrap my arm around Jude's shoulders, dragging him close.

Evelyn raises her brows. 'You mean Jude?'

She doesn't appear particularly freaked out.

She smiles. 'You think they're going to take his word over mine? A drunk boy who's obsessed with you? Over me? Evelyn Tait?'

Jude lifts a hand. 'Excuse me. Obsessed?'

I was also caught on that sentence, but chose to ignore it in light of our present situation. 'Evelyn, your plan is ... is ...'

Totally going to work.

Shit.

I change tack. 'Uh, maybe we could talk about this before we do anything rash.' I glance over the side of the boat, arm still wrapped around Jude's shoulders as I drag him down further against the hull, sinking below the sides. I think it's about time to jump ship.

Right then Evelyn kicks the edge of the longboat and it tilts dramatically, water washing over the side. She hisses, 'You're done, Lottie. Admit it. You've been playing some sick game with me. You're trying to take away everything, *ruin* everything that's mine.' Her voice rises, her face red beneath the hot sun, sweat gleaming on her skin. And her eyes glitter. Like they're filled with tears.

Which can't be right.

I don't get much time to ponder this because Evelyn kicks the boat again, more water slopping over the edge, sloshing around where I'm huddled down in the hull with Jude. River soaks into my hot sweaty sneakers, into my dress and hair. It's actually kind of nice and cool, and Evelyn must think so too, because she kicks the side again, viciously, right when we come into view of the main fairground.

Someone shouts, and a crowd of people converge on the riverbank. All staring. Pointing.

At Evelyn.

'Cos she looks crazy.

The boat has drifted to the side, caught in the reeds as it slowly spins just along from the fairground, next to a large tangle of eucalypts that overhang the water at the river bend, submerged logs and overreaching branches gone green with slime beneath the surface. We spin and the huge carved wooden figurehead blocks me and Jude from view, huddled together low against the inner hull to avoid getting thrown out.

Evelyn is rocking the boat with her whole body weight now, the wood creaking. Groaning. Water spilling over the edges.

Uh oh.

'Um, Evelyn?'

'What?' she snaps. She still hasn't realised she's got an audience and I'm starting to enjoy myself again.

I smile at her sweetly. 'I think the boat is going to sink.'

'Don't be an idiot. It's a Viking longboat. They're sturdy, Lottie. Made for sea-faring.'

I snort. 'Evelyn, this boat was not made by Vikings. It was carved by some random Australian dude in some random Australian town. And it's going to sink.'

She flinches as the boat spins, water spilling over the side where she's weighted it down with her foot. She flings herself back, but it's far too late. The boat is so filled with water that it's like sitting in a floating bath. We're definitely going nowhere fast, drifting slow and languid in circles towards the river bend downstream. Water slops up to my ribcage and I laugh. I can't help it, the sound bubbling from my chest and spilling over.

She's so screwed. Finally she's noticed all the people on the riverbank. As we spin I catch a glimpse of Grace with her hands over her mouth, and some angry old dude in full heavy armour shaking his fist at Evelyn and shouting obscenities. I can only imagine he's the one who carved this sturdy Australian long-boat. I catch sight of Sebastian and Celeste, too, and press lower into the hull to avoid being seen.

Jude's hand is clasped around my arm like a vice, his face so pale it's like a bunch of freckles just floating in midair. He looks pretty ill. I pat him on the head as the water sloshes around our elbows. We're curled together in the bottom of the hull, sitting in cool water while the summer sun blazes overhead, the boat drifting and spinning aimlessly on the far side of the river. We draw closer to the bend where the fairground clearing ends and the bush begins again, gum trees thick and draping into the water. The boat spins slowly around the river bend, overhanging tangled bush hiding the fairground from view.

Shouts slide across the river surface and I'm pretty sure that about fifty people, Celeste, Sebastian and Grace included, are all tearing their way into the thick bush to yell at Evelyn. I want to be out of here before they arrive.

'You can swim, right Evelyn?' I check, because I'm not a murderer.

'What? I ... yeah, but ...' She's distracted, attention on the bank and the thick copse of eucalypts that now hide the fairground from view, waiting for her doom to come bursting from the foliage. She turns back to me with wild eyes. 'Don't leave me,' she whispers.

I snort, dragging Jude upright as I attempt to unclench his bloodless fingers from the neck of my dress. 'Are you serious? You just tried to frame me.' I throw her a slow grin as the boat spins close to the far side of the bank. 'You're on your own.'

And with that I lean against the wooden side and the ship tips erratically, Evelyn screaming as I plunge into the river, dragging a yelping Jude in behind me. He straightaway chokes on the muddy brown water, coughing and spluttering, but I don't care. Drinking some water right now will be good for him. His plastic helmet floats away across the choppy waves.

I grab my own stick crown before it disappears, and then kick ground. The water, it turns out, is only rib-deep. We're about four metres from the riverbank, surrounded by reeds and overhanging branches, right next to a huge thick copse of twisted gums and wavering yellow grasses. Perfect for hiding in.

Jude sloshes around in front of me, while Evelyn and the half sunk Viking longboat spin away and finally connect with a sandbank further downriver, right in the middle. She cries out as the boat shudders and it becomes clear that her journey has ended. That's when she bursts into tears, head in her hands, sitting in a pool of water inside a half-sunken boat.

My heart tugs a little.

But only a little.

Jude has realised he can stand by now. He rubs river water over his face, his hair wet and hanging into his eyes. 'Well, that was weird,' he mutters.

'Yeah,' I agree, glancing at him. Not as weird as him kissing me. The water seems to have shocked him back to himself, drunk Jude gone. Water drips from his lashes, wet hair hanging low and sodden t-shirt sticking to his skin. I frown and turn away. His gaze is clear and blue like the sky.

I flick my head towards the shore. 'Come on. We should stay out of sight.'

As we disappear into the heavy overhang of trees, shouts waft from the distant bank.

Poor Evelyn.

'What are we gonna do?' whispers Jude.

'Let's go dry off a bit, and then just re-join the fair and … I dunno, look normal. Okay?'

He nods solemnly. 'Okay.' He pauses. 'Except how are we going to do that, exactly? We're on the wrong side of the river.'

I roll my eyes. 'This isn't medieval times, Jude! There's an actual bridge with an actual bitumen road. We passed it in the car.'

'Oh. Right.' He grins at me, sudden and wide.

Slipping beneath a fallen tree, I stop in a tiny clearing between a tangle of twisted thorny bramble and two monstrous eucalypt trees. We're all alone, just us and the wind and glimpses of sky peeking between the twisted branches overhead. I wring myself out, sodden velvet dress clinging to me in every way possible, my hair dripping beneath the crown of thorns. Jude keeps touching his head.

'It floated away,' I tell him. His helmet is long gone.

Just like Evelyn's super ability to appear composed and perfect all the time.

I giggle, unable to help myself. 'Wow, did you see her face? I can't believe she did that.'

Jude frowns. 'She's going to be in so much trouble.' He looks guilty.

'Come here.' I pull him closer, turning his head this way and that, examining his face. The grass smells fresh, dappled light and blazing sun beating down to dry us. I've decided I'm going to forget the kiss thing. Jude clearly has. And there's no way I'm going to let one drunk kiss ruin our long and glorious friendship.

'Uh, Lottie? What are you doing?' Jude's cheeks flush and he can't meet my eyes. But then he obviously realises he's staring at my clinging velvet instead, which makes him blush harder. I let it slide because I've decided we're going to be normal again, and also because he's having a rough day.

'You don't look drunk anymore, so that's good.' I force a grin. 'I think you drank half the river though, so maybe that's why. How do you feel?'

Jude wrinkles his nose. 'Kind of bad ... for Evelyn. Do you think she's going to be okay?'

I sigh and let him go. 'Imagine if her supremely dumb plan had worked. It'd be us sitting downriver getting screamed at by an Australian Viking right now, and your dad would find out you're a big drunkard and he'd forbid you from ever seeing me again.'

Jude blinks. 'But I didn't do anything.'

'Jude,' I say with pity. 'You got drunk as. And anyway, that's just the way life works. Being innocent never saved anybody.'

He looks upset, and heaves a great big sigh.

I bite my lip. 'I guess we should get out of here. The sooner we get back to the fairground the better.'

Jude nods, and the two of us creep through our little nature sanctuary away from the river. We have to crawl under the most enormous fallen tree trunk, rippled black bark hanging off it in shreds as we wiggle through lush thick grass, sun pouring between the canopy of twisted branches high overhead. Birds call and the river water gurgles and Vikings yell loudly in the distance.

Peaceful.

A bitumen road looms ahead and we stagger up a dry grassy bank to reach it, one way leading back to the far off city and the other towards the main fairground. We walk in silence, sneakers slapping wetly on the hot tar, my hair and clothes slowly drying under the beating sun. I'm feeling awkward again, mind wandering to places it shouldn't go, and by the time we re-enter the fairground I'm twitchy.

We plunge into the melee, stalls covered with shimmering swords and curling smoke from cooking fires, even a woman picking at a harp. I'm finding it hard to meet Jude's eyes, and that's when I notice that people are staring at us. Running my hands over my dress, I don't know what's wrong. I'm mostly dried out.

'You want something to eat?' Jude asks abruptly. He's stopped walking, staring at me hopefully.

No. Of course I don't want something to eat! Evelyn nearly drowned me (sort of) and we're meant to be meeting Celeste any minute now and the boy I grew up with just kissed me. And I have no idea where Sebastian is and I feel like I should care about that more. Yet Jude is watching me with shimmering blue eyes, staring, and I wonder if this is his way of trying to make things right again between us.

'You buying?' I ask suspiciously.

He snorts. Loudly. 'You wish.'

So definitely no apology then.

But he grins too, weaving off into the crowd. So I follow. Complaining loudly about people who offer food and then take it away. I'm getting so worked up that I only narrowly avoid slamming into a dude dressed as a full-blown medieval knight, with a metal helmet and everything. Even in this heat. Jude laughs at me, grasping at my elbow, and honestly, it does feel kind of normal again. Like my shoulders are beginning to relax after Jude coiled them so tight I thought my muscles would burst. A smile tugs at the corners of my mouth.

Everything is going to be fine.

Right then a hand hooks onto my elbow and I'm yanked sideways into a dark open space, a smelly stable thing, Jude's clasp on my elbow yanking him in right behind me. I slam into Grace, who's so short she goes staggering and then Jude bodily hits me from behind and I go staggering too.

When I right myself I realise we're standing in a wooden shed with piles of smelly hay in the corner and loads of metal tools hanging off every surface. I blink.

'Hi Grace,' says Jude.

She gapes at us. 'What the hell are you two doing?'

'Um, getting food?' I shrug. Grace looks crazy, all wild-eyed and sweaty.

'Celeste is looking for you,' she breathes.

'So? We're going to meet her at the van. Like she said.'

'Well, you're super late and you look like shit!'

Now it's my turn to gape. How insulting. Until Grace adds, 'You have weeds in your hair and your face is covered in mud.'

I turn to Jude, glaring. He looks fine, a bit bedraggled, but fine. And he didn't think to mention this to me? He blinks serenely back.

'If Celeste sees you like that, there's no way she'll believe you weren't on the boat,' says Grace.

My heart beats jagged against my chest. I don't want to get caught. For once I didn't actually do anything wrong. I can't quite catch my breath. 'Evelyn tried to frame me,' I blurt.

Grace's mouth grows tight. 'Yeah, I saw.'

I open my mouth to say *I told you so* but Jude suddenly grasps my hand, pulling me in towards him. He shakes his head, glancing at Grace who's still hovering beside the door, peeking out into the sunshine. That's when I notice her face is pale beneath her pink hair and her shoulders coiled tight. And something about her eyes is strange. Has she been crying?

The words die on my tongue.

It occurs to me then that Evelyn might be my mortal enemy, but she's Grace's girlfriend. Though maybe she's not anymore. For some reason, looking at Grace's pale face, this idea doesn't make me as happy as I thought it would.

I clear my throat, the smell of hay and horse dung thick in the air as I walk to Grace's side and touch her shoulder softly. 'Are you okay?'

For a moment she leans her head against my arm, closing her eyes. Then shouting from outside snaps her back. She peers out of the thin gap in the door. One of the raised voices belongs to Celeste, yelling about safety and unchaperoned longboats, and the other is deeper and male. And the way he's screaming makes me think he has some very personal stakes in the argument.

I touch my mud-streaked face. 'She can't find me like this.'

'Quick,' Grace hisses. She launches from the door towards

Jude and pushes him back towards a dark corner of the stable, shoving him behind a stack of shelves covered with horsey things. He goes stumbling hard into a rattling wooden table, the surface strewn with metal horse shoes that clink and shift in the dust, raising a cloud that sets him coughing. I'm following already but Grace shoves me after him for good measure.

I slam into Jude and everything clinks again, dust pooling in the air, catching the sunlight and sticking to my sweaty skin. I attempt to back the hell away, holding on to my thorn crown, except Grace launches herself right behind me, her back shoved against mine, and I'm thrown forward into Jude again, the table wobbling and all the little horse shoes clinking wildly.

Jude slings an arm around me for balance and everything is going downhill fast. His hand is way too near my bum so I arch my back to glower at him. Immediately he throws his hand in the air, cheeks flushed beneath the dust settling on his skin. Grace presses me inwards from behind, and any normality I'd scraped back between me and Jude is thoroughly and completely stripped away. I suck in my breath.

'Hey, Grace?' I try to twist, my forehead hitting Jude's temple, the sticks of my crown scraping his skin. I rip it off my head. 'Grace!'

She just shoves back into me. 'Shut up,' she hisses. 'I'm trying to save you idiots! Celeste is out there searching for you and you both look dirty and guilty right now.'

Well. She does have a point. No one's going to believe we weren't involved in the longboat's sinking if we turn up looking like bedraggled shipwreck victims.

So I stop moving. Sort of because of what Grace said, but mainly because the longboat guy's shouts have increased.

Louder than ever. I imagine Celeste as the ringleader of a horde of Celts, their patterned cheeks shimmering in the sun as they swing their sharpened iron swords. I imagine the longboat guy as a knight in heavy armour impaling me with a lance like they were doing to those watermelons. I imagine my head exploding in a shower of pink juice and black seeds.

It sure as hell beats facing the reality of what is happening right now in this stifling shed.

Jude is leaning back against the table, both hands behind him on the rough splintery wood. And I'm squeezed like a piece of sandwich filling between him and Grace, face to face with Jude, or at least my face to his throat because he's got his chin raised as high as it will go. The dust has settled, clinging to his skin and hair, great streaks of dirt running across his throat and jaw.

'Are you certain this is really necessary?' I ask. 'I think I ...'

'Shut up,' Grace hisses, shoving her elbow into my back. Hard. I wince.

The only sound is the argument outside and Grace's breathing. And Jude's.

His chest rises and falls in quick shallow bursts, throat slick with sweat and streaked dirt. Head up, he turns slowly to the other side, grazing his chin against my forehead.

He smells like sweat and muddy river water and horse dust.

And he smells like Jude.

I move my face slightly, my mouth practically touching his throat. I grimace in the dark. All I see is skin, skin, skin and his jaw, tight and gritted. A beat pulses beneath his throat, breath from his mouth ruffling my messy hair.

Weird.

All of it is weird.

Jude clears his throat softly, drawing my attention to his mouth. He's leaning his head away, blue eyes trained very purposely onto the cobweb-shrouded ceiling, and I'm fascinated by the way his mass of freckles extend across his cheek like a thick flood only to stop at the very edges of his jawline.

I'm staring, but whatever.

It's not my fault we're squished together.

Finally the noises die down and Grace backs off me. I immediately dislodge my body from Jude's and he slowly unwinds from the stretched tight position, shoulders losing their tension and hands unclenching. He stays sitting on the table and his chin lowers to stare at me, his eyes practically glowing in the dark they're so bright.

I might be staring as well.

Quickly I turn my back on him.

'Thanks for that, Grace,' I say, scalding. 'This place is just charming. I particularly love the horse shit in that corner.' I point at it for good measure, seething suddenly, beyond irritated.

She shoves me in the hip, and I can see the way she's pretending to be fine, a wide grin plastered onto her face. 'Whatever. I just saved your bums!'

I scowl because she didn't. Celeste was never going to come in the shed. I'm about to tell her so, when Grace says, 'Hold up, I'll go check if the coast is clear. Don't come out until I say so.'

'Graaaaaaaaaaace,' I whine, but she's gone, slipping from the crooked wooden doors out into the burning sunshine beyond.

I stand awkwardly looking after her, then swing around to glare at Jude. He stands tall, straightening his shoulders. I shove my crown on my head and turn my back on him. Crossing my arms over my chest I plonk myself on a tree trunk stump, the smell of hay heavy in the air.

Jude lumbers to my side and lowers himself onto a stool nearby, brows raised as he watches me. The atmosphere is thick and weird. My skin prickles.

The silence is eating me alive.

We don't have to wait long. Grace pokes her pink head back inside the stable and gestures for us to follow. I burst into the sunshine, the wind hot and heavy, and people, people, people everywhere, most of them hovering around a bunch of musicians beneath a striped tent. Court music trills through the air, with tin whistles and softly banging drums.

I take deep breaths of fresh country air while Grace reaches on tippy toes to fuss over me. She's pretty excellent really, smoothing my hair and making sure my crown sits nice and straight. She pulls river weed from the back of my dress and flaps my flowing skirts until the mud is gone, using bottled water to clean my dirt-streaked face under the baking sun. Not much can be done for my squelching sneakers.

When she's done she gestures with her chin towards Jude. I sigh dramatically, just so she knows I don't like it, then turn him around in circles as I smooth his hair and shift his crumpled t-shirt so it sits right, kicking at the mud caked on his sneakers, none too gently. He breathes, 'Thanks, Lottie.'

I roll my eyes at him.

Then Grace positions me and Jude outside the music tent among the crowd, places steaming medieval hot dogs into our hands, and darts away into the crowd. Within five minutes she's casually leading Celeste and a squealing Leo back towards us, with a satisfyingly bedraggled Evelyn trailing behind. I glance at Jude as we prepare ourselves for this 'chance' meeting, and that's when Sebastian appears behind Evelyn. His ocean eyes lock onto mine.

Sebastian. I forgot about Sebastian.

At first Celeste is pissed that we never showed back at the car when we were meant to, but I tell her our phones both mysteriously died, which of course they did, though that might have had something to do with our swim in the river. I guess we seem fairly innocent, because when she asks Jude if he's drunk and he blinks at her silently, she totally buys my entire story about him eating a bad Middle Ages taco and feeling a bit ill. And no, no way, we were nowhere near the river and have no idea whatsoever what she's talking about.

I'm pretty triumphant as we all trail back towards the van. Grace is clearly ignoring Evelyn. Evelyn is close to tears, which is a vast improvement on her normal smarmy self, and Celeste is doing the quiet livid thing, where you know the second we drop the others home she's going to explode.

Evelyn is in for a world of trouble.

And I couldn't be more pleased.

Though a tiny seed of guilt blooms in my stomach at Grace's tight expression. Despite the fact that, for the first time ever, none of it was actually my fault.

We reach the van and Sebastian leans close, whispering in my ear, asking where I was. I think he's disappointed, and he says real low so no one else can hear, 'I feel like the whole day was wasted because I didn't get to spend it with you.'

I think maybe it's the most romantic thing anyone has said to me, but somehow it doesn't settle deep inside my chest the way I expect it to. Sebastian looks at me with his ocean eyes and his tousled hair and his pretty smile. And I don't feel what I want to, my head too filled with worry over Grace, and with excitement that just this once Evelyn is the one who screwed up. Everything twists and turns inside my skull, with no room at all for his sweet words and pretty smiles.

No room for drunk kisses in the river reeds, either, but I'm still hyper aware of Jude when we all climb in the car. We say nothing to each other yet I can feel the space between us like it's solid, and it's filled to the brim with river water and tangled reeds, beating sunshine and horse dust. Tangled like a thick solid rope tying us together.

Me and Sebastian get shoved in the very back of the van and he spends the whole drive home talking about his friends at school and his plans for the summer holidays, which are looming close. I tell him my family are all going to Ireland to visit my nana for New Year's and then spend the rest of the drive listening to him waffle while I wonder what exactly constitutes moon eyes.

I glance at the back of Jude's head, at his shoulders and tense neck, and wonder if what Jude is currently giving my little brother in the seat beside him are moon eyes.

And when he turns and flashes me a hurt look over the car seat, I wonder if those are moon eyes, too.

17

HEALING MY LIFE

On Sunday, Sebastian comes over. He just turns up. Evelyn is under house arrest so she's sulking on the couch with Leo when I bring Sebastian in. Dad raises an eyebrow at me and Celeste smiles warmly, and I have no idea how I feel about him being here at all, but still lead him to my bedroom just to get away from all the staring.

'Let me guess, this side is yours?' Sebastian grins and gestures towards my half of the bedroom, where the walls are plastered in metal posters and the desk is dotted with band stickers, massive speakers tottering beside the bed. He steps towards my corkboard to examine the words and quotes stuck all over it, murmuring, '"Deeds will not be less valiant because they are unpraised."' He turns to me. 'What's that from?'

I clear my throat, trying very hard not to think about river reeds or muddy country water or dust settling on skin. '*Lord of the Rings.*'

Sebastian grins. 'Oh, cool. I like it.'

I grimace. 'I don't. I hate it.'

'Why's it stuck there then?'

I collapse onto the edge of my bed heavily. 'I don't know.'

Sebastian sits carefully next to me, sunshine from my open window flaring across his face, his eyes burning bright like sun reflected off water. The bed dips beneath his weight and he's suddenly sitting a lot closer than he should be. He doesn't move away though. He isn't smiling anymore, either.

Electric nerves tingle inside my chest and I clench my fingers tight. 'Why are you looking at me like that?' I whisper.

'Because you're pretty.'

I gape at him. Because I'm pretty?

It makes me feel good that he thinks that. Of course it does. Sebastian the unattainable, the boy I've loved forever who didn't notice my existence, now thinks I'm pretty. It's marvellous. Wonderful. Extraordinary.

I stand abruptly, coughing. Walk away across the room.

Sebastian grins. I guess he thinks I'm shy but, honestly, I don't think that's it. My stomach is rolling like the ocean and my fingers are tingling and I have this strong solid idea in my head that I definitely don't want Sebastian to kiss me. Not here in my bedroom, not today when I'm feeling sick and weird. Not when my head's filled with tangled river reeds and horse dust smeared on skin.

Maybe not ever.

I bite my lip.

But it's Sebastian Lewis.

And I've loved him forever.

Or, at least, I think I have.

He steps closer, still smiling his easy smile, all white teeth and ocean eyes, his hair soft and streaked with light. He's going to kiss me. He is.

His fingers touch my face, pressing into my hair, and my

heart beats jagged against my chest, my breath turning shallow and uneven. I can't believe this is happening. It's like a dream, like a story, like it's happening to someone else.

I wish it was happening to someone else.

I'm about to shut it down and pull away when a *crack* sounds, wood slamming against plaster, from the door being flung open hard. Sebastian and I flinch. Evelyn stops dead when she sees us standing by the window. Her gaze runs over Sebastian's hands in my hair and his body close to mine and her expression turns sharp and vicious.

Sebastian must notice, because he lets go of my face and takes a step back. Immediately I feel lighter, clearer, better, until my stepsister shuts the door behind her and says sweetly, 'So, did you hear that Lottie kissed Jude yesterday?'

Sebastian gapes.

I do, too, more than a little embarrassed. Immediately I blurt, 'That's not true! Jude kissed *me*!' I cringe. Just to hear the words out loud flushes me hot and strange. 'But he was drunk. It wasn't real,' I stammer. 'He probably doesn't even remember.'

Sebastian turns to me and he is *pissed*, brows low and mouth tight. He makes a sound low in his throat. 'He remembers. You didn't think to maybe mention this to me?'

'Well, I did ...' I stumble over my words. 'But then I didn't.'

He scowls like he'd like to say a whole lot more, but Evelyn is still hovering beside the door with a massive smile smeared across her face. Finally Sebastian leans in real close, right against my cheek to hiss in my ear, his breath warm against my skin, his fingers curling around my hand. 'I like you, Lottie. But you're killing me with this shit.'

When he draws back I can see something new blooming in

his expression. Hurt? 'I'll see you at school,' he says, and then he leaves, the bedroom door closing again behind him until it's just me and Evelyn left alone.

She smiles sweetly and flops onto her bed, making herself comfortable. She reaches for a book.

Slowly I lower myself onto my mattress, gaze never leaving her face as I whisper, 'Why do you hate me so much?'

She flinches, gaze frozen on her page. She doesn't lift her head. 'Because you keep stealing from me.'

I shake my head. 'No. Before that. When you first moved in you hated me. Before you even knew me.'

She sits sharp and fast, flings her book against the wall. It slaps against the plaster and thumps onto the floor. There's silence, then words scrape from her mouth all at once, hissing and spitting like a fissure, as if she doesn't want to say them. 'I don't belong here. In this family. With all of you.'

I grit my teeth. 'You think you're better than us? You have somewhere better to be?' Her words are like needles, pricking my skin. I don't think she belongs here either, but it still offends me she believes she could do better.

Evelyn stands up. 'Yes. Anywhere is better than here with you.' But her voice shakes, like it isn't what she really wants to say, or what she really means. She leaves the room, but quietly this time. No slamming doors. No screaming.

Her words hang in the air after she's gone.

I sit for a long time before using the landline to call Grace to meet up, my own phone still waterlogged and useless. I need to talk to someone. Everything's swirling inside my brain like a cyclone. There are too many tiny pieces and I can't see how they fit together.

Celeste and Leo are sleeping on the couch and I creep by them silently to approach Dad in the kitchen. Evelyn is sitting out on the iron balcony, her back to us, hunched and small with the glass doors shut. She's in direct sunlight and the day is burning hot. Too hot to sit on black metal with no shade. I watch her through the glass and wish for the very first time that I could see inside her head. Understand who she is.

But I can't see anything.

'Tell Evelyn to come back inside,' whispers Dad, voice low so as not to wake Celeste or the baby. 'She'll burn if she stays like that.'

I stand still at the kitchen bench for a long moment, then I say, 'I don't think she'll listen to me, Dad. Can I go out? I'm gonna meet Grace.'

He pats my head affectionately. 'Yeah. Go. It's too quiet here anyway, am I right?' He smiles and I wonder if he's really oblivious to the tension in our household, to the barriers between me and Evelyn, and me and Celeste.

Or maybe he knows, and he's just doing the best he can.

I trip over D'Angelo on the way out and watch as she scratches at the carpet beneath Dad's study desk. And then I slip out of the flat before she pees and Dad orders me to clean it up.

At the river I sit beneath the stretching limbs of a lush fig tree, my feet dangling over the side of the wharf kicking the air above the churning water. A hot thick wind rustles the branches above, birds hanging off the tree and screeching as the waves beneath my feet swell and splash against stained concrete. Beneath the surface shapes glide in the dark. Jellyfish. Pale and soft.

'What are you staring at?'

I flinch at Grace's voice, sudden over my shoulder. I throw her a tight smile. No one else is here. The day is too hot and the whole wharf is deserted, the concrete baking and sweat sticking my t-shirt to my back.

'Nothing,' I say. 'Just the jellyfish.'

'Oh. I thought maybe you'd seen a dolphin.' Grace sits on the cracked concrete beside me, flinging her legs over the side, her rubber thongs hanging precariously off her toes above the waves. She heaves a backpack onto her lap and pushes sweaty pink hair from her eyes.

'What's that?' I point at the bag and she grins.

'Some special contraband. Swiped from my dad's special cabinet.'

I'm alarmed. 'Won't he notice?'

'He didn't notice the last one.'

'Yeah, but if there's none left at all he might start to catch on,' I point out.

'Maybe,' agrees Grace. She pulls out a glass bottle of brown liquor and unscrews the cap. Despite my initial protests, when she offers it to me I grin and gulp some down.

I screw up my face and gasp. 'Disgusting!'

'I know, right? He loves it.'

I hand the bottle back. 'You're going to get in so much trouble.'

Grace shrugs. 'Nah, I'll just tell them you did it.'

I don't appreciate the joke. 'They'll believe you, too. Please don't do that.'

She smiles, but this time I think the edges are frayed, and her eyes stay sad. She nudges me. 'So, what's going on with you and Jude?'

I turn away, peering downriver where the bridge stretches over the water and gulls wheel in the sky above. 'Nothing.'

'Pfft, whatever. Come on, Lottie. Your best friend kissed you!'

I mutter, '*You're* my best friend. Not him.'

She shakes her head, disbelieving. 'How are you so calm? If he kissed you it's a big deal. This is a *big deal.*'

'No, it's not,' I snap. 'He was drunk.'

'So? It's still going to change everything.'

I bite my lip, embarrassed at the fear swelling inside my chest, at the way my eyes pinprick. I swipe at my cheek and continue gazing downriver, this time at the gaping factory that spills from the industrial estate, red scuffed brick and cracked glass windows, tin streaked rust-red with age.

'What about you?' I change the subject. 'Did you and Evelyn break up?'

Grace swigs from her bottle, offering it back to me. 'You'd like that, wouldn't you?'

I turn to her in surprise. 'What do you mean?'

'I know you hate her. I know you think she was just using me.'

I take the bottle and say nothing, lifting the glass to my lips, taking another gulp of the fiery liquid. I cough.

'Maybe you were right,' says Grace quietly. 'Maybe she was just with me to hurt you. I dunno.'

She seems so small all of a sudden, fragile and tiny and wounded. And I want to tell her that Evelyn didn't do that but I can't. Because I'm pretty sure she did.

But I don't feel like saying *I told you so* anymore.

'I'm sorry, Grace,' I say instead.

'Me too,' she whispers. She drinks, blinking back tears, and then slams the bottle against the hot concrete with a loud clink, startling me. 'But you know she's messed up, right? Like, you should cut her some slack sometimes, Lottie.'

I gape at her. 'Some slack? Are you serious?'

Grace shrugs. 'She's having a hard time. And it wouldn't hurt if you were a little nicer.'

I frown. 'Why do you do that? Why do you stick up for her?'

'Because I like her,' Grace says simply. 'And I think she's in trouble. Maybe she used me, maybe she didn't.' She takes another drink and her face turns determined. 'But I'm going to find out.'

I'm surprised. 'You mean you didn't dump her yet?'

Grace grins wickedly, like she knows I'm going to find her next words very disagreeable. 'Nope.'

I shake my head, peering at the white ghost jellyfish, so slow and languid beneath the waves.

'But I'm not talking to her right now,' Grace admits into the silence.

'That's definitely the mature way to handle it,' I say. 'Well done. Very clever of you.'

Grace raises her brows. 'Oh, so you've had a nice long chat with Jude about how he kissed you, have you?'

I scowl at her and she laughs. Loudly. I think the alcohol is doing its job, setting her tongue loose. Her shoulders are relaxed and her back is uncurling.

I feel fire in my belly and chest, my own limbs unwinding and my muscles loosening. My head is spinning. I squint at the bottle. It's very strong. I take another swig and splutter. It's disgusting.

'Why do you think he kissed me?'

Grace shifts beneath the hot sun, wiping sweat from her forehead. 'I don't know.'

I nod. I don't either. It's hard to imagine Jude feeling anything more than friendship for me, because things haven't changed between us over the years. We've always been the same. Always been close. Always had fun together. Always told each other everything.

I start, realising that's not quite true. Because lately things *have* changed. Just a little.

Hardly noticeable changes, like not wanting him to see me in my undies when we went swimming at the beach, or like him giving me the silent treatment, and not telling me what's going on with his parents. I had to drag it from him, and I still feel like he's holding back.

It's like the world was the same, everything was the same, Jude was the same, but our relationship was slightly askew. Just the smallest bit. Barely noticeable.

Until Jude kissed me in the river reeds next to the muddy water and now I've definitely noticed.

My head is fuzzy, my thoughts loose. Grace is lying flat on the hot concrete, groaning and sweating up a storm. I nudge her. 'You wanna go for a swim?'

She grins.

'Oh, and by the way,' I add quickly. 'Sebastian came over today and tried to kiss me.'

I'm on my feet and running away along the wharf before she can sit up, her scream of '*What?!*' echoing behind me.

It feels good to run, Grace screaming my name and chasing me down the empty wharf. We slide together giggling onto one of the bobbing pontoons, an abandoned red brick mill rising behind us, barbed wire fences and floating discarded plastic tumbling across the concrete beneath the sprawling fig trees. I kick off my thongs next to the water and scream when Grace shoves me towards the edge. I sidestep her and then we're both stripping to our undies because no one's around except the cars occasionally crawling over the river bridge in the distance, too far away to see.

I dive-bomb into the water, hoping no jellyfish are nearby. And Grace follows with a scream, plunging into the cool waves beside me.

And we swim and giggle until my throat turns raw and my muscles ache and when it gets dark we walk home along the wharf, empty boats bobbing on the choppy waves as we pass the looming sheds, streetlamps seeping orange light across the pathway.

Gulls wheel overhead in the darkness and I try my best to stop thinking about moon eyes.

But I can't.

18

LATIBULE

I can't sleep.

Soft shouts swell outside my window, bleeding through the flyscreen from the warm night outside. Evelyn's breathing in her bed across from mine is heavy and steady. The room is silent except for the sounds she makes in her sleep, sheets tangled where she's kicked them. Darkness spills from beneath our beds, creeping across the floor, seeping from the corners near the ceiling. Filling the spaces up.

I sit and press my ear against the wall, running my fingers over the cracked plaster beneath my posters, waiting for the shouting to stop. It doesn't. Faint and half-lost on the wind, but filled with tension and raw voices. And fear.

I throw back my sheets and pad to the window, listening closer. And finally I slip from the bedroom and leave dreaming Evelyn behind to move quiet as a ghost through our dark flat. I slide the balcony door open and step into the night, the black sky stretching above the buildings and the streetlamps on the road flickering and pooling orange across the pavement. I shiver, though it isn't cold, pulling my long black t-shirt tighter around my body, feeling small and fragile because of the dark.

Because of the shouting.

I make my decision and climb precariously between our balconies, across the interstice, flashing my undies, not that anyone's here to see. The whole world is sleeping. Pushing my hair from my eyes I crouch on Jude's balcony and peek into his bedroom.

It's empty, a lamp on beside his bed, yellow light dancing across the ceiling. His bed sheets are tangled. I push awkwardly at his window pane and then freeze as the shouting begins again. From the lounge room? The voices swell from within, louder and sharper, and I climb inside, trying not to make too much noise.

My bare feet land on Jude's polished wooden floor, and I stand alone in his bedroom, listening. Fragments of words. Sharp, biting things. Words his father will regret in the harsh light of morning, spoken now slurred and wet, from between gritted teeth. My body winds with tension, muscles contracting in my neck, coiling and pulling.

And then I hear the distant crack of the front door, slamming with shocking finality, and footsteps stomp towards Jude's door. I flinch as it flings open, but it's only Jude, standing in the open space blinking at me.

'You shaved your head,' I blurt. And he has. It changes every-thing about him, suddenly harder and sharper despite the freckles smattered across his skin, his eyes deeper and darker. His expression is hard, too. Different.

He steps inside his bedroom. Shuts his door slowly, like he's thinking about it.

'We woke you.' It's not a question.

I nod. Feeling awkward. Because things are different between us now. Because he kissed me. And late night visits are maybe not the thing they once were, filled with innocence and sweetness and video games.

Did we grow up? Is that what this is, this problem between us? I hate it.

'Jude,' I start. Then stop. Because I don't know what to say. I settle with, 'Why did you shave it?'

A ghost of a smile touches his mouth. But then it disappears again, as quick as it came. 'My dad's gone to stay at a hotel. Or so he says. He'll probably find a four am TAB bar instead.'

My fingers curl around the bottom of my t-shirt, filled with tension. 'I'm so sorry.'

He stares at me. 'It doesn't matter.'

He keeps staring, not looking away, until the heat of it makes me uncomfortable. I turn, sweeping my attention across his room, searching out the royal doll with the cracked face, the homework piled on his desk, even the empty juice glasses still left from the last time I was here. Everything familiar. Everything where it should be. I glance back at Jude. He's still staring.

He's wearing trackies and a thin t-shirt, and because his hair is gone he seems like a stranger. I can't help staring back, trying to find the Jude I know in this new hard face.

I can't find him.

I turn away, step towards his desk and run my hand over the surface, the air thick and tight with tension as I rustle the papers with my fingertips, trying to think of something to say, anything to break the awkwardness that's growing in my stomach. I've never had to fill the silences with Jude before. Never.

But tonight I don't know him at all.

I'm about to say something stupid, about chemistry home-work, that's how awkward I'm feeling, except when I turn around the new unrecognisable Jude is standing right there, close, so close I could reach out and touch him if I wanted to. I flinch, because I hadn't expected the proximity.

My fingers curl into fists at my side, the breath leaving my body because of the *look* he's giving me. Are those moon eyes? Does he stare at me this way from his window, when I'm out on the balcony in the sunshine mucking around with my tomato plants? Is this what his dad meant?

The stranger leans close, until his mouth is near my cheek, until his breath touches my throat, my hair. Across my skin. And he's breathing shallow and fast, chest rising in time with it, his body held close. So close. But never touching. 'Tell me to stop,' he says. But I say nothing at all because I can't think straight. So his mouth presses slow against my jaw, long and deliberate.

My eyes flutter closed. I don't mean them to but my skin is sizzling where he's kissed me and everything is odd and strange and tilted. When Jude pulls away from my body I can't recognise him at all. The boy I've lived beside my whole life is gone, just disappeared. Swallowed whole by this person who is different, who holds himself differently, who breathes heavy and fast like he can't help himself. He's watching me, face close to mine, nose almost touching but not quite, his hands held at his side. Moon eyes burning bright.

I stare back. Can't move. Can't breathe. Everything is turning and still at the same time and I want to stop this from happening but also I don't. Slowly he reaches for me, one hand bunching my t-shirt against my thigh, tugging me closer, and the other moving into my hair behind my neck, fingers splayed against skin and mouth sudden and hard against mine, pressing me back, back, back against the desk, against his body, and I cling to him to keep from falling, or because I want to hold on, or to stop the desk sliding as it rattles beneath our weight, paper rustling to the floor. And I hold him as tightly as he holds onto me, my fingers clutching at the neck of his t-shirt, touching skin on his throat, on his jaw, moving across his buzz cut and his face. And it's not enough to be pressed back by him, I surge forward, push him too, kiss him back, not thinking straight because it isn't Jude. He makes a noise low in his throat when my fingers touch his skin, and then he's leaning me back against the desk again, kissing me deeper. Longer. Harder. Until I think my brain is gone and this is all there is, being shoved against a desk in this dark bedroom being kissed by Jude.

By Jude.

Jude.

My eyes flick open.

I shove him back. Hard. He staggers and then rights himself, expression shutting down, closed and wary, chest heaving.

I turn towards the window. My mouth feels bruised and my hands streak through my hair, smoothing it down, trying to pull myself in, stuff everything back where it should be. Where it should've stayed. I can't look at him. 'This isn't ...' I stammer. 'I didn't mean for ...'

'You didn't mean for it to happen?' His voice is low and hard and warning, and I turn towards the sound in the dawning light.

His mouth is tight and hands clenched. I shake my head. 'Jude,' I start, but he cuts me off.

'No. Don't you dare pretend you don't know.'

I blink. 'Know what?'

His eyes blaze, standing frozen in the centre of the room in front of his tumbled bed, his shoulders tight. 'You know,' he says in the new hard voice. 'You know how I feel.'

'I don't … Jude, please.'

'Don't pretend. You know! You always have.' His expression is accusing and sudden anger boils inside my belly.

I snap, 'How could I know if you don't tell me?'

'I *did* tell you.' Hurt blooms in his face, sudden and hot. 'I told you. I told you not to date that dickhead Jonathon Lee.'

I freeze. That was a long time ago.

'And I told you I hated you behind the shopping centre.'

It takes me a moment but then understanding blossoms inside my chest, spilling into my toes, into my fingers.

The game of opposites.

I stare.

'And I kissed you, didn't I?' he breathes. Moon eyes again. Shimmering in the lamplight. 'At the festival.'

'You were drunk,' I whisper, shaking my head.

'But you still knew.' Except now he sounds less certain. 'You always knew and you brushed me off. Because you weren't interested.' Silence blooms between us, filling all the spaces tight with tension. Finally he breathes, 'I thought you knew.'

I swallow. 'You never told me.'

But I'm uncertain. Did I really not know? Did I never notice anything in the way he was around me, the way he looked at me? The way he did anything I asked, came running whenever I needed him?

Had I truly not noticed what's so obvious now, shining transparent in his face?

Or was I afraid of it? Of things being different.

Of losing what we already have.

Jude steps closer, almost close enough to touch, but not quite.

And then he stops.

Even though his shaved head makes him different and his jaw is sharper than I remember and his shoulders wider, the new hardness in his face suddenly slips and a glimmer of the old soft Jude seeps through. 'I'm telling you now,' he murmurs.

My pulse quickens, cheeks flushed hot, and it's laid out bare between us. He did that. And I have no idea how I feel, a tangle of emotions trembling inside my chest, twisting and churning.

I think I'm afraid.

'You said you didn't want things to change,' I breathe. Back behind the shopping centre, the night we played the game of opposites.

'I made a mistake.' So much is visible within his eyes, surging beneath the surface. 'I was wrong.'

I step backwards, more a stumble. Because it's all too new, too much. I can barely take it in, my heart pounding and my blood roaring in my ears, the memory of him a taste on my tongue. My head aches and my skin where he touched me is alive with burning and all I want right now is to be at home, to be safe in my bed beneath my covers in my room with Evelyn. To have time to think.

'It's too much.'

I don't realise the words have escaped my lips until he flinches. Until he steps back just to be away from me, sucking in his breath quick and turning his back to me.

'That's fine, Lottie. It doesn't matter.'

'Jude—'

He cuts me off, his voice choked. 'You should go home. Before your dad wakes up.'

But I don't want to. I want to feel easy in his company again. I want to slide onto the floor beside his bed and play videogames, or do homework, anything, anything at all to bring things back to the way they were before he kissed me.

I glance at his desk, at the pens and papers strewn across the floor, and I think things have gone much too far for returning. My eyes prick. I swipe at them so he won't see, and quickly climb out of his window. No more words as I pull my body over the spaces between our homes and step back onto my balcony. Slipping inside the house just as Leo begins to stir.

In my bedroom I lie still beneath my sheets and my heart beats loud and jagged in my ears and I hear nothing at all through the wall. Only silence.

And then it's morning and Evelyn throws a pillow at my head to wake me for school but I'm already awake.

19

BEING HIGHLY INEFFECTIVE IS A SKILL

Monday at school is long and slow and Jude isn't there and I avoid Sebastian and Grace like the plague and hide in the library all through lunch. I pretend to study when really I can't think of anything except muddy river water and the desk in Jude's bedroom.

And how he's ruined everything.

On Tuesday morning I snap at Celeste when she offers to make me breakfast, my mind filled with mistakes and whose fault was it and the stranger that is Jude. My brain bursting with it. And with anger too, because everything is destroyed and I've never felt more confused. His name beats through my chest nonstop like a drum. *Jude Jude Jude.* I shake it out and snap at her, 'I don't need a new mother, Celeste. I can make it myself!'

'Lottie!'

Dad glares at me, but I turn my back, facing the sink and ignoring Evelyn who is hovering nearby to watch the show. 'What? It's true. She's not my mother,' I spit.

Dad's voice turns low and dangerous. 'Your mother isn't here, Lottie, and that's not Celeste's fault. Your mother made her choice. And it's Celeste who chose to be here, with us. And she's trying.' His voice softens when he says the last bit and he places his hand on her shoulder, an apology in his eyes.

It only makes me angrier, all this fire and confusion in my gut with nowhere left to go. 'Well, I didn't ask for it. You guys just shoved it on me. Forced it! No one bothered to ask what I wanted!' I'm yelling now and even Evelyn is taken aback at my outburst, the cat running around manically, stirred by the loud voices.

But I can't stop. I think I'm about to cry, only just managing to swallow the tears back down, my voice shaking and cracking, and too late I realise I'm screaming at Dad, 'I hate her! She's stupid. All she talks about are her dumb office stories and no one cares! They're boring and stupid. Everyone thinks they're stupid.' The tears well over, sliding down my cheeks, but the fury still burns in my belly, out of control.

Leo wails, his cries escalating into high-pitched screaming, the cat gone now, probably around the corner out of sight so she can pee on the floor in peace. Dad opens his mouth to reprimand me but Celeste gets in first, angrier than I've ever seen her, her fake facade slipped away.

The true Celeste come out for all to see.

She bounces Leo on her hip and her voice shakes, thick and hot. 'I'm sick of you criticising me, Charlotte. I know what you think of me. I know you make fun of me. I'm sick of it! I enjoyed my job; why is that so hard for you to understand? Why make fun of the things I care about? What kind of daughter are you?'

'Not yours! I'm not your daughter,' I yell back. 'And you do the exact same thing to me! You make fun of my music. You act like it's stupid, like I'll grow out of it. I bet you make fun of it with your friends. You're such a hypocrite. You make fun of the things I care about all the time. All the time!'

Celeste blinks at me, mouth opening and closing and I'm breathing heavily, trying hard to hold back the wave of tears but choking on them instead. And Dad's expression has turned bright and hot, anger flaring into every space. He points towards the door. 'That's it. Go to school. And come straight home afterwards and apologise to your stepmother. Do you hear me? You're grounded.'

I roll my eyes, still seething. 'Whatever,' I spit. 'Great counselling, Dad.' I give him the thumbs up. 'Being grounded sounds perfect! Where am I gonna go after school, anyway? To Jude's?'

Even just saying his name makes the tears harder to hold back, my voice cracking, and I see Celeste watching me carefully, a strange look on her face that I hate. A soft look. Pity. Or understanding.

But she's wrong. She doesn't understand me at all.

I glare back at her. 'Oh, and by the way, Celeste, your daughter gave the finger to her science teacher yesterday and got detention. Maybe she forgot to tell you?'

And then it's chaos, Leo screaming and Evelyn yelling and, as Celeste rounds on her daughter, I split from the flat as fast as possible, before anyone's attention can return to me.

I hate everyone and everything.

All of it.

I pound down the stairwell with my chest heaving, pulse racing as I kick the door at the bottom, shoving it open to burst into the sun, swiping tears from my cheeks.

Evelyn. Celeste. Jude.

I hate everyone.

Well, except Grace, obviously.

I just feel sorry for her. She's stupidly depressed now without Evelyn, because after ignoring her for a couple of days, they finally broke up. And she's so sad now I can't bear to tell her about Jude.

Besides, I don't want to talk about him at all.

Still. It's eating up my insides.

At school I take deep breaths in the music room. It's still early, before classes have started. My hands are shaking. I'm nervous.

'Are you ready?' Mr Smith asks.

I bite my lip and nod, hoping I don't look as sick as I feel, hoping it won't be obvious in the recording. Mr Smith flicks on the video camera, which sits on a tripod near the upright piano, and then he gestures for me to begin.

And I don't know why I'm doing this. Winning the music scholarship was just a way to destroy Evelyn, to take back something that she cared about, but I've already done that. After the longboat incident Evelyn was in huge trouble with our parents. And after Monday, when Grace dumped her and Evelyn was upset enough to lash out in science class, she got in trouble at school, too.

So what's the point of doing the video?

What's the point of winning the scholarship?

I just wanted to make Evelyn mad. I wanted her to be in trouble like I always am. I wanted to win.

I got everything I wanted.

But I don't feel happy.

The game is off, anyway, because after my outburst at home there's no way I'm going to be able to fool Celeste and Dad that I've changed for the better. Not anymore. And Jude still hasn't come back to school, which means his dad probably hasn't come home, so no one's around to make him do anything he doesn't want to, and I feel worried and bitter all at the same time.

So what exactly is the point of this?

Except the red light is blinking on the camera and Mr Smith is waving for me to begin, and my fingers pluck the perfectly tuned strings of the sticky school guitar and I think maybe I want this. Not just to win some game. Maybe I care about it. The guitar. Even the classical music. Maybe I want it just for me.

My attention flicks to Mr Smith's face and he smiles at me encouragingly from within his wiry beard, waving me onwards like a conductor.

So I play. And maybe it works like therapy, because as the music pours from the acoustic my head feels lighter, like my troubles are dancing from my fingertips along with the notes.

By the end of the song I'm dreaming about muddy river water and the moon and I think I press those dreams into the notes, too. I hear them inside the music, swelling and blooming and waiting for me to decide.

Despite everything, I'm excited by the time I knock on Mr Virk's door. Maybe because Mr Smith says I did well on the recording, that I actually have a good chance of doing well with the guitar. Mr Virk's secretary is away, thank goodness, so I don't have to deal with her glares today. When he calls me inside and I catch sight of his shiny balding head and the threadbare couch, I realise I haven't been here in ages.

'Long time no see, Jerry,' I say.

He smiles. A genuine one. Not even a little bit exasperated. 'Indeed. And how have you been, Charlotte? Mr Smith's been telling me some very good things about your efforts. Is that the application form?' He gestures towards the folder clutched tight within my hands.

'Yeah. He helped me finish it today. I printed it so I could sign it.'

Jerry reaches across his desk to take the papers. 'I'll get Geraldine to scan it for you. Mr Smith already sent her the video file.'

'Thanks, Jerry.' I hesitate. 'Did Evelyn give you her application yet?'

'No, not yet. Why?'

'Oh, nothing. Just wondering.'

Old Jerry stops his paper rustling and cocks his head to the side to peer at me over his glasses. 'And how are you and Evelyn getting along these days, Charlotte?'

I clear my throat. 'Oh. You know. Fine.'

He nods absently. 'I hope you'll keep an eye on her. I'm sure you already know she's been struggling quite a lot lately.'

I frown. 'You mean because of the finger-giving incident in science?'

'Well, yes. But I meant that Mr Smith said she hasn't been practising her music very much. Or at least, not as much as she used to. Mr Smith used to be very good friends with Evelyn's dad, you know, so he does take an interest in her progress. And of course she's a very talented flutist.'

I blink. 'Evelyn's dad?'

'Mmmh. From when he worked in the conservatorium. Her dad managed the scholarship placements during the two weeks and he'd conduct the orchestral performance at the end.'

I stare. 'What, Evelyn's dad did?'

Jerry does seem a bit exasperated. 'Of course.'

'Oh,' is all I can manage. I feel strange all over. 'I didn't know that.'

Old Jerry is certainly acting impatient now. 'Don't you and Evelyn live together?'

'Yeah.'

'Then talk to her!' He says it like it's obvious. Like he thinks I'm being ridiculous. But I don't get annoyed because I'm too busy thinking about Evelyn. And her dad.

Mr Virk attempts to shoo me out, because clearly having me standing around being mute isn't working for him. Before I go, though, I notice the tomato plant on his window sill, lush and green. Its springy stalks have grown quite a bit since I saw it last.

Jerry catches me looking and smiles. 'Yes, it's quite healthy, isn't it?' He gets up from behind his desk to show me the little hard tomatoes blushing red beneath the wide soft leaves. And then he tells me about his wife's tomato curry, and how she's nearly due with their second child. And I blink at him and listen for once instead of talking, wondering about this entire half of his life I never thought about before. And wondering about Evelyn's dad, who I never thought about before, either.

The word for it is *sonder*.

I know because I look it up. And when I get home I'll pin that word onto the corkboard above my bed, too, just so I don't forget.

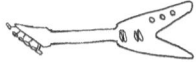

I do a pretty good job of avoiding Sebastian. Until school's let out and I'm walking to the train station under the beating sun, alone for once because Grace's mum and dad picked her up to go shopping. The ocean smells like salt and the jacarandas are spilling purple flowers across the ground like a coloured carpet. Lorikeets hang from the spreading fig trees cracking through the bitumen road and there he is, standing right ahead of me in the shade of an overhanging jasmine vine.

'Lottie,' Sebastian calls, smiling wide in his easy way, confidence rolling off him as he strides towards me to take my bag. 'I'll carry it for you.'

I hold on tight to the straps. 'I've gotta make my train. I'm grounded so I can't miss it.'

Sebastian raises his brows. 'That doesn't sound like something my Lottie would say. Since when do you care about curfew?'

My Lottie?

I blink at him and think he doesn't know me. Not really. And that's why I can't tell him any of the problems I have, can't share any of it with him.

And it sticks this great big barrier up between us, bigger even than before, when he never noticed me at all.

Sebastian is going slightly pink, his cheeks flushed, from the sun or because of me I have no idea. But eventually he bites his lip and says, 'Listen, Lottie, I know this is weird. I know it's weird for me to like you but here I am.' He smiles. 'And I really like you. And I'm willing to do this, even after what you did with Jude.'

My stomach sinks. He's so pretty in the flickering shade of the jasmine vines, stems and blossoms curling around his face, sunshine streaming through the leaves to catch on his shining hair and ocean eyes. None of it is right.

'Wow,' I breathe. It's hard to know what to say. I don't get confessed to very often. And Sebastian's confession was a lot clearer and less messy than Jude's.

That strikes me fairly hard.

What happened between me and Jude, was that a confession too?

It was. Jude confessed to me.

That he felt ...

That he felt *something* for a long time. Since we were fourteen at least.

Longer?

I can't get my head around it. I never thought of it as a confession until now. It makes me feel strange, my mind twisting and twirling.

'Lottie?'

I crash back to reality, to the sunshine and the jasmine vine and Sebastian. He's nervous now, like maybe this isn't going how he thought it would in his head. He presses, 'Wow, what?'

'Um, wow like what you said was so ...' I pause and clear my throat awkwardly, trying to figure out how to say this. 'Sebastian, I liked you for years, but I don't think you know that. Back then I was dreaming you'd say something like this to me.'

'Oh. Phew.' He grins wide. 'For a minute there I thought you were about to turn me down.'

I say nothing, just stiffen.

Sebastian's eyes widen.

'Oh,' he says. Silence stretches out, jasmine scent wafting in the hot summer air, sunlight flickering across his face.

Then he turns his head to the side suspiciously. 'Because of Jude?'

'What? No!'

My response is too fast and his mouth tightens. 'Alright. I get it.'

'Get what?'

He sighs. 'Nothing, Lottie. Or at least, nothing that I want to talk about with you.' But then he must change his mind, because he adds, 'I told him, outside your house. Just before the festival.'

I shake my head. I don't understand what he's saying.

'I told Jude that I liked you. And that he should back off. I told him he had zero chance.'

Oh. Well.

I blink. That's not very nice.

I'm thinking of that night, of Jude's face as he stormed up the dark stairwell after Sebastian was gone, of the tension in the air and how I was so sure he was going to tell me something. Until his drunk dad came home and broke the moment.

He kissed me that weekend.

'What did Jude say?' I whisper.

Sebastian just smiles at me, and he doesn't answer.

I don't know how to react to any of this, until Sebastian finally breaks the awkward silence. 'You better run if you want to catch your train.'

I nod dumbly. And then I do what he says, running the entire way to the platform, sun beating on my back, salt sharp in the air. I make it just in time, collapsing through the last carriage doors as they slide closed.

I'm gasping and covered in sweat, wiping it from my stinging eyes and pushing my hair back from my forehead and that's when I lock gazes with Jude. He's not wearing his school uniform and his skin is streaked with dried salt, his t-shirt damp with the ocean and sand clinging to his cheek. His hair is still buzz-cut short and it's even more severe in the daylight, changing the panes of his face.

I look away. And we don't talk the whole way back to the Port, and when we get off the train we walk home on different streets.

20

HOW TO LIVE YOUR BEST LIFE, OR WHATEVER

I make it home just before curfew. Dad's still at work and Evelyn hasn't come home from school yet so it's just me and Celeste and Leo in the flat. D'Angelo gallops around vigorously underfoot, her tiny paws thundering up and down the lounge room. Lost in one of her manic moods.

I don't say anything to Celeste, but it seems like she wants to say something to me because she's hovering. Presumably she wants to discuss the insanely huge argument we had. Presumably she wants to go into excruciating detail about that lovely moment when I screamed in her face that I hate her. Which is why I am supremely glad when the landline rings.

'I'll get it,' I announce, pouncing on the phone. 'Hello?'

'Charlotte?' The voice sounds tinny and small through the receiver.

'Mum!' I'm so relieved to hear her voice that my own cracks. I quickly turn my back to Celeste, embarrassed. She's moved with Leo into the lounge area to give me some space, but the flat is just one open room and privacy is hard to come by. I cup my fingers around the earpiece and whisper into the phone, 'I tried to call you last night.'

'I know, sweetie. I'm sorry, things have been hectic here. You know John got that promotion and we have the wedding scheduled for New Year's Eve now.'

'New Year's?' My voice turns low and I twist again to further hide my expression from Celeste. I hesitate, my heart beating faster. 'When did you decide that?'

'A few weeks ago, hon. Didn't I tell you?' Her voice crackles on the other end, like the reception is bad. She sounds very far away. 'I'm positive I told you.'

She didn't tell me.

I take a deep shaking breath. 'You said you wanted me to come to the wedding, though.'

'Of course we do! Absolutely.'

'But it's when we're going to Ireland. To see Nana. Dad already got the tickets. For all of us.' I hesitate again, force myself to lose the pleading edge in my voice. 'I already told you about it.'

'Of course, honey. I remember, and you know how much we'd love it if you come to the wedding, but if you can't, I understand.'

I press closer against the wall, fighting tears. Because she *shouldn't* understand. She should want me there. Enough to move the date. Enough not to make me choose between her and Dad. I say nothing.

'Was there something else you needed to talk about? In your message last night you sounded upset.'

I find my voice. 'No. Nothing. Everything's fine.' I glance behind me towards Celeste, but she's feeding Leo now, ignoring me. 'Mum, I'm really sorry but I've gotta go. Grace just got here and we have, like, so much homework.'

'Okay, honey. No problems.'

She sounds relieved.

I have a sudden urge to fling the phone across the room but instead I shove my finger against the disconnect button because I can't bear to tell her I love her. I can't bear to hear her say it back when I don't know if it's true.

When I've hung up I stay leaning against the wall, calming my expression, blinking until my eyes are dry again.

Celeste calls softly, 'Lottie, can I make you a coffee?'

I turn around and I'm about to scoff and tell her no, tell her I don't need coffee, that I don't even *like* coffee, except something else comes out instead.

'Okay,' I say. And I think right now I'd drink bitter disgusting coffee if it means I don't have to be alone.

Celeste's face lights up and she places the now soundly sleeping Leo into his rocker and steps lightly into the kitchen. She motions towards one of the kitchen stools for me to sit.

I do. And I watch her as she boils the kettle, as she pushes her crazy frizzy hair from her face and pulls two mugs from the cupboard, the wrong ones, the ones I don't like, and spoons instant coffee into both. 'Sugar?'

I nod. Who knows?

'Milk?'

'Why not?' Will it make the drink more or less disgusting? I don't even care.

She smiles as she places a steaming ugly mug on the counter between my hands. It's boiling outside, sweat prickling across my skin and the woman feeds me the hottest drink ever, made from literal boiling water.

So stupid.

I'm peering at the murky brown liquid when Celeste sits carefully on the stool beside me, clearing her throat. 'Lottie. I have something to say.'

I glance at her, fear leaping into my throat. What? Is she going to send me away? Is she cancelling the holiday trip overseas? Is she going to burn all my metal posters and t-shirts?

'I was unfair this morning,' she says instead, her voice small. 'You were right. I was being a hypocrite.'

I stare at her, astounded.

'I remembered what I said about your t-shirt. When you were about to come shopping with me that time. Do you remember?'

I shake my head.

'Never mind. It wasn't nice.' She's nervous. Biting her lip and playing with the handle of her mug. She coughs, awkward. 'I realised I never tried to understand the things you liked. And I acted as if you liked them because you're young, or because it's a phase you're going through. And I never respected them. Or you.'

She's gazing at her hands. 'And when you said all of that this morning, it made me realise that how I felt about you making fun of the things I like, how I like going into the office, and I like the work I do and the people I work with, must be the same as how you feel when I dismiss the things you like.'

I am so still. Like a statue. 'You mean, like metal?'

She nods.

'And my t-shirts?'

'Yes. And your nail polish. And make-up.'

I stare at her.

'I wasn't being fair.' Celeste takes a deep breath. 'I'm so sorry, Lottie. I won't ever do it again. That's a promise.'

I glance at my chipped black nail polish, at my fingers clutched around my mug. Suddenly it's like I'm underwater, like Celeste and her calm voice are all that's piercing through. I think about Mum on the phone, her voice crackling through the receiver. She doesn't care if I come to her wedding or not. She doesn't care. And now Celeste is apologising and the world is the wrong way up, inside out, curling at the edges. And more than anything in the entire world, more than I wish things would return to normal with Jude, I wish that it was *my* mum sitting here apologising to me instead of Evelyn's.

I swipe at the tears leaking down my cheeks, embarrassed and flushed hot because I don't want her to see me crying over something so stupid.

Except Celeste reaches for my arm, just a soft touch, and I can't help it, can't stop it; I burst into tears. She wraps her arms around my shoulders and holds me tight as I sob and feel stupid.

Because of Mum. Because of Sebastian.

Because of Celeste and Evelyn.

And because of Evelyn's dad.

I stop crying abruptly, gulping back sobs and staring at Celeste, blinking fast as the words tumble from my mouth. 'Did your husband die?'

It's so out of the blue that Celeste flinches. She's clearly confused but she says, 'He did. But we told you that before I moved in, didn't we? Me and your dad?' She seems worried now, like maybe they'd forgotten to do it.

I shake my head. 'No. You told me. I remember. But ...' I hesitate and bite my lip hard, frowning. 'I dunno. I knew about it but I never thought about it. Not properly.'

I glance across at her but actually I'm thinking of Evelyn,

of her shoulders shaking in the night, of muffled sobs that I'd dismissed as being something else, anything else. I take a deep shuddering breath. 'I'm really sorry he died.'

'Oh.' Now Celeste is fighting back tears too. 'Thank you, Lottie. I was ... it was hard. For me, and especially for Evelyn.' She watches me. 'Did she mention it to you? Is that why you're asking?'

I shake my head. 'No. We never talk.' I look across at her and guilt swells because of that, too, enough to make me whisper, 'I'm so sorry.'

Celeste misunderstands. 'It's okay, Lottie. It still really hurts but it was a little while ago now. When Evelyn was ten. Her dad got very sick. But all of us knew what was coming and we did the best we could.'

I squeeze my mug and words blurt from my mouth, because I can't help myself, because that's who I am. 'How do you think he'd feel about Leo? About you marrying my dad?'

Celeste blinks at me and then recovers. 'I don't know,' she says finally. 'I hope he'd be happy for me.'

I chew my lip, my mind racing. 'Are you nervous about meeting my nana in Ireland?'

Celeste laughs, raising her eyebrows. 'Should I be?'

'I dunno,' I admit. 'I haven't met her either. I've never been overseas before.'

'And are you looking forward to it?' She asks this carefully, like she's thinking about my mother's wedding. It occurs to me that maybe Celeste already knew about the changed date, maybe my dad already knows and told her. Maybe no one wanted to tell me because they didn't want to hurt my feelings.

'Well?' Celeste prompts. 'Are you?'

Finally, I say, 'Yes.' And it seems my decision is made. I'll still go. Celeste beams and something else occurs to me, that maybe she actually prefers if I go with them, all of us together, instead of me being left behind.

I smile at her, small and shy, an expression that is completely wiped from my face with her next question.

'So what's going on between you and Jude?'

I gape at her. 'Nothing!'

Celeste rolls her eyes. Like for real. 'Lottie, I'm not as stupid as you think I am. I know you're always sneaking over there, at all hours too, I might add.'

I gasp. 'Does Dad know?'

Celeste grins. 'No. And I'm not going to tell him if you don't.'

I breathe easier.

'I get the impression things aren't going very well lately?' Celeste adds. 'Which might have something to do with your new friend Sebastian Lewis perhaps?' She takes a sip of coffee, eyes on me the whole time and a smile twitching her lips.

I groan and press my forehead against the counter, doubled over like a deflated balloon. 'I hate them both.'

She laughs. 'Unlikely.'

I roll over, my cheek still pressed against the laminate counter. I watch her carefully. 'Do you want me to tell you what happened?'

It's obvious how excited she is. How badly she wants to scream, *Yes! Tell me! Let's share mother–daughter bonding time!*. To her credit she holds herself back, giving only a small dignified nod of her frizzy head. 'Sure. If you want to tell me.'

I don't mind that she thinks we're bonding. It doesn't stop me. In fact, I feel like I'm unravelling as I explain it to her, about Sebastian and Jude being weird and about what they've both asked me. Or in Jude's case, asked without asking. I don't mention anything about my plan to destroy her daughter, though, which I think's for the best.

When I'm done Celeste excitedly slaps her hand against the bench, startling the cat, who's just ventured into the kitchen to find food. D'Angelo quickly thunders away into my bedroom. Leo stirs too, but only for a second, and then his steady breathing sets in again.

'Phew,' breathes Celeste when he's asleep again. Then she smiles. 'Okay, I've got a game for you.'

'I hate games.' I wrinkle my nose, thinking about Jude's game of opposites.

'No, this is a good game,' insists Celeste. 'It'll give you clarity. Ready?'

I sigh and nod.

'It's a word relation game. So when I say a word, you have to tell me what you think of first, as quick as you can, with no hesitation.'

I groan. 'That sounds like something Dad would make me do.'

Celeste smiles. 'Well, yes, he taught me the game.'

I lean my cheek against the laminate countertop again and whisper, 'Oh no.'

Celeste just continues, 'So let's practise first. Here we go. *Leo!*'

I say nothing, just blink at her.

'Come on, Lottie. Tell me the first thing that pops into your mind when I say his name. *Leo!*'

'Gross,' I answer, quick as lightning this time. Then I grin at her wickedly. 'Like that?'

Celeste frowns at me, but her eyes are sparkling too. 'Cheeky girl. Again. *D'Angelo!*'

'Piss.'

She nods like that answer is completely acceptable. 'Alright, we're ready to go. This is the real thing now. *Grace!*'

I smile. 'Friend.'

'*Evelyn!*'

'Sour.'

Oops.

Celeste frowns and I wave my hand in protest, saying, 'I meant to say lovely. Lovely.'

'I think we'll deal with that one a little later. Let's continue then. *Sebastian!*'

'Pretty.'

'Oh, interesting. Unexpected.' She grins. '*Jude!*'

I open my mouth to say ... nothing.

It's too vast. Muddy river water and childhood scraped knees. The salty ocean. His stupid desk in his stupid bedroom and his stupid shaved head. And a million other thoughts rising in waves like I'm rolling on the ocean. There isn't one single word for all of that. No way.

I shrug. 'It's too hard.'

'That's okay, but we did learn something.'

I frown. 'What?'

She flicks her frizzy halo of hair and pouts at me, exactly like an annoyed mother should, like she's about to scold me. 'You *cannot* date a boy just because you think he's pretty, Lottie. I forbid it. There has to be some substance there too. Agreed?'

'Sebastian has substance,' I protest. 'It's just that I don't know him all that well yet. That's why I was just focusing on the pretty thing.'

Celeste shakes her head like it's all settled, ignoring me. 'Absolutely not. I forbid it.' She clears the mugs and carries them towards the sink. That's when my brother wakes and starts screaming. This time I offer to change his nappy for Celeste and she sits back on her stool and beams and beams and beams.

Stuff doesn't seem any clearer after our conversation, but I do feel a lot better. A lot lighter. My mind less twisted and heavy.

And in the end my word association was dead on. Leo really is very gross.

21

PICKING THINGS APART AND PUTTING THEM BACK TOGETHER

Me and Grace get the train home from school, just the two of us alone. Evelyn stayed back to practise with Mr Smith and though Jude's back at school he's avoiding me just as hard as I'm avoiding him. I gaze out the dirty glass at the river as it flashes by. At the factories with the glass windows like jagged teeth, the sun reflected on the water, and the rotting jetty above the waves.

The carriage is packed, rocking back and forth, crowded with kids from school and adults, too, all living their huge lives, walking around experiencing the world in their own ways. I glance at Grace and murmur, '*Sonder.*'

She peers up from her phone, the fading sun reflected across her skin, blazing like her pink hair. 'What?'

'*Sonder.* It means to understand that everyone around you is living a life as complex and vivid as your own.' I bite my lip and turn to the window again, thinking about Jude. Thinking about his dad. Wondering what's going on. Wishing he'd never kissed me so I could call him and ask.

But also ... not wishing it, too.

I stiffen in my seat, hands clenching my school skirt, shocked at myself. Thoughts of river reeds and his bedroom desk race through my mind, and soon my heart is beating harder against my chest, my blood roaring in my ears. I relive the moments in my head, over and over, examining them from every angle. His hands in my hair, against my skin. His mouth on mine.

Maybe it wasn't so bad. Kissing Jude.

My cheeks burn the whole train ride.

Grace doesn't talk much on the walk to my house. She's still upset, though she doesn't mention Evelyn. Back at the flat Celeste's head perks up over the back of the couch, the room cool and dark after the blazing sunset outside. My stepmum offers to cut us slices of watermelon and shyly I say yes, smacking a big wet hello kiss onto Leo's fat cheeks. My voice when I tell Celeste about our day actually sounds normal instead of sarcastic, and Grace raises her brows at me as we walk into my room. I just shrug.

Things at home are changing.

In my room I stand beside my bed and stare at the words on my corkboard.

Why are so many of the words I collect sad ones?

Like *hiraeth*. And *saudade*.

Tacenda. Kalopsia.

One by one I pick them off my board, screwing the paper into my fist and chucking the pieces into the waste paper basket beneath my desk.

I leave the word *sonder* where it is. And *anguilliform*. *Tarantism* and *kalon* stay too. And Jude's movie quotes. My fingers hover over them, touching the curling edges of the paper.

I turn to find Grace watching me. She smiles softly and we both settle side by side on my bed, backs against the wall.

We're facing Evelyn's side of the room. Her neatly made bed. Her orchestra posters and the little porcelain animals lined up on her window sill. It's the first time I've thought my room appeared empty without her in it.

Celeste comes in with the sliced watermelon and after she's gone we eat in silence, juice running down my chin and hands. Finally I announce, 'So I think Sebastian tried to ask me out.'

I haven't told Grace everything about Jude, not about what happened between us in his bedroom, but I know she's been talking to him. She won't tell me what he says. She keeps pushing me to go ask him myself. But I can't.

Even now my heart races faster just thinking of it, like I'm on the edge of a precipice. I need to pull back and maybe, just maybe, things will eventually return to normal. Or at least a weird stilted version of normal.

Or I can step off.

Grace sits straighter. 'Whoa. Really? What'd you say?'

'Nothing really. But I think he got it. I mean, it was really nice but ... you know.'

She sighs. 'Yeah. I know.'

I frown, lost in the memory of Sebastian's confession. 'I mean, it was sort of sweet? But also a little condescending.' I pause. 'Huh. Actually, he said he knows it's weird that he likes me.' I turn to Grace with wide eyes. 'He said it's *weird*! What's that supposed to mean?'

She looks pissed off on my behalf. Just as a good friend should.

'And you know what else?' I'm warming to the subject now, wiping watermelon juice on my skirt. 'I remember him saying that if I liked Jerry there must be something wrong with me!'

'Who's Jerry?' Grace muses.

'Mr Virk.'

'Oh.' Her mouth is full of watermelon. 'What a jerk.'

I sigh and shrug. 'Nah. I think Sebastian's okay. Mostly. You know, as a friend he's okay. That's what I mean. He's sort of great but also sort of not great.'

'Right,' Grace agrees as I lean my head back against the wall, running over all my previous conversations with Sebastian, picking them apart and putting them back together. Thinking about them differently now.

Maybe Celeste is right. Maybe being pretty isn't good enough for me. Maybe I want something a little ... *more*.

I lean over and nudge Grace with my elbow. 'What about you? Have you talked to Evelyn yet?'

She shakes her head.

'Are you going to?'

She sighs. 'I dunno.'

'You know, I found out something about her the other day. Like Mr Virk brought it up.' And I tell Grace about Evelyn's dad. About what Celeste told me.

Grace's eyes bulge. 'Well, duh, Lottie,' she says. She shakes her head in disbelief. 'You knew her dad died. What did you think it meant for her? You're only feeling bad about it now?'

I feel a little scolded. A little stupid. I mumble, 'I guess I never thought about it properly before.'

Grace crawls off my bed and stands next to my corkboard to tap her finger hard against the word *sonder*. She raises her brows at me, pulling a face as if she finds me unbelievable.

'I know, I know,' I protest. 'That's why I put the word up there. To remind me. I'm not proud.'

'You shouldn't be.' She shakes her head and flops back down beside me. 'You really are an idiot.'

'I know,' I mumble.

'Is that why you're asking me if I've talked to her? Because you feel sorry for her now?'

I shrug. 'Maybe.' I hesitate and then add, 'She seemed sad this week.'

'It's different between me and her,' says Grace softly. 'I mean, it's good if *you* can manage to get along with her now. But she did something really bad to me, Lottie. And now I can't tell if she liked me or if she just did it all to get back at you.' Her voice shakes so I take her hand and squeeze. But then she says, 'What about you and Jude?'

I let go of her hand, cheeks flushed as I sit straighter. 'I don't want to talk about Jude.'

'Lottie, come on—'

The door swings open and Evelyn is standing there. She blinks at Grace, surprised to find her sprawled across my bed. Her face turns pink. 'Sorry,' she mumbles and then she turns right around and walks out.

Grace leaves soon after that, her own cheeks burning, and when I come back upstairs from walking her out I can't find Evelyn anywhere. I mean, I don't search that hard. She's just not in our bedroom. But Celeste must notice because she coughs to get my attention and then gestures towards the glass doors and the balcony. She turns back to the dishes, clinking away at our watermelon plates, Leo drooling happily on the rug in the lounge area.

I hold my breath and slip outside into the heat, sun shining onto the black wrought iron of the balcony, everything hot to the touch. I sink down beside her.

Evelyn blinks, surrounded by my lush tangle of tomato plants, hard green fruit growing among the thick leaves, sagging the little plants towards the rough wooden planks. Scents of tabouleh and coriander rise from the restaurant below, savoury and filled with spice. 'Are you okay?' I whisper.

'What do you care?' Evelyn's voice is acid, sharp and spiteful. Her eyes are red.

'Have you been crying?'

She glares at me. 'No!'

I bite my lip. I have absolutely no idea how to do this. Being nice is hard. I glance across at Jude's balcony. If he was here he'd tell me what to say.

'So,' I start, 'how are you settling into our house?' I fumble over my words, awkward. 'I mean, obviously I know it's been ages, like, well over a year, but I just realised I never actually asked you when you first moved in and I never asked you where your dad was or what happened to him and I guess I knew because I'm sure my dad told me but I didn't think about it properly and now ... I still don't ...' I stop talking, sucking in a deep breath.

Evelyn's brow furrows, her hair wavering in the hot wind. Sticking to her neck with perspiration. 'What the hell are you talking about?'

'Nothing.' I sit stiff and tense beside her. I try again, 'I just ... I was thinking, you know.'

'Oh great. Marvellous. The brilliant Lottie was thinking. Glad to hear it.'

I frown, trying not to get annoyed. But seriously. She's

annoying. I clear my throat, and imagine Jude here to pinch me every time I'm about to get snappy. Be nice. Be kind. Be brave. Isn't that what he said?

I try again. 'Look, Evelyn, the thing is, I was thinking about you, and I was thinking that my name is Lottie Murphy, and my dad is Donal Murphy and there's Leo Murphy and Celeste Murphy but you're still Evelyn Tait. And I thought ... I thought maybe that was hard. For you, I mean. Like maybe it feels like you're left out.' I trail off, awkward.

Evelyn sucks in her breath, snaps, 'I don't want your stupid name! I've got my dad's.' She stands and she's obviously *pissed*, so maybe I haven't handled this very well. 'I don't need your dad or your name or you, Lottie! And I don't know what you're trying to do right now but it won't work! I'm not going to get tricked by you.' She turns on her heel and slams open the glass sliding doors, disappearing inside.

Leaving me alone on the hot balcony.

And she doesn't talk to me again for the rest of the evening, not even once, not during dinner, not while we all sit awkwardly watching television, not when D'Angelo pees in the kitchen again.

But when we're getting ready for bed I catch her glancing at me, furtive and quick, a strange expression on her face that I can't quite read. And before I flick off my light I say goodnight to her.

She doesn't answer, but I hear her shifting on her bed long after the room is dark, long after the flat has gone quiet and our family have all gone to bed.

And when she does sleep I hear her whisper a name into the darkness.

'*Grace.*'

22

THERE'S MAGIC IN LISTENING

The rest of the week passes in a blur, and stuff with Sebastian is weird but okay. He's still hanging around us but it feels different, like he's not so focused on only me, and instead he starts talking to Grace heaps, who seems to be warming to him now.

I guess maybe he wasn't really that into me after all, because surely he'd be more upset. He doesn't seem to be, doesn't seem to care that things ended between us before they began. When I examine my feelings, I admit to myself that it pricks at my pride a little, how totally okay he is. Yet at the same time I guess I'm pretty okay too. More than I would have thought, back when I used to dream about him all the time, lying in bed at night thinking about his pretty face.

It makes me fairly certain I never liked him the way I thought I did.

With Jude, on the other hand, it's different. There's a lump in my throat I can never seem to swallow, a sharp tang on my tongue that never goes away. Thoughts of him curl through my mind when I'm awake, seeping into my dreams when I'm asleep.

And I miss him.

Sometimes during lunch Jamie Gorecki and Obi Okocha come over too, all of them sitting at our table and hanging out with us. It's pretty weird, but also nice. Our little group swelling at the seams, people popping in and out.

Evelyn doesn't comes back, though, and Grace spends a lot of her time glaring at Jamie Gorecki across the lunch table. At first I think it's because of that thing from first year when he made fun of her pink hair, but then I remember he used to go out with Evelyn. I think Grace might actually be jealous.

Time passes and eventually even Jude ventures back to sit with us, though he keeps his distance from me, talking only to Grace and never meeting my eyes. He sits quietly to the side with shadows clinging to the panes of his face, like he hasn't been sleeping, and I hate the way we don't talk to each other and I hate the gaping interstice between us and I kind of hate him, too.

Sometimes.

Other times I catch myself staring at him. My chest pounds when he comes too near and I keep glancing at his freckles, at his buzz cut, at his smile when he grins at something Grace said. I keep staring at him. I can't seem to stop.

I'm pretty sure no one notices until one day when Sebastian grins at me, raising his eyebrows, flicking back and forth suggestively between me and Jude. I burn red and ignore him, spending the rest of lunch reading a book and refusing to talk or look at anyone.

That is until Grace calls Jude's name across the table. Everyone else is still talking, their voices loud and overlapping. I listen for Jude's response and feel strange, like I'm underwater. Like I'm far away. Like I'm over here and they're over there. Grace asks, 'Did your mum come home?'

Grace knows she did. Because I already told her I saw Jude's mum get out of a taxi yesterday, Jude dragging her suitcases upstairs. I watched them from our balcony and that night I listened hard for screaming, but there was nothing. Only quiet.

I wait. Holding my breath. Will he answer? I'm desperate to know how things are in his home, how *he* is. I'm pretty sure that's why Grace has asked him now, at the table in front of me. So I can hear.

Jude keeps his eyes lowered as he says quietly, 'Yeah, she came home.'

Grace nods, pressing gently, 'And do you know what's going to happen?'

'Yeah. I know. My parents are getting a divorce. My dad's moving out.'

Silence.

Even the other boys' conversation trails off, though I don't think any of them were listening. And I'm right, because the next moment Sebastian says loudly, 'Who's moving out?'

Grace answers, 'Jude's dad's moving out. His folks are getting divorced.'

I wince. Did she have to be so tactless? I feel Jude flinching, though I'm not near him. I want to grab his hand and drag him away. He doesn't need to be subjected to this.

Except right then Sebastian says uncertainly, 'Dude. That's rough.' He hesitates and then leans closer, his voice low. 'That's screwed up. My parents have always been solid, you know, and I can't imagine what it'd be like if … I'm really sorry, man.'

Jude blinks. 'Oh … Um, thank you.'

Too weird.

Jamie Gorecki pipes up next. 'My parents got divorced last

year. It sucks. I had to pick which one I got to live with. They made me choose. They making you choose?'

Jude blinks again, opens his mouth to answer when I stand abruptly, grabbing Grace's arm and dragging her behind me. 'Yeah, yeah, we're all from broken homes. How sad. We've gotta go.'

'I'm not from a broken home,' says Grace helpfully. 'My parents love each other very much.'

Jude rolls his eyes, but a smile creeps across his mouth, and I think somehow the tension at the table is gone. I watch him shrug it off, like he's glad it's over, as if his confession wasn't such a big deal after all. The other boys keep talking, laughing and joking now, this time drawing Jude into their conversation.

I pull Grace all the way down the hall, away from them all, and when she tries to talk to me about Jude I shush her.

'Where are we going?' she whines.

I ignore her until we reach the music room. I press my finger to my lips and point at the closed door, leaning close to listen and gesturing for her to do the same.

Inside Evelyn performs her piece for Mr Smith. And when I glance through the small grubby window I see the video camera is flashing red as Mr Smith records her flute solo for the scholarship. Grace and me press our ears against the door and I realise it's the first time I've listened to my stepsister play. Like, *really* listened.

The tone of her instrument is breathy and sweet, clear like a bell as she trills and soars through her intricate classical piece, every note precise and perfect. I'm loath to admit it, but it sounds beautiful.

When she's finished Mr Smith's voice rumbles through the

door. 'That was perfect, Evelyn, perfect! Next term we'll focus on more than just technique, though. Emotion is important too. Like how Lottie plays the guitar. Not so perfect, but with feeling.'

I shove my hand over my mouth, biting back a laugh, imagining Evelyn's sour expression. Grace slaps my arm. 'Stop that,' she hisses.

I roll my eyes, but I do stop. Who knew anyone ever compared Evelyn to me? I thought it only happened the other way round.

It makes things feel more even between us, and when Mr Smith leaves the room I grab Grace's hand and force her to follow me inside where Evelyn is sitting wiping down her flute. She glances up, her face red. When she sees me she snaps, 'What?' But then closes her mouth fast when she realises Grace is behind me.

I lean against the piano. 'We heard you play. You sounded good,' I admit.

Evelyn's rosebud mouth tightens suspiciously.

Grace coughs, glancing at my stepsister. 'Yeah. You sounded good.'

Evelyn stares back.

I roll my eyes at them. 'So, are we still going to that metal gig you set up or what?' I address the question to both girls but get only blank looks in return.

'From before,' I exclaim, exasperated. 'You said there was an all-ages gig in the city. You said you wanted us all to go together.' I wrap my arm around Grace's neck and raise my brows at Evelyn, challenging. 'Well, *we're* going. Are you coming or what?'

I swear Grace is holding her breath.

That would be because I told her what Evelyn said in the deep of the night when she was sleeping. I think it went a long way towards healing my best friend's broken heart. Which means my stepsister owes me big time. I grin wide at her, and slowly Evelyn nods, still blank, like she hasn't quite figured out what's going on. But that's fine. She'll figure it out soon enough.

Four days later Mr Virk calls both me and Evelyn into his office, our names announced over the school's intercom and blasted into every classroom. Which is embarrassing. I catch Jude's gaze as I leave class, and he stares back with blue eyes shining, making my heart beat harder.

Grace shakes her head at me as I pass her desk and I mouth a contrite, 'But I didn't do anything wrong!'. She just shrugs like she doesn't believe me.

But I really haven't.

I follow the hallways to the second floor where Mr Virk's office is, slipping inside and giving my most charming smile to his secretary. She just screws up her face in return, sour like a lemon. Sour like Evelyn, who already sits waiting on the cracked orange chairs outside the principal's office.

We go in together and old Jerry waves us to his threadbare couch. I sink into the familiar cushions but Evelyn is much less comfortable, fidgeting and shifting in her seat like she's never been here before. And maybe she hasn't.

'So, girls,' Mr Virk starts. 'First, congratulations on entering the scholarship program at the conservatorium. I know Mr Smith is very proud of all your efforts and may I say that the school is too. Well done.'

He pauses, peering at us over his glasses, his balding head shining in the sunlight. We wait expectantly, Evelyn fidgeting beside me, clearly filled with nervous energy. Me, I'm calm as anything, totally relaxed.

'Unfortunately ...' Jerry hesitates and I lean forward.

'Unfortunately what, Jerry?'

He sighs. 'Unfortunately it seems there's been a bit of an incident.'

'An incident?'

He frowns at me. 'Yes, Charlotte. One of sabotage, I would suspect.' He raises an eyebrow. 'You may or may not be shocked to hear that one of your applications has been erased from our system.'

Evelyn gasps. 'But it's due today!'

'Indeed it is.' Mr Virk glances at his watch. 'In a half-hour to be exact.' He waits expectantly, as if hoping for a confession.

He'll be waiting a long time.

I hold my hands up, proclaiming my innocence just as Evelyn rounds on me, hissing, 'What did you do?' I think she's about to throttle me.

Mr Virk waves his hands in the air, attempting to calm things down. 'Evelyn, Evelyn! Stop! Your application is fine, it's already been sent.'

She stops dead, gaping stupidly.

I smother a grin and then attempt to appear innocent. 'Mine was deleted?' I frown. 'That sucks! I worked so hard on that.'

'Yes, yes, very sad. Believe me, we'll be putting all our efforts into figuring out how this breach occurred.' He pauses. 'For instance, Geraldine has already changed the password to her computer.'

I blink at him innocently. 'Is it a bit more complicated now, Mr Virk?'

He frowns. 'Why, yes it is, Charlotte. It's no longer stuck on her screen, either.'

'You mean with a post-it note, Mr Virk?'

Evelyn watches me, her face frozen as Mr Virk removes his glasses and sighs loudly. 'Yes,' he says. 'It's much more complicated now. I can assure you we won't face this same problem again.'

I nod and climb to my feet. Evelyn copies me, her expression still blanched.

I say, 'I think maybe you need CCTV in your office, Mr Virk. I asked Geraldine last week and she mentioned you don't have any.'

He purses his lips. 'Yes. Well. That would be nice, wouldn't it?' We walk towards the door, Evelyn just ahead of me, her face ashen. Except just before I leave Mr Virk calls me back, 'Oh and Charlotte?'

I turn. 'Yes, Mr Virk?'

'It seems to me you could have just asked.'

'Asked?'

'Asked us not to submit it.'

I blink. 'I don't know what you're talking about, Mr Virk.'

He waves me away, rolling his eyes. As I shut his office door I catch him looking at the tomato plant blooming lush and green upon his window sill, the fruit blushing pink. Wondering if it's worth it, I suppose. Teaching is such a thankless job.

I wander out of the office, beaming another charming grin for Geraldine who scowls back at me as I step into the hall, sneakers squeaking against the linoleum. After sliding the office door shut I whip around and almost bang right into Evelyn, who is hovering behind me.

'Why did you do that?'

I frown. 'Do what?'

'Seriously, Lottie. *Why*?!'

I don't answer. Just walk away along the hall. Evelyn follows, scurrying at my heels.

'Did Grace tell you about my dad?' Her voice is accusing, filled with hurt. 'About him working at the conservatorium?'

I stop walking and turn back. 'No,' I say quietly. 'Grace didn't tell me anything you told her. If they were your secrets she'd never tell. Not even to me.' I scoff. 'Even though I'm her best friend in the world and she should. Even though she told you *my* secrets, I might add, like how I used to be crushing on Sebastian.'

Evelyn blinks. 'Oh.'

Silence draws out between us until finally I feel compelled to admit, 'Mr Virk sort of mentioned your dad used to work at the conservatorium.' The halls are empty, classes still in session. 'It made me think about him. What it might be like for you.'

She pauses. 'That's why you said that about my last name? Not because of Grace?'

I shake my head. 'I said it because of *me*. Because I felt bad.'

She bites her lip, glancing at her shoes. Then she tosses her head, scoffs. 'But I would have won anyway. You didn't need to delete it.'

I roll my eyes. 'Don't be so sure. Mr Smith said I play with feeling, remember?'

She glares at me. 'There's no way you'd get in just playing with feeling.'

I grin. 'You're right. But wait until next year, Evelyn Tait. Next year I'll really destroy you. Next year I won't hold back, even despite your dad.'

She snorts. 'As if you could beat me.'

'I will! I'll get technically good and totally beat you into the ground. Everyone will be screaming my name, chanting it.' I make cheering noises, like a large crowd hissing.

Evelyn sniffs, falling into step beside me as we walk back towards our classes. 'That sounds more like they're booing you.'

'They're definitely not. They love me.'

She scowls and stomps away towards her next class, in the opposite direction to mine. I grin after her.

Everything is changing, bit by bit.

Falling into place.

Or nearly everything.

I walk back to class humming technical guitar riffs, my fingers dancing through the air like they're flickering across an imaginary fretboard. And I'm dreaming of Jude that day in the ocean, long hair dripping in his eyes and salt streaked skin. Freckles turning darker beneath the sun, eyes as blue as the sky.

It occurs to me then, sudden and hot, that being afraid doesn't suit me.

I can be braver than this.

23

TO BE HONEST, I JUST WANT TO BE NEXT TO YOU

'What do you think?' I push my hair back and turn my face to the light so Grace can see better. I'm crouched on the floor and she's cross-legged on the edge of my bed, make-up spread out on my bedspread.

She's helping me get ready for the metal gig, and I commissioned her to do my eyes as black and thick as she could, with winged eyeliner and light lip gloss. I think it looks pretty flash. I squirm a little closer. 'Is it even?'

Evelyn comes to stand over Grace's shoulder, peering at my face critically. 'It's not even. You look stupid.'

I roll my lovely kohl-rimmed eyes at her as Grace asks my stepsister shyly if she wants help with her make-up too.

I make puking sounds and crawl off the floor, leaving them to it. They still haven't got their act together, but I can feel them dancing around it, coming closer and closer as the days ebb by. Judging by the way Evelyn is staring at Grace I can't imagine they'll make it through tonight without some drastic relationship changes. And despite having my blessing I still think they're gross. Or to be specific, just Evelyn is.

But maybe that's just how sisters feel about each other.

I dunno. I've never had one before.

I adjust myself in the mirror over our shared dresser, black hair out and long, ironed straight and shiny, black t-shirt displaying my favourite band, short denim cut offs and shimmering stockings with cool boots. I feel fairly nice tonight. Fairly confident, too. I edge out of the bedroom and into the main flat. Dad and Celeste are on the couch with Leo, watching him like he's the most wondrous, gorgeous thing in this world, when really he's just a fat baby. I lean close over their shoulders, startling them. 'Watcha doing?'

Leo drools long strings of baby spit and smiles his toothless happy smile at me. I lean across my dad to pinch my baby brother's cheek softly. I guess he's a bit cute. Sometimes. When I'm not changing his nappy.

'Lottie, do you have a sec?'

I glance at Dad, immediately suspicious. 'Why? We have to go soon. You said we were *allowed* to. I told you it's an all-ages gig, so they'll put wrist bands on us and everything. We're not going to be drinking!' None of that is technically true, but I've decided that being too good doesn't suit me. A healthy balance is needed.

He just chuckles, holding his hands up in surrender. 'Of course you're going, of course.' He laughs again but I'm still suspicious.

'What then?'

'Come on,' he extricates himself from the couch, from Celeste who smiles at me serenely and nestles back in with their slimy baby. 'Let's go to the study.'

'Daaad,' I whine. The stupid study.

I sigh and follow him across the room, settling heavily into the stupid velvet chair as Dad sticks his bum on the corner of his desk like always. I have zero idea why he likes his 'study' so much. Perching on the table can't be comfortable. And besides, the tomato plant I gave him is there, taking up a lot of room, so there's a lot less for him now. His desktop is a jungle of lush leaves and winding green stalks, the scent of the plant fresh and sweet. Dad clicks his fingers because apparently my attention is wandering.

'So, Evelyn told me you're getting pretty good on the guitar.'

My eyes flick to his, surprised. 'Oh.'

He nods, a smile slowly spreading across his face. 'She also suggested that perhaps playing metal guitar is quite similar to classical. She may have mentioned that a lot of metal guitarists are classically trained.'

I say nothing, my heart beating a little faster. What is going on?

'Celeste and I discussed it, and if you do still want to, and you're willing to get a part-time job, we'll match whatever you save towards an electric. And we'll pay for the lessons, like we do for Evelyn.'

I'm breathless. 'Really?'

He grins. 'Yeah, really.'

My mouth falls open, mind racing. 'But what about an amp? And a pick-up? And a pedal? More than one pedal. And can I get a Razorback?'

He frowns. 'I don't know what those things are but I suppose we can discuss—'

I launch myself at him, wrapping my arms around his neck. 'Thankyouthankyouthankyouthankyou.'

'Alright, alright, you're choking me.' But he's grinning, too.

He hugs me tight and kisses my cheek, murmuring, 'You deserve it, Lottie. You've done well. It's been hard and I'm proud of you.'

I pull away. 'What was hard?'

His smile tightens. 'Your mum leaving. A new family moving in. Me and Celeste having Leo. Things are different now.'

I pause, considering. 'But they're okay.'

'Change is scary,' he says. 'But it's good. I'm happier now. I hope you are, too, Lottie.'

I think about it. Am I happier? Than I used to be?

I don't know. It's hard to say.

I think of all the words to describe wanting things as they were. *Saudade. Hiraeth.* Longing for the past. Nostalgia and homesickness, like staring back through rose-coloured glasses. I think of my mum, of the family we had or didn't have. Or at least the family we had in my memories. I press tears from my cheeks, smiling. 'You're making me mess up my eyeliner, Dad.'

He smiles. 'That certainly wasn't my intention, daughter.'

I grin, blinking rapidly as I shrug. 'I like things now,' I finally relent. 'They're okay.'

And that seems to be enough. He squeezes my shoulder and smiles, a real smile filled with warmth and his own happiness, before he steps away to join Celeste on the couch.

I stay perched on the ugly velvet chair, looking out the dim glass into the night beyond our balcony. Thinking. I liked Jude before too. With his soft face and his sweet smile and his long hair. Yet ...

Resfeber.

New beginnings are good too.

Buzz cuts and sharp features and sure hands. I like those things too.

I get up and clomp in my boots through to my bedroom, making sure I knock loudly before venturing in. Grace and Evelyn are exactly how I left them, Grace painting bright red lipstick carefully onto my sister.

'I'm gonna go get Jude,' I announce.

Grace blinks. 'He didn't want to come.'

I shake my head. 'Nah. He's coming.'

'Well, good luck.' She shoots me a secret grin before turning back to my sister. 'We're almost done. We'll meet you downstairs in a sec.'

I go back out and organise to meet Celeste in the car park with the others. She gets up and gathers baby Leo's mountain of travelling stuff because apparently he's coming for the ride. Celeste says the car helps him sleep.

While everyone is busy organising themselves I slip from the flat and walk across to Jude's door, pounding my fist relentlessly against the wood until the lock clicks open on the other side.

'I thought that was you, Lottie!' Jude's mum smiles at me and then drags me in for a warm hug. The woman is different in every way to her son. Tiny and dainty where he's stocky, with dark thick hair and dark clear skin, not a freckle in sight. 'I haven't seen you since I got home.' She seems genuinely distressed by this so I guess Jude hasn't mentioned how weird things have gotten between us. Which I am totally cool with. The less she knows the better.

I smile sweetly. 'Is Jude here? We're going out to a gig in the city.' I follow this very quickly with, 'It's all-ages so no drinking and Celeste is driving us,' so she can't protest.

'Oh. Jude never mentioned it.'

His voice shouts from deep within the cavernous space of

their home. 'Mum, who is it?' His footsteps draw closer and then he stops dead behind her, at least a head and shoulders taller than his tiny mum. He's staring. And I think I must be staring too, because his mum clears her throat.

'Lottie's here to take you out, sweetheart. You ready?'

'Take me out?' he repeats, his voice raw and slow, like he's still three steps behind.

I nod with determination. 'Yup.' I forge forwards into the flat, pushing him aside and leaning down to find his sneakers from the shoe rack. 'Here, put these on.' I shove them towards him. 'And where's your wallet? Your phone?'

His mum swipes his phone from the top of a cabinet beside the door. 'Oh, here it is.' She locks eyes with me and smiles. I take the phone and grin back at her, ignoring Jude's protests.

He doesn't want to go. It's too late. He isn't dressed properly. His t-shirt has a cartoon logo on it and he'll be laughed at. He doesn't know where his wallet is.

I dismiss it all and grasp the sleeve of his t-shirt and tug him out the door as his mum hands me his wallet, recovered from the depths of the flat. She shuts the door firmly behind us as I drag Jude into the deserted concrete stairwell.

The lights are dim and blue, fluorescents flickering weakly along the stairs. It's hot and heavy and my boots thunk loudly against the concrete. Jude's breathing fast from all the rushing, from trying to keep up. He tugs his t-shirt out of my grip and stops walking.

I stop too. Turning back to glance up at him from a few stairs below.

'Lottie,' he breathes warily, confusion written across his face. 'What are you doing?'

I smile at him slowly. Then take two deliberate steps towards him until we're level again, darkness shrouding the ceiling, seeping from the winding staircase overhead.

Blue lights flicker in the dark, colours staining his skin. I smile, reaching close to shove his phone in the side pocket of his jeans. He doesn't move, staring at me. Then I push his wallet into the other side. I press my fingers against his chest and push him back, one step, two, three steps, fluorescent blue flashing across his teeth, clinging to the shadows of his face.

His mouth is open, surprised as his back hits the concrete wall behind him, my fingers pressing into his thin t-shirt. My mouth on his.

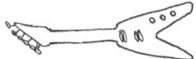

The car ride into the city is nice.

The window in the back is open and my hair flies in the wind, squished next to Leo's baby seat. The city lights rush by, sparkling in the night as we drive towards town, passing trains flashing and cars humming on the highway, streetlamps flooding yellow across the busy buzzing streets.

Evelyn is in the front, talking animatedly to her mum about the scholarship she's won. Organising the details. And Grace is in the little back seat, gazing dreamily out the window, her pink hair changing colours as the lights outside the car flash red and green and orange.

Jude sits on the other side across from me, leaning his head against the glass of his window, staring with a small smile on his face. He looks confident now. Relaxed. Different with his shaved head and sharp lines, sharp jaw, sharp eyes.

Different but good.

He's not staring at me.

I watch him. Which is much more interesting than being watched.

Moon eyes, huh?

He's got moon eyes for my baby brother right now, reaching out to press his finger against Leo's pudgy baby cheek. Leo is delighted. Best thing that ever happened to him. I almost feel jealous. Then remind myself that's ridiculous. I don't own Jude's moon eyes. They don't belong to me.

I watch them both as the car rumbles onwards through the city.

I guess it's okay if my brother and I share them.

I lean over Leo, stretching my body across the spaces between me and Jude, my brother softly kicking my arm. I reach for Jude, tug him close until my mouth nears his ear, whispering so only he can hear, 'I really hate you, Jude Carillo.'

I grin when I pull back, raise my eyebrows in the flashing lights, waiting for him to understand. And he does. Little by little an uncontrollable smile creeps across his mouth, skin flushed beneath his freckles. He watches me with his elbow propped against the window, hand over his smile, moon eyes shining.

At the gig we all sway to the music and I forge to the front to shake my head so my hair surges across my face, letting the sound fill my body, pump my blood and turn me soaring with energy. Sebastian and Jamie turn up and they joke around and make fun of the metal heads, me included, and Grace and Evelyn disappear into a dark corner just the two of them.

In between songs I explain to Jude again the differences between death metal and black metal. 'See they have painted faces. That's corpse paint. Pretty much just black metal bands wear that stuff. And the sound too, it's different. Death metal is tighter, with more technical guitars and drums, and the vocals would be deeper and more guttural. More like a growl.'

Jude nods. 'Uh huh.'

He's listening but he's not listening. I'll probably have to explain it to him all over again tomorrow.

But I don't mind it.

'These guys are good, actually,' I continue. 'I looked up some of their old stuff and wasn't so into it, but this is cool.'

Jude leans close, mouth near my ear. 'Well, the flower that blooms in adversity is the most rare and beautiful of all.'

I blink at him. 'You mean the band?'

His face is serious as he nods.

I gesture at the three musicians on the stage, getting ready to begin a new song, jagged black and white paint slathered across their faces and long messy hair. 'Jude, did you just compare those dudes to a flower?'

'Yes.' He's trying hard not to laugh now. It's in the shape of his mouth.

I shake my head. 'It's from a movie, isn't it? Which one?'

'Definitely not. I made it up myself.'

And no matter how hard I press, he won't tell me. He writes it on a piece of paper the next morning, handing it across our balconies so I can pin it on my corkboard. By then I've already googled it so I know he's full of shit, but I still pin it up anyway. It's a pretty sweet quote to add to my collection. And I like the idea of Jude smiling to himself in his flat, thinking he's fooled me.

In the afternoon, as the sun is baking and the house has grown quiet, too hot for anyone to move about with any energy, I step outside onto the balcony to examine my tomato plants. They're all growing well, ripe red fruit weighing down the curling green leaves, heavy towards the wooden scuffed floor. I spend ages checking them all, examining their leaves and how many tomatoes are growing among the wild tangled plants, carefully selecting the best ones.

Picking up two pots, I hesitate, looking back at my collection, which is getting thin now. There are hardly any bushes left. My neck aches from dancing the night before, my muscles hurt from smiling and my throat is raw from yelling over the music. But it's a good ache.

I carry the most perfect two plants into the house and place them on the kitchen bench, silver shimmering across the black laminate countertop.

D'Angelo sniffs around my feet while I search through the kitchen drawers for a texta, and I freeze momentarily, thinking she's about to pee beneath the fridge again. Instead she just rubs her fluffy body against my shin and slowly ambles off towards the laundry, where her litter tray sits, unused for weeks. Scratching sounds drift out from behind the door, mixing with the steady hum of the washing machine, and eventually D'Angelo re-emerges, her business done. She launches herself onto the couch, curling into one of the cushions and purring.

I watch her, a small smile playing across my mouth. And then I resume my search, until, texta in hand, I lean forward to write a name on each silver tin with looping curling script.

Celeste Murphy.

Evelyn Tait.

ACKNOWLEDGEMENTS

It is very exciting to have this opportunity to write another round of acknowledgements for a second novel, an absolute dream come true!

Once again, I have to thank first and foremost, you, for reading this book. I am so very grateful for your time and so hopeful this story made you happy. I don't even know how to express my gratitude to all the readers who sent me comments and messages about my debut (people even told me they had read it twice!). You are all the absolute best. A special thank you to Emmey, for your endless support and enthusiasm!

A belated (and very grateful) thank you goes to Jo Case, who missed out on being acknowledged for her hard work in delivering my previous novel to the world (I always feel so bad about this!). Thank you, Jo, for this time and for last time!

Huge thank you to the rest of the Wakefield Press team, including Michael, Liz and Maddy, as well as all the others who work behind the scenes.

An ENORMOUS thank you for Margot Lloyd, publisher and editor extraordinaire. I love working with you and you've made my dreams come true. Thank you, Margot.

A massive thank you for my lovely and hardworking agent, Jane Novak, for always being available to give advice, answer my million questions and provide thoughtful feedback on endings. Thank you so much, Jane!

A crazy big thank you to all the booksellers, bloggers, reviewers, authors, Instagrammers and readers who have shown me such an unexpected and overwhelming amount of support, both via the online #LoveOzYA community and in real life. Particularly thank you to Amelia, Mhairi and the rest of the YA Circle from Adelaide Dymocks (I'm so grateful to have so many bookish friends). Thank you also to the rest of the Dymocks Adelaide staff for being so lovely!

Thank you to my wonderful friends who have all supported me on this publishing journey. It's really overwhelming how lovely everyone has been. HUGE thank you to: Kirsty and Nicole, Janine, Clair and Richie, Teegan, Mo Yang and Ngaire, Julie and Mauro, D'Angelo, and everyone else – you know who you are.

Thank you to the authors who have gone above and beyond supporting me and who have given me all of the happy feels: Vikki Wakefield, Allayne Webster, Danielle Binks, C.G. Drews, Jodi McAlister and so so many others.

Thank you to my local YA author group. To the exceptionally talented writers, S.J. Morgan and Kristy Fairlamb, thank you for listening and sharing and generally being such cool people. I'm so glad I connected with you both!

Thank you to my wonderful writing group, Adelaide's Novelist Circle, both present and past members. You have all made my work so much better than it could ever have been without you!

Thank you to my wonderful family, here in Australia and over in Ireland (a special hello to my sisters Ozi and Ima!). Your support and enthusiasm has been so amazing and I am eternally grateful.

Thank you to my mum and dad for everything. I'm especially grateful to my dad for the cover illustration and because he always goes out of his way to do everything for me. I am truly a lucky daughter.

And finally, thank you to my husband Gus. You look after me, believe in me, and make me happy. I can't imagine anything better than that. I love you.

Wakefield Press is an independent publishing and
distribution company based in Adelaide, South Australia.
We love good stories and publish beautiful books.
To see our full range of books, please visit our website at
www.wakefieldpress.com.au
where all titles are available for purchase.
To keep up with our latest releases, news and events,
subscribe to our monthly newsletter.

Find us!

Facebook: www.facebook.com/wakefield.press
Twitter: www.twitter.com/wakefieldpress
Instagram: www.instagram.com/wakefieldpress

www.ingramcontent.com/pod-product-compliance
Lightning Source LLC
Chambersburg PA
CBHW020633260626
47157CB00008B/2724